TWICE

A GUILTY PLEASURES EDITION

ROMEO PREMINGER

CONTENTS

PART I

1

SAL SLIPPED OUT of the 6:55 a.m. Niagara Rainbow at Beacon while it was raining cats and dogs. He'd hoped to make it all the way to Buffalo, but the conductor was catching up to him, puttering through the cars, checking tickets, since they left Grand Central. Sal knew the tricks for getting a free ride from Secaucus to Penn Station on New Jersey Transit, but Amtrak was a different story. He didn't know the conductors' patterns. He couldn't hide between cars or hole up in the toilet and expect no one to notice for nine hours. He had sixteen dollars in his pocket, and he wasn't about to blow it all on a ticket when that money had to stretch for who knew how long?

Adding to his bad luck, the sky had opened up like it was time to build an ark. He ducked into a glass-paneled wait station on the platform, but not before he was sopping wet. When he'd jetted from New York, Sal had filled his Army/Navy backpack with anything he could grab, pulled on his Western boots, and thrown on his snap cap and his suede jacket. Five seconds running down the platform, and he was soaked through.

He dug a soft pack of Camels out of his jeans. The case was damp, and he tossed away three smokes before finding one that wasn't drenched. Sal lit it with his Zippo, which mercifully still worked, and he sucked in two big lungfuls of cancer. After, he glanced out of the glass enclosure. He was thinking he better figure out real soon what the fuck he was doing.

He could try hopping on the next train, jump out again if a conductor spotted him, and put more distance between himself and the city. Sal took another long draw of his Camel. That was risky. Now that he was soaked through, he'd stick out like a sore thumb and leave a trail of water wherever he went. Sal didn't trust those Amtrak stiffs. Commuter rail workers couldn't be bothered to do more than write up a citation for fare evasion if they caught you, but Sal had heard the big rail companies got the heat involved. He had an outstanding warrant for failure to show up to court after the pigs nabbed him doing business at the West Side pier. It went back five years, but he wasn't keen on taking chances and ending up in the back seat of a police car for a free return trip to Manhattan and the downtown pen. He also had a prior that a public defender had pled down to loitering and a sentence of forty-five days in the clink.

Rain flushed down the walls of the enclosure, blurring his surroundings. Sal took hard, angry drags on his cigarette, inciner-ating it down to the filter. He felt like screaming. He was too old to be dealing with this bullshit. Twenty-eight. With no place to rest his head. Having to give it a try making it some place he knew nothing about. Starting from zero. The only thing he had that was worth a dime was one of Joey's gold watches. He could get seventy, maybe eighty dollars for it at a pawn shop. *Fucking Joey.* Thanks to him, Sal would be living like a street punk again. He wasn't a kid who could get by in that situation anymore.

He smoked down a second cig, and the downpour gradually eased. Sal could make out the train station and its surroundings through the glass. He was in the country now. Trees, budding green, were everywhere—in thick thatches along the river side of the tracks, throughout the town's wide grid of streets, and beyond in rolling hills untouched by human development.

The little town looked deserted at eight thirty in the morning.

Across from the station, Sal saw a block of marginal businesses and vacant storefronts. A newsstand. A Western Union. Some abandoned red brick factory. A single traffic light was strung over the cross street by the station. One of those flashing red lights that was the same thing as a stop sign. No cars to be seen in any direction.

Sal had never been farther upstate than the Bronx Zoo. He'd heard of Woodstock. Back when, some kid he used to know at Port Authority said he'd been there in 1969. The punk couldn't stop talking about it, some days claiming he'd been in the front row when Jimi Hendrix played the national anthem, sometimes claiming he'd taken part in an orgy in a camper van with a group of girls from Vassar. The kid was an acid head, so who knew if it was true?

This town, Beacon, didn't look like a hippie haven. It looked like some of the places Sal had passed through on the bus to Asbury Park: desolate, depressed, like the whole town was in foreclosure. That could mean there was a scene Sal could work his way into. People outside of the city were friendlier and more trusting. *That's right, Sal. Think like the savvy entrepreneur you are, and don't get stuck on the past.* Opportunities were everywhere. He'd need to lose the suede fringe jacket and his expensive boots so he blended in more, but these things could be figured out.

He shook out his snap cap. One way or the other, he was going to have to make his present situation work. Beacon looked like a shit town, but he'd ended up there for a reason. Sal was hardly the religious type who believed God had a plan for him, but when you'd been punched in the face by life for as far back as you can remember, you didn't have much to hold on to besides karma and superstition. The rain had let up for the moment. The morning sun strained against the cloud cover, casting everything in an ethereal light. The desolate town was looking more alluring in a weird way.

Sal scanned farther down the street along the train station. He spotted an old-fashioned motor lodge with a diner. The Beacon Motel. Sal hadn't seen that style of roadside motel in years. It reminded him that the farther you got out of the city, the more outdated everything was. It was 1978, and this town looked like it was stuck in the 1950s. Uphill, by a throughway, they had a Pepsi-Cola billboard that must've been there for over a decade. A pin up girl with the stupid slogan: More bounce to the ounce! *Jesus.* The locals probably hadn't heard of disco.

Well, that Beacon Motel looked like a good place to get a cup of coffee and a buttered roll for a dollar with free refills. Sal could kill some time, dry off, and think about his next step. He shook the sleeves of his jacket, replaced his cap over his wavy shag of hair, and headed over there.

The diner was a narrow, eaved appendage to the faded, sandy brick, L-shaped motel. Three cars were in the parking lot: a cream-colored VW bug, a blue Ford sedan, and an old, rusted pickup. All New York State plates. That stood to reason. It was hard to figure that a motel got much business in the middle of nowhere. The diner, in tarnished chrome, didn't look like a top destination, either. It had a Help Wanted sign in one of the windows, which gave Sal his first funny thought of the day. Was the owner looking for kitchen staff or crying out for help more generally? *Help me out of this fucking place.*

Sal opened the glass paneled door, triggering the jangle of a bell overhead, and he stepped in. He quickly clocked three customers. An elderly couple in one of the turquoise vinyl booths and a woman in drab custodial gear sitting on a stool at the far end of the counter. She was alternating between tugs on her cigarette and dabbing a triangle of toast in the yolk of her fried eggs. Nobody was tending the counter, and Sal spotted the ancient cash register. He steadied himself. Desperate as he was, robbing a diner was a low odds proposition. Especially since he didn't have the means to get out of town quickly. Sal sidled over to a stool at the counter, threw off his rucksack and jacket, and took his cigarette pack out and emptied it in front of him. Maybe he could dry out his squares or even find one in his wet pack that was smokable.

He noticed the other customers glance his way, which made him self-conscious for a moment. Sal slyly pocketed the diamond stud from his right ear. He didn't need another reason to stand out. If Beacon was anything like the small town he came from, a guy could get jumped for looking like a fairy. Not that Sal couldn't defend himself. He just didn't need more trouble that day.

He gave the old-timers a nod, and they smiled back at him, real friendly. The maid, with her stiff, long-haired perm, didn't look his way again. She seemed like the type who minded her surroundings but was also content to mind her own business. She probably cleaned rooms for shitty wages to support her kids in some shitty apartment. Sal was familiar with people like that. Nothing to worry about with her, so long as he stayed out of her way. He went back to laying out his squares to dry on the counter. He knew these kinds of places. A rundown diner was a rundown diner whether in upstate New York, midtown Manhattan, or Northern Jersey where he'd grown up.

A good five minutes passed, and no one emerged from the back rooms. Through the kitchen order window, Sal saw the top of the cook's head and his hair net a couple times, but whoever tended tables was nowhere to be found. He would've liked a cup of coffee. They had a regular and a decaf pitcher in the coffeemaker just across from him, and he could really use a hot drink to warm up. Well, at least he was out of the rain and out of New York, and the fact was, he had no place special he needed to be.

Joey Delvechio was dead. He'd warned Joey what could happen, but it was still a shock to Sal's system. Sal cursed himself. What had he always said? Don't get too comfortable. He should've come up with an exit plan months ago. He should've gotten out the first time the Castelli brothers came by to lean on Joey for the money he owed them.

Bells jangled from above the door. Somebody came into the diner with a heavy gait. Sal took care to keep his cool, not swing around and stare like a mook. When the guy stepped up to the counter, Sal stole a careful peek.

Reflexively, his heart rate spiked. A police officer with a big star badge on his black, double-pocket shirt was peering straight ahead at the kitchen. Sal darted a glance over his shoulder. A squad car was parked in front of the diner. It didn't look like the cop had brought anyone else along.

The officer clopped the bell by the register. "Hey. Can a fella get some service 'round here?" He turned to Sal with a chummy grin. "Ain't like it used to be, is it? Them Jimmy Carter commies got us living like Russkies on a bread line."

Sal didn't have an opinion about that, but he could fake a knowing grin. The cop took a fuller account of Sal and the wet cigarettes in front of him.

"Stinks to get caught in the rain." He brought out from his shirt pocket a pack of Marlboros, tugged one out and handed it to Sal. He even lit it for Sal with his disposable lighter.

"Thanks," Sal said.

The copper pointed a finger at him and winked. "Next time I get caught in the rain, you can pay me back."

While the officer perched around to try to see what was going on in the kitchen, Sal gave him a little once-over. His name plate read Lieutenant Hogan. A jolly copper with a paunch and a ruddy complexion. Late thirties or early forties. No wedding band on his left-hand ring finger. He had a holster with a pistol.

"Hey Eddie," the cop called out to the kitchen. "My buddy taking a nap?"

He glanced at Sal and chuckled. Sal smirked along and took a drag of his cig.

"Where you from, pal?"

Sal straightened up in his seat. "Jersey." He put on a rueful grin. "I picked a hell of a day to come up here and see a friend about a car."

Hogan looked over his shoulder to the diner's big glass window. "You must've missed the weather report. It's s'posed to be off and on all day, but it'll pass. You know what they say about April showers."

Sal nodded along. The cop slid an ashtray down the counter for Sal.

"Must be a good deal to make the trip all the way from Jersey. He meeting you here?"

Sal skipped a beat.

Hogan grinned like Sal was slow. "Your friend. He meeting you here at the diner?"

"Oh. Yeah, yeah. But he don't get off from work for a coupla hours." He drew up another hard luck smile. "If I had brains, I woulda taken a later train. I misread the schedule. I never been this far upstate before."

The swinging door from the backroom flew open, and Hogan's attention turned to the fellow who'd come out behind the counter. That was a relief. Sal dropped his gaze while the two men conversed.

"What'll it be, Lieutenant?"

"It's Danny to you. I keep telling you that."

"So you do. George screwed up the order from the bakery, so we're out of cherry pie. You got a second choice?"

"You know I only come here to see that handsome face."

Sal peeked up. He only then got a good look at the fellow behind the counter. Hogan was right. The kid shone like a fucking diamond. Movie star blue eyes, the face of an angel, and thick blond hair. Sal had a hard time looking away. Beneath his apron, the kid's starched, white shirt was open a button, and Sal glimpsed a swath of his smooth, pink chest and the gold chain cross around his neck.

"Yeah, right," the kid said sarcastically. "How 'bout a grilled muffin? We've got bran and blueberry."

"Blueberry sounds great. And a cup of coffee. The way you know I like it."

The kid—he couldn't have been more than twenty-five—scribbled it down on his order pad, and he passed the sheet through the order window to the cook, apparently Eddie. Then he went straight to the coffeemaker, ignoring the fact that the lieutenant looked eager to chat him up. That intrigued Sal. The kid didn't like the cop. He didn't seem nervous, though. More like bored and annoyed. The kid had probably had his share of disappointments in life. With his good looks, he could be doing better than tending a dump in the middle of nowhere, so there had to be an interesting story there. He filled out that apron, shirt, and trousers damn well.

The young man grabbed a paper cup and poured in coffee from the regular carafe and tipped in a glass canister of sugar for a count of five. He stirred it with a spoon, put a cap on it, and brought it over to the lieutenant.

"Eddie'll have your muffin ready, pronto."

The lieutenant's eyes were fastened to the kid. Sal hadn't expected that kind of flirtatiousness from a Mayberry pig. Unless he was misinterpreting things. Maybe upstate men didn't know from queer and just acted like that around each other.

"You got other customers," Hogan said. "This guy came all the way from Jersey. You gonna offer him a cup of coffee?"

The kid glanced at Sal like he was being put upon. "You want a cup of coffee?"

Sal found himself being much more polite than he might've been in other circumstances. He gave the kid a big, good-natured smile. "Best offer I had all day."

The kid filled a white mug with coffee and gruffly set it on a dish in front of Sal. Sal hid a grin. The kid was uppity but smooth. Most people wouldn't have noticed the flash in his eyes from his appraisal of a wet, sketchy stranger who had blown into his diner. Sal even caught the kid's quick glance at the earring hole in his right ear. Meanwhile, the maid cleared out in a hurry. Seemed she wasn't too keen on the young bossman.

The cook set the cop's grilled muffin on the order counter, and the kid put it in a paper bag and handed it to Hogan. Hogan scrounged out a beat-up, overfilled leather wallet, picked out three dollar bills and handed them to the kid.

"Keep the change, killer."

The kid gave him a tiny smile and punched open the cash register.

Hogan beamed in delight. "There it is. I knew I could pry a smile outta you."

The kid shut the register with a ding and faced the lieutenant deadpan. "You keep the juvenile delinquents from marking up the back of the building, and you won't have to do any prying."

Hogan pointed a finger at him. "You got a deal. Hey, give my regards to George. He back in town?"

"Yep. Just last night."

Hogan smiled from some private amusement. "Well, let him know I came by, and as always, I left a happy customer." He tipped his cap to Sal and strolled out of the place.

That relaxed Sal some, and then the old couple came over to settle their bill. Once they left, Sal was completely alone with the young beauty. The kid cleared the couple's table and deposited plates, cups, and utensils in a wash bin behind the counter. He wasn't big on friendly conversation. Sal noticed he had a heck of a nice diver watch with a bright orange dial. A real Seiko. That didn't match his cheap, cross necklace, which every working class Catholic boy got for his first communion. Sal took a sip of his coffee.

"Mmm. That's good stuff," he said. "S'pose I could get two eggs on a roll?"

"It's a dollar forty-five."

"I gotta pay 'fore you make it?"

"Just letting you know. The coffee's forty cents."

Sal rubbed his jaw. "Guess I'll have to take your word, seeing as I never got a menu."

"You want a menu?"

"Nah, you look like the honest type. How long you worked at this joint?"

The kid ignored that question. "How do you want your eggs?"

"Scrambled. You charge extra for that?"

The kid took his order pad out of his apron, and scribbled things down. Sal noted the nameplate on his shirt. Will.

Will passed the order through the kitchen window and drifted down the counter to page through some kind of real estate daily. Sal had much bigger issues to contend with, but none were as fun as ruffling the kid's feathers. Sal told him, "Y'know, I ain't some vagrant looking to bum a meal."

"Oh yeah?" Will glanced at Sal's Marlboro butted in the ashtray. "We've got a cigarette machine by the john. You don't need to be mooching off my customers."

"I ran into a little problem with your town's precipitation. You gonna hold that against me?"

Will gave a little shrug. He went back to reading his paper. Sal pulled out what he could.

"You get a lot of customers 'round here? 'Sides your queer cop friend and the local retirees?"

Will's eyes flared, and then he scowled dismissively. "Hogan's not queer."

"I thought he might be." He delayed the kid again. "I was sayin', you get a lot of customers? I'm genuinely interested."

"We're not the Plaza Hotel, but we do all right." He crossed his arms in front of him. He had handsome arms. His junior biceps showed better with his shirt sleeves pulled taut like that. The way he said plaza with a hard "a" made Sal grin.

"The *Plah*-za Hotel," Sal remarked. "You been to New York City?"

"Yeah. You?" Will passed a glance at Sal's suede fringe jacket, which he'd draped over a neighboring stool to dry.

"I ain't been to the Plaza, but yeah, I been livin' in the city for a while." Sal picked out one of his cigarettes in front of him that looked dry and lit it with his Zippo.

"Sorry to disappoint you, then. Guess you're used to fancy dining in Times Square."

Sal smiled to himself. The kid was trying to take a dig, but he was green. If he really knew Times Square, he'd know it wasn't a place for fancy dining. It was a place for junkies, hustlers, and prostitutes.

"What's so funny?"

"Nothin'."

"You told Hogan you're from New Jersey. So, what is it? Jersey or New York?"

"Same difference. It's just a hop, skip, and a jump on the train." The kid was looking at him skeptically. "So, what does a fella do for fun up here?"

"You should've stayed in the city. There's nothing to do in Beacon." The kitchen bell dinged, and Will brought Sal's egg sandwich over.

"I been to all kinds of places," Sal said. "I grew up in a little town that don't look so different from here."

"You a drifter?"

Sal took a pull on his cigarette. "You this pleasant with all your customers or is it my lucky day?"

Will finished writing up the bill and placed it on the counter face up in front of Sal. A dollar and ninety-five cents. Underlined, twice. "When you're ready." He stepped away to clear the counter where the maid had been sitting.

Sal had an impulse to throw his plated egg sandwich against the wall. Who the fuck did this country pretty boy think he was? He controlled himself and took a chomp of his eggs on a roll. Sal washed it down with some coffee and measured his bites. He wasn't going to wolf his meal in front of the kid like he was some low class nobody. His teeth were in the fight now. The kid wasn't the kind of mark he was used to, but he was committed, and he was going to come out on top.

When Will passed by again with the maid's dishes, Sal fixed a glance on him. "You got a nice place here. You lookin' to hire? I saw your help wanted sign."

Will set down his dishes. "We need a handyman and custodian. To do some fix-up work and clean the toilets."

"Oh yeah? How much does a gig like that pay?"

"You know somebody?"

"I was thinking of applying myself."

"You're from the city, and you're lookin' for a job in this dead-end town?"

"The concrete jungle ain't all it's cracked up to be. I got nothin' against new experiences." Sal ashed his cigarette. The wise guy was getting too cocky for his own good. From what Sal had seen of the cheap motor lodge, if they were down a custodian, Will was doing that shit work himself. The pretty boy couldn't enjoy scrubbing toilets.

"We're not a charity. It's hard work," Will said.

"I ain't expectin' a handout." Sal flexed his bicep in the damp, clinging sleeve of his silk button down. "I got some muscle. Wouldn't you say?"

Will rolled his eyes.

"So, how much does it pay?"

"You're serious?"

"You serious 'bout needing the help?"

"It's minimum wage."

"Well, I bet that goes a lot farther up here than in the city."

Will swept a glance over Sal and nibbled his bottom lip. "If you're really serious, I can see if the owner's available to meet you."

"You ain't the owner?"

"I'm the manager. The owner likes to meet potential hires himself."

Sal cracked a smile. "Well, then, that'd be fantastic if you could for-sill-a-tate an introduction."

"Facilitate," Will corrected him.

"FUH-cilitate," Sal enunciated. "Guess I'm lucky the job don't require impressin' the customers like a smart guy like you." Sal shrugged. "I got other skills. How 'bout we see what the owner thinks? Unless you're worried I'll make a bad impression." He pulled at his collar to air his damp and wrinkled shirt.

"At least he'll see you don't mind getting your hands dirty."

Sal hid his anger with a toothy smile. "There's a dryer in the bathroom," Will told him, and then he turned his back to wipe up around the coffeemaker.

"I got caught in the rain. It ain't a federal offense, is it?"

That came out hotter than Sal wished it had. The kid could take it, though. He didn't flinch, and when he turned to face Sal, his face was blank. Sal liked that. He was tougher than his pretty looks might suggest.

"I get it. It happens sometimes."

Sal's stomach rumbled. He hadn't eaten since yesterday's dinner, and he'd only taken a few bites of his egg sandwich.

"S'pose I finish this up, hit the bathroom, and you bring me over to meet the big man?"

"I'll look for him now. He'll meet you here." Will stepped over to the cash register and locked it. "Take your time. The 'big man' likes to move at his own pace."

They exchanged a glance, and then Will stepped into the backroom.

SAL STOOPED AND contorted himself beneath the bathroom hand dryer. It wasn't his first time cleaning up in a public bathroom, which is not to say he relished it. At least he had privacy. The places he was familiar with had junkies and petty thieves you had to keep an eye out for. Compared to that, the diner bathroom was luxurious. He had it to himself, and he was making progress drying his hair and shirt. His jacket and boots were kind of hopeless, but at least he'd be able to face the owner without looking like he'd rolled in from napping on a park bench in the rain. If they even had park benches in Nowheresville.

Applying to work at a motor lodge, maybe sixty miles north of the city, hadn't been Sal's plan, but here he was. At first, he'd only asked about the job to get under the kid's skin. Now, the idea was growing on him. He needed money, and the sleepy town could be a good place to hole up for a while. He was still spooked about the Castellis. Mobsters didn't like loose ends.

Laying low in a small town was actually genius. If he'd made it to Buffalo, sure, he might've had more opportunities, but he also might've been tempted into the wrong kinds of opportunities. Sal was over stringing together small time grifts just to have the cash to rent a room for a week and buy a couple of meals. He hadn't had to do that in two years, and his other specialty, tricking, turned his stomach just thinking about it. He thought he was out of that game for good. Here in Nowheresville, he was safe, and if this motel job worked out, he'd have a little income and rebuild from there. What he needed was a situation where he could make real cash and buy himself some peace of mind and security.

Sal looked at himself in the mirror. *You're an aging punk, but you're still a smart punk.* He'd barely stepped off the train from Beacon, and already he was working angles. No doubt, he'd lost a good set up, but Joey Delvechio had never been the kind of person he could count on forever. Even if he hadn't gotten himself killed by the mob, he'd been headed for disaster. Every queer with money was the same. They couldn't help themselves from self-destructing, and they never meant it when they made a promise.

In the beginning, Sal thought Joey was different. When he strolled over to Sal's spot at Haymarket and offered to buy Sal a drink, he looked too young to have serious baggage. Sure, he was flashy in his Armani suit, gold rings, and expensive cologne, an Italian prince of Bensonhurst. But his natural good looks—that baby face—cut through that costume of class and clout.

Joey made conversation without getting filthy or taking a grope of the goods he was buying. He wasn't hung up about being queer, on the outside at least. He wasn't married. When he brought Sal back to his apartment above a nightclub, his place was flush for a guy in his early thirties. Sal fucked him on his king-size waterbed while some trippy lightshow played on the ceiling and the Moody Blues crooned from quadrophonic speakers. Joey was clean and kept himself in shape. He wasn't into anything weird. He paid Sal twice his usual asking price and was a perfect gentleman.

And he'd fallen hard for Sal. Joey came back to the bar looking for him the next night, and after that, Sal gave him the phone number for the rooming house where he was living. They must've gotten together four, five nights in a row, and things got more personal. Joey told Sal he owned the club below his apartment. He was a step-nephew of Vito Castelli, who'd set him up with the business. Honchos was a new queer strip club Sal had heard about. Legit, to the extent that any New York shake joint was, and bringing in a good crowd. Sal had also heard of Vito Castelli, who was a bigtime mob boss. That should've put him off the grift, but Sal had never had a sugar daddy treat him so right.

Joey sent town cars to pick him up. He bought Sal nice clothes. He took him to dinner at restaurants with real tablecloths and wait service, not giving a shit about people seeing the two of them together. He told Sal he was gorgeous, and he worshiped him in bed. With all that going on, Sal started sleeping over at his place. He was getting compensated better than he'd ever been, and he couldn't see a reason not to do it.

One summer weekend, Joey drove Sal to Montauk in his Lincoln convertible, and they stayed at a motel right across from the sand dunes and the beach. Over a candlelit dinner, Joey gave Sal a wrapped jewelry box, inside of which was a big diamond stud to replace the stainless-steel ring in Sal's ear. He asked Sal to move in with him and make things exclusive. He told Sal he'd take care of him. Again, looking back, that should've gotten sirens flashing in Sal's head. Any hustler who'd survived the game for more than a few months could tell you that moving in with a john was the quickest way to turn gold to shit. But Sal thought he could handle Joey, and grabbing a bit of the good life was irresistible.

As cover for their relationship, Joey said Sal could help him manage the floor of his club and get on the payroll for five hundred a week. Sal had no experience managing a business, but he wasn't going to turn down an opportunity like that. Nobody had ever had faith in him for that kind of responsibility, and Sal had faked it to get paid many times before. Besides, he knew the scene. The place just needed someone to make sure only paying customers were getting the kicks and Joey's employees weren't being disrespected.

The club was fucking rolling. They had a velvet rope for the line of queens waiting to pay the ten-dollar entrance fee each night, bouncers in suits, a bonafide deejay with a killer sound system, a slick stage with lights, the hottest strippers in town, and a VIP lounge where guys paid hundreds of dollars to get the full deal from the performers in curtained booths. Joey was hands-off managing things, and he sure needed the help so the club stayed profitable and nothing got out of hand. Sal used to joke that he was a zookeeper, but the truth was, he loved the job.

At twenty-six years old, he was finally out of the hustle, which he'd been doing since he left home at seventeen. It was one of those life changing experiences. Sal could've found his way into the club's safe and treated himself to a couple weeks of living like a big shot. Fuck, as a younger punk, he might've settled for stealing Joey's gold jewelry. But Sal realized it was time to play things differently. He was getting old for the game and needed to think about setting up a future for himself. It helped that he liked Joey. He had a big laugh and a way of not taking anything too seriously, including himself. To say Sal loved Joey might've been too much, but they had some good times.

All that changed, sooner than Sal had wanted to admit. It definitely was no honeymoon after the first six months. Joey's every-now-and-then partying with coke turned into an all day, all night habit. He was dipping into the club's till to pay his dealer, and his jealousy flared up like a nuclear bomb when he was loaded. Sal wasn't even fucking around. He was finally in a good situation and had no reason to fuck around. But Joey went paranoid, and their arguments got messy.

Still, Sal stuck it out. When Joey went off, Sal could get the upper hand with him, whether that was just being the louder of the two or knocking some sense into Joey's hopped up brain. Two, three times a week, the night ended with one or both of them cleaning up a bloody lip or nose, and Joey bawling and begging Sal not to leave him. Sal thought he could straighten him out and get him focused on running the club the right way. For a while, it was manageable, and living in a madhouse was better than going back to the streets.

Naturally, Sal was fooling himself. He knew there's no reforming a cokehead, but he was too stubborn to give up before everything went up in flames. Joey got way behind with his bills. He kept saying Sal just needed to be patient while he caught up with his receipts, and meanwhile, he was using the club as his personal funhouse. Every night, he was doing blow with strippers up in his apartment. The staff didn't respect Sal no more because they knew Joey didn't care what they were doing. Sal found out he was paying one of the strippers hundreds of dollars to fuck him, buying his coke and giving him expensive gifts. Half of his staff were ripping him off one way or another. The place was bringing in crazy cash, and it was walking out the door every night.

The Castellis needed Joey out of the way so they could reap those profits. Sal couldn't blame them. Toward the end, a wino from the Bowery could've run the business better than Joey. Sal's problem was he was guilty by association. People could figure out how Sal had gotten the job managing the club. He slept in Joey's apartment every night. The strippers who knew about Sal's past spread rumors he was the one who got Joey messed up and he was stealing money and riding the gravy train into the ground.

One night, when Sal was closing up the place, a bartender who tricked with Fabio Castelli tipped Sal off. While Sal had been handling traffic in the VIP Lounge, Joey left with a carload of the brothers, and they were going to make him disappear. At the least, Sal was going to be tossed out on the street. He didn't want to stick around to see if they had worse plans for him. The Castellis ran everything from 34th to 59th Street, and they didn't earn respect from being nice guys. In the past, Sal had tricked at a video store on Eighth Avenue. The owner had a jagged scar across his face and a lame leg from what the brothers did to him when he didn't have their cut on the first of the month.

Two years he'd spent trying to help Joey keep the place in business, and Sal had been run out of town with less money in his pocket than when he'd met the fucking disaster of a person.

Sal slapped himself to break out of his pity party. You can't trust nobody, and when you're feeling comfortable, you probably should've bailed at least a week ago. Now, Sal had to make lemonade from lemons, or some shit like that. He took one last look at himself in the bathroom mirror, fixed his gelled hair just so, and convinced himself he'd achieved a respectable appearance. Well, probably not in the snotty kid's eyes. Pretty boy had read him well, and that gnawed at Sal's ego and got him riled up to prove Will different. Sal grabbed his backpack and jacket and ventured out to the diner.

He heard the owner's booming voice before he saw him. The guy was loud and brash, some kind of immigrant? From what Sal could tell, he and Will were having a peaceable conversation, though the guy had a way of talking that sounded like he was arguing. A Greek accent? Sal summoned his charm and presented himself.

"Good morning."

The owner took Sal in with far less scrutiny than Will had. He had a generous smile on his mustached and bearded face. A full head of hair that was more than half gray. Well-fed, the guy was. His blue button-down strained against his belly. He walked around the counter and shook Sal's hand.

"George Filapoussis."

"Sal Minovich."

At closer range, Sal noticed George's gold chain necklace, his silver Seiko watch, the dime store cologne he'd thrown on liberally. He was a stocky fella, but shorter than Sal by a few inches. Coffee breath that could stun an elephant. He didn't wear a wedding ring.

"What brings you up from New York City?"

Will must've told him that. It wasn't good to have two stories running at the same time. Sal smoothed things over. "I was telling Will, I'm looking to give it a try in a new place. A fella can make good money in the city, but you figure in the noise, the pollution, and the cost of living, and it don't add up so well."

George smiled approvingly. "I grew up in Queens. Worked as a stock boy at a Gristedes when I was a kid. Gristedes still around?"

"Sure is."

"You done time?"

George said it like it was something to get out of the way.

Sal chuckled. "No sir."

"How old are you?"

"Twenty-eight."

"A good age," George said with a wink. "Young enough to bear hard work, and old enough to know the value of it. When I was twenty-eight, I gutted and rebuilt this entire property. I could work all day and close the bar down the street at two o'clock in the morning. Get up the next day and do it all over again."

"He doesn't want to hear your old stories, George," Will said. "He's just looking for a job."

Will had planted himself by the back counter, refilling napkin dispensers. George shrugged off his comment with a grin. "What was I saying? You're twenty-eight. You haven't run off on some girl? Left her to fend for herself with a houseful of little Sals?"

"Oh no, sir. That was my dad's beat. I ain't looking to follow in his footsteps."

"You like girls?"

Sal noticed Will watching him. "I like 'em fine. They ain't so partial to me, so far."

"You're a good looking fellow. Holding out for the right woman, I bet."

Sal scoffed. "I dunno. Could be."

"You have papers?"

"Christ George, does he sound like he's off the boat?" Will snapped.

There was an odd vibe between the two men, and Sal couldn't place it, just yet. George had to be twenty years older than Will.

He owned the motor lodge. But Will scolded him like a senile father. They sure didn't look like they were related.

George turned to Will with a little bite in his voice. "I just like to know." He faced Sal. "I keep things off the books, so it's not a problem for me one way or the other. Would that be a problem for you?"

"Works out best on both sides, in my experience," Sal said.

"Will says you've done repair work before?"

Sal lowered his gaze to stop himself from looking at the smug troublemaker who had now propped himself up on the back counter to watch. Sal never told him that. He improvised an answer. "I done fix-up jobs back in New York. Mostly at hospitality type of joints."

"Really?" George glanced at Will. "It'd be a big help to have someone with that kind of experience." He turned back to Sal. "You work anyplace I might've heard of?"

"No place special. I mean, nowhere a respectable businessman like you would know." He looked at George squarely. "But hospitality's hospitality, ain't it? I know how to keep a place in shape."

"I don't doubt it." George scratched his ear. "And you might be surprised by the kind of joints I'm familiar with in the city." He smiled at Sal. "We can talk about that another time. I was a single, young fella in New York myself. You use dope?"

That got Will studying Sal again.

"No sir. Never been my thing."

"You drink?"

"Now and then. Special occasions, mainly."

George's face widened in amusement. "Special occasions! I like that better than those preachy people who go door to door with their pamphlets." He glanced at Will. "What do they call themselves?"

"Jehovah's Witnesses."

"That's it. Where the hell did they come up with that?"

"It's from the Hebrew bible. Jehovah is another name for God."

George looked at Sal jollily. "Will's always teaching me some-thing. He's the smart guy around here. You knew about that?"

"No, sir."

"We've got a bunch of those weirdos in town." George caught himself. "Hope I'm not offending you, Sal. You religious?"

"I was raised Catholic. But I ain't been to confession in a long time."

George grinned. "You've got a sense of humor. I like that. I think I like you, Sal. But one more question. You play cards?"

Sal peeked at Will for a cue. The kid didn't give anything away.

"I know crazy eights."

George burst out laughing. "Crazy eights. That's what they're playing in the city these days?" He waved his hand. "I'll teach you. We play pinochle Sunday nights. I think you're hired, Sal. Just got the easy stuff to work out. It's one twenty-five a week, and you get a room in the back, meals included. If you've got your own place, I'll make it one hundred fifty. It's Mondays through Saturdays, and we open at seven in the morning. You get this place spic and span, sweep up outside, do some light repairs, and help Eddie with the dishes when you've got the time. Sound all right?"

Given Sal's recent turn of fortune, it sounded pretty decent. Sal only needed ten, twelve dollars a week to buy cigarettes. He could use his first week's paycheck to pick up T-shirts, underwear, and his basic bathroom stuff. He worked out the numbers in his head. In the scheme of things, it was shit wages, but room and board helped. He'd have almost half a grand saved up in a month. That was decent traveling money. Besides, the motor lodge couldn't need much upkeep. How many guests could they get in the middle of nowhere?

"Sounds great." George reached out his hand, and Sal and George shook on it.

George glanced at Will. "This guy here will go over the routine. He's been after me to bring someone in to wash the graffiti off the wall out back."

Will slid down from the counter. "You need to rent a pressure washer, cheapskate."

"Some WD-40 and a steel brush works just as well." George looked down at his watch. "I'm late. I've gotta see a guy across the river about a jukebox." He turned to Will. "See there. I'm keeping my promises." He tossed Sal a grin. "This one gives me my marching orders too."

Sal was getting the picture about them two. He tried to not let it show on his face.

"Will can take you to your room so you can get settled in."

George gave Sal a parting grin. He headed to the back room, and as he passed by Will, he clasped the back of his neck and gave it a light squeeze. Sal watched the kid tuck his chin into his neck and darken in the face. To the average person, it would've seemed like an affectionate gesture, as a father saying goodbye to his son. But Sal saw through things. He smiled to himself. This was going to be real interesting.

2

LATER THAT WEEK, however, Sal was already questioning his decision to give honest work a try. He'd never worked harder for a measly one hundred and twenty-five dollars a week. He got up each day at six o'clock, mopped the diner and scrubbed the bathrooms, and then he grabbed a broom to sweep the walks from one end to the other of the two-story motel. He also had to pick up trash and cigarette butts in the front and rear parking lots and tidy the strips of lawn. When he finished, he had deliveries to haul into the kitchen. Crates of groceries on Mondays and Thursdays. Refills for the soda machines on Tuesdays. The bakery truck came by every Wednesday and Friday, and there were daily deliveries of milk and eggs and special deliveries of paper goods, cleaning products, and back-breaking jugs of water.

Add to that, Will had an endless list of projects that kept Sal busy late into the day. Will wanted to pretty up the curbside yard in front of the motor lodge, so he told Sal to turn over sections of the lawn for flower beds, no delight with a handheld garden claw in weedy, barely thawed ground. Light bulbs needed to be replaced around the building. Windows needed washing. Curtains got fucked up, and there were touch up paint jobs inside and outside the rooms. When a sink or toilet got clogged and needed plunging, that was Sal's job too.

The worst was trying to remove the graffiti from that back wall. Someone had marked up a spot in the corner with the banner: "Murray Does Rush," which seemed like a reference to huffing unless the kids in town were up to date with progressive rock bands. Sal would lather a small section with greasy WD-40 and scrub it with a steel brush until his hand and arm throbbed, and he didn't accomplish more than a puke-colored blur of spray paint. It wasn't that Sal was too high and mighty for physical labor. At Joey's club, he'd carted cases of beer and liquor up from the basement and taken care of ice deliveries when they were short-staffed. But this racket George had suckered him into went on from the crack of dawn till eleven o'clock at night by the time he finished helping Eddie close out the kitchen and haul bags of garbage to the dumpster.

Sal had no one to shoot the breeze with, either. In New York, he could walk up to anyone and kill some time just talking shit and get the latest gossip on the streets. Prior to his gig at Joey's club, he'd done the square thing before, briefly, cleaning up a meat packing plant overnight. What made that shit work tolerable was the smoke breaks when guys could bitch about their jobs and feel a sense of solidarity. He was curious to find out if the other help knew a thing or two about Will and George's relationship. Eddie seemed like a decent guy, but he was Portuguese and his English was terrible. The maid, Loretta, spoke English fine, but she kept to herself unless she needed help hauling a bin of laundry to the washers in the basement.

All of this made Sal feel like he was working off a sentence of community service. He thought about finishing out the week, collecting his one hundred and twenty-five dollars, and buying a train ticket to Buffalo like he'd planned, but he kept getting turned around. He wouldn't have admitted it back then, but he had it bad for Will.

There was nothing rational about it. Will treated him like dirt.

Forget about the simple courtesy of a hello when they crossed paths in the morning. Will avoided his gaze, ignored his attempts at small talk, and only spoke to him when he had some job for Sal to do.

Still, Sal was fascinated by the kid. He was beautiful, and he didn't even know it. Sal caught customers checking him out at the diner, and Will just skirted their glances and tended to business. He wasn't a prima donna, neither. He showed up at the diner by seven every morning, and waiting on customers was only part of his job. Sal saw him in the back office, calling in orders and managing the books, and he had to cover the front desk to check in and check out motel guests, answer the phone, and give directions for getting back on the thruway. The pretty boy was no phony about bettering the joint. In his downtime, Will tidied up the little motel lobby, and Sal heard him haggling with vendors like he was running a Las Vegas casino.

Meanwhile, George rarely made an appearance. He drove off in his Oldsmobile most days and didn't return till late at night. Sal noticed the two had neighboring second-floor rooms in the back of the motel, not far from his own room on the ground floor. When he took the garbage to the dumpster at the end of the night, Will's room was dark while George's had signs of life. Strains of Greek music traveled from that room. Sal heard animated voices, though he couldn't make out what was going on. The Greek music cut out every night at midnight on the dot, and the room went dead.

Friday afternoon that week, Sal ran out of paint to touch up one of the motel rooms, so he strolled over to the motel office to talk to Will about it. Really, the hot shot's office was just a little windowless room behind the front desk, crammed with file cabinets, broken equipment, and a chipped bureau stacked with mail. The kid was sorting receipts into an accordion folder. Sal knocked on the open door before he presented himself, and Will didn't even look up at him.

"You're gonna have to get another bucket of white paint if you want me to finish the bathroom in 213."

Will's eyes didn't leave his work. "We've got an account at Harvey's Hardware. Make a right out of the parking lot, along Railway Road, and it's three blocks up Center Street. Tell the owner you work for George, and he'll give you a gallon for four dollars and twenty cents."

"I gotta make the trip?"

"If you need the paint. It's only a fifteen-minute walk."

Sal hung around the door. "How's the owner gonna know I work for George?"

"This isn't the city. He'll take your word."

Sal picked at a callus on his finger. "You know your town. I ain't arguin' with you, but I'd be more comfortable if you came along. Bein' that I'm new 'round here."

Will looked up at Sal in his put-upon way. "I don't have time to babysit the staff. I can call ahead, but I'm telling you, it's no big deal."

Sal stepped closer to Mr. Wonderful's desk and fixed an earnest gaze on him. "I ain't looking to make your job harder, but George never said running errands was part of the deal."

"You might've noticed George doesn't take much interest in how things operate around here. Why do you think I'm stuck tending the place day and night, seven days a week? *I'm* the only one who gives a shit about keeping us in business." Will stood and opened one of the steel file cabinets behind his desk, sorting through folders. Sal's eyes were drawn to the fit of the kid's khaki Dickies around his buttocks. *Jesus, Joseph and Mary.*

He swiped his face. "I get that. All's I'm saying is fair is fair. If he wants me running errands, I oughta get paid for that."

"I'll talk to him about it." Will turned around and laid a five-dollar bill on his desk. "Bring back the change." He went back to sorting through the file cabinet.

It was time to let the kid know who he was dealing with. Sal took a cigarette out of the pocket of his utility shirt, lit it, and leaned his shoulders and one foot against the wall.

"How long you and the bossman been fucking?"

Will swung around to face him. "You got a lot of nerve saying that to me. Get out of here before I can your ass."

Sal held up his hand. "It ain't a problem for me. Just took me by surprise up here in Squaresville. I ain't looking to spread your business 'round. I just like to know what's what."

"What's what is do your job. Capiche?"

Sal bowed his head. Blood coursed through his veins. He knew he was playing with fire, but the problem was, that was Sal's comfort zone.

"I'm just making conversation. You allergic to that, sweetheart?"

Will's face flushed. "I'm not your sweetheart, and you don't talk to me that way in my fucking office."

Sal couldn't help grinning. The kid had a mouth, but he'd probably never thrown a punch. He took a long, deliberate drag on his cigarette and exhaled. Then he gazed boldly at the kid, staring down his body to his crotch.

"Get out," Will snapped.

Sal didn't.

Will put on a tough guy front. "You want to know something? George never should've hired you. What's your game, Sal? You looking for an angle to shake George down for money? You're not gonna find it. And if a penny goes missing around here, you can bet you'll be at the top of the list of suspects."

"I ain't a dirtbag," Sal burst out. "Last job I had, I was makin' half a G a week, and that place had some class." The kid flinched. Sal took a deep breath to control himself, and he crushed out his cigarette in the ashtray on Will's desk. "I'm sorry. I shouldn't have shouted at you. But you got it all wrong 'bout me. You been treatin' me like a disease since the moment I walked in here. Ain't I showed I'm willin' to do the work?"

Will snorted dismissively and kicked the file cabinet drawer closed with a clang. "I don't have time for this." He stepped around the desk, but with Sal there, he had a narrow path to the door, unless he wanted to try it sideways. "You gonna get out of my way?" Will said. "I've gotta catch the mailman when he comes by."

They held a standoff, inches away from each other. Will puffed out his chest, and his nostrils twitched with breaths. The steam from his body lapped Sal's skin. The threat of violence set off a potent intoxication in Sal's brain. Before he could think better of it, he clawed his fingers through the back of Will's thick hair and pried open Will's mouth with his.

Will took a second or two to react to the situation, but then he fought his way out of the kiss, nicking Sal's lip with his tooth. His eyes were wide and trembling with anger. Then he cracked his open palm across Sal's face.

"You pack your shit and get the hell out of here."

Fireworks throbbed in Sal's vision. His lip stung, and he tasted blood in his mouth. That slap must've broken some blood vessels. It also brought his cock to a stand. He tried getting a hand around Will's forearm to bring him close, but Will ripped it away.

Sal eyed him with a bullying grin. "Don't you got to talk to George about that?"

"First chance I get."

"What you gonna tell him? I mean, you probably shouldn't mention nothin' 'bout you and me."

"There's nothing to say about you and me, asshole."

"Well then, what did I do?" Sal moved in a little cozier. "I been doing my job all week. Ain't been late or loafed off once. You gonna make shit up?"

Will took a half-step back. "Cool it." He glanced at the office door. He'd have to push through Sal to get to it. Sal could guess what was going through his head. He'd lowered his voice. Was worried about someone overhearing. Particularly George whose comings and goings were unpredictable.

"You gotta have just cause to fire somebody." Sal drew up to him again, gauging the kid's reaction. Romancing a live wire was right in his sweet spot, and their proximity was doing things to Sal. He leaned close and spoke into Will's ear. "I think we got just cause for George to fire me, but who says we gotta let him know?"

Will snorted, arrogantly. "I don't go that way, and even if I did, you think I'd be interested in a grifter like you?"

He didn't back away. Sal widened his stance, surrounding the kid seductively, no physical contact yet, just mingling the heat from their bodies. "Let's see." Sal scooped his hand between Will's legs, feeling around, real sexy, and finding his sultry stuff. He sweet-talked in Will's ear. "I think you're interested, and you know we could make it really hot."

Will leaned away, but only so much. Sal had him captive, and he licked his scored upper lip, savoring the needles of pain there. He ran his teeth against Will's neck. "I'll make it hotter than your old man. I wanna fuck you till we're both drenched, and then I wanna fuck you again."

Will tried to still Sal's hand, but his resistance was weak. Sal looked into his eyes, wolfishly. "You gonna slap me again or call out for help? It don't matter. I'm so hot for you, nothing's gonna stop me."

Sal sealed their mouths together. This time, Will didn't put up a fight, and it was deep and humid and wanting. Sal drank in the scent of him, his aftershave, the fear steaming from his pores.

The bell rang from the front desk beyond the office.

"Anybody around?"

That voice shocked Sal to his senses for a moment, and Will pushed away from him. "That's the mailman," Will muttered. He wiped his mouth, smoothed out his clothes, and adjusted himself. Then he shoved past Sal to get to the door. Sal grabbed his arm.

"That wasn't so bad, was it? Think 'bout it, okay?"

Will yanked his arm away from him. "There's nothing to think about. You're history. I'm talking to George as soon as he gets back."

He left Sal in the office. Things hadn't gone as well as they could have, but in the afterglow of that steamy kiss, Sal felt like it had been worth it, even if it got him canned.

3

COULD BE WILL meant what he said about reporting Sal to George. He steered clear of Sal for the rest of the day and glanced away the few times their paths crossed in the diner. Could be Sal was out of a job, and George wouldn't even pay him for the week. Now that he'd come down from Cloud Nine, Sal was antsy.

Sal was who he was, and he made no apologies for that. But he had to admit he came in too hot. Will wasn't like the men he was used to. The kid played like he'd been around the block, but he was still a small-town boy.

Sal cursed himself. After he'd barely escaped the mess with Joey, he shouldn't be taking risks. He had lucked his way into a job with room and board, and he ought to be focused on making it work for at least a month or two, living on the cheap. When he had a bundle saved up, he could go anywhere. Maybe Sal could've had a little fun with Will while he was working the gig, but he should've studied the situation to pick up cues. As he'd suspected, Will didn't mind getting down with guys, but Sal scared him and probably left him even more assured Sal was a low-class punk on the make. Not to mention, he should've kept in mind how complicated the situation was. What had he been thinking? He could sex him out from under George after being there for a week? George was probably Will's meal ticket, and Sal was nothing.

It had been an excruciating day. When George showed up, the odds were good he'd be out on his ass, and then what was he going to do? He'd busted his balls all week, and he'd be leaving with nothing to show for it. He couldn't go back to New York. His reputation was shit now. People would think he screwed Joey over, and the Castelli brothers had their hands in every hustler bar and bathhouse from the Battery to the Bronx. Sal would have to go back to turning tricks on the West Side Highway, renting a room at a boarding house, going to bed every night with a switchblade in his hand. It was making Sal physically sick thinking about it, and he barfed up the couple of bites he'd had of a chicken salad sandwich during his dinner break and hunched over himself in the bathroom stall. He couldn't go backward like that. He'd fucking die.

Sal pulled himself together in front of the bathroom sink. What he should do is talk to Will. He would play things apologetic. He really hadn't meant to scare the kid. He didn't want to get Will in trouble with George, and he just had to persuade him keeping George in the dark about what happened was the best thing for both of them. He'd promise to be respectful moving forward. Sal snuck two little bottles of mouthwash out of the stock closet across the hall, gargled both of them for a count of thirty and spat out in the sink.

That would be the wise thing to do, but saying he was sorry didn't come easy to Sal. Yeah, he'd made a mistake, but he'd only been asking the kid to give him a chance. Didn't he deserve respect too? He'd done everything the kid asked, never complaining. Sure, Sal had crossed a line, but really, he'd just been trying to get to know Will, and Will knocked him down every time he tried. The motel lodge was lonely, and they could both use a friend, couldn't they? Sal never had a friend like Will. Besides being a knockout, the kid worked hard, had a good head on his shoulders, and he didn't take shit from nobody.

Sal's thoughts turned and twisted in his head. This job was supposed to be an easy, temporary situation, and now it was fucking with his brain. He had no business going soft, particularly for some pretty boy who thought his shit didn't stink. If Will was going to get him fired, he should be figuring out how to grab some cash out of the register and say goodbye to the shit motel and the shit town. But Sal couldn't commit to that, either. There were times a person had to go for broke, but Sal hadn't been around long enough to get a read on things. He could be pulling the trigger too fast. Will might've been bluffing. If things worked out for just a couple more weeks, he'd be a lot better off than landing his ass in jail for petty larceny.

So, Sal muddled through his routine that night. He washed dishes in the diner, and at closing time, he helped Eddie scrub up the kitchen. When they were done, he went out the back entrance toward his room. Before he'd taken two steps, he spotted George's Oldsmobile Cutlass pulling around to the backlot of the motel.

He considered heading George off, flattering the bossman some way to get on his good side, and working into conversation there'd been a misunderstanding between him and Will. Then Sal had second thoughts. George had no reason to believe him over what Will was going to say. He'd probably end up looking like a troublemaker. Sal took the long way around the building so he wouldn't run into George, and he shut himself inside his little room. *What a fucking mess.* He'd spent the whole day trying to figure out how to fix the situation, and he kept coming up empty.

Pretty soon, Sal was standing at his screened window, trying to listen to what was going on upstairs. After George went up to his room, Sal heard a muffled conversation, and then that Greek music came on. Sal couldn't hear anything through that. Carefully, he stepped outside to see if he could make out what was going on above him. He snuck to the corner of the building where he had an angle to see upstairs. Lights were on in George's room, but Will's room next to it was dark.

The town was eternally quiet at night. All you could hear was the wind swelling against the trees and, now and then, a car speeding by on the distant thruway. Sal thought he caught a little of George's booming voice. Was he angry? Drunk? Sal couldn't tell.

The music cut out, and George's apartment plunged into darkness. Still, Sal listened, wondering about confidences being shared, or tensions brewing, or maybe, horribly, the two rolling around in bed.

The apartment was dead still. Meanwhile, Sal sensed he wasn't alone. He glanced behind him and saw a stray cat down the walkway. He was appraising Sal warily, a ginger tom, and he let out a mewl.

Sal went into his room and found a can of tuna he'd taken from the kitchen. He opened it from its tab and set it out on the walk. He'd always liked cats, and street creatures needed to look out for each other. Sal squatted and gave the hungry boy a scratch behind the ears. *What would you do in my situation, fella?* Sal smirked to himself. The place was driving him so bonkers, he was looking for advice from alley cats.

SATURDAY MORNING, WILL showed up at the diner while Sal was wiping down the front window. Eddie came in just after seven o'clock, and a family of four showed up for breakfast a little later. Will wasn't any more or any less bitchy than he'd been all week. George didn't show up, which was typical too. Unless Sal was dreaming, Will hadn't said a word to him. Why else would he be acting so casual? Later, when the family cleared out, Will asked Sal to clean the laminated menus, and he was happy to grab his spray cleaner and rag and hop to it.

So went Saturday, and Sunday morning, Sal woke up and found an envelope that had been slipped under his door. Sal tore it open, worrying he might find some kind of legal letter terminating his employment. He found instead three crisp bills: a Benjamin, a twenty, and a five. His first week's pay. Sal coughed out a laugh. He'd been stressing over nothing.

He took a long hot shower. He had dodged a bullet, and whatever Will's reasons were for not asking George to fire him, he
should count his blessings and leave well enough alone. One
hundred and twenty-five dollars! It was hard earned cash, but it
was all his, and he had the day off. Sal wrapped a towel around his
waist and looked at himself in the mirror. With all the physical
work he'd been doing, he was as lean and wiry as a marine. He
decided he deserved to treat himself a little after the shit week he'd
been through. He'd go into town, buy himself a nice, big breakfast,
pick up a few clothing items, maybe see some sights. He wouldn't
blow all his cash. He'd be thrifty about it.

Sorting through the few clothes he had, he stepped into a pair
of hip huggers, pulled on a ribbed T-shirt, and stuck his diamond
stud back into his ear. If the local prisses couldn't handle a hot
macho faggot, they could go fuck themselves. He wedged his feet
into his cowboy boots, threw on his suede fringe jacket, and
shaped his hair in the mirror. Then he stepped out of the motor
lodge and into town, picking up his strut from the days he used to
cruise Christopher Street.

He soon discovered, however, Beacon was a ghost town on a
Sunday. Sal walked three blocks of the main strip, Center Street,
and every single business was closed. Not that there was much in
the way of businesses to start. A rinky-dink novelty shop. A sub
and pizza place that didn't open till five o'clock on a Sunday. A
clothing store with outfits in the windows that looked like they
could be on the costume rack for *Leave it to Beaver*. Sal hadn't
expected Fifth Avenue, but it was goddamn depressing. There were
more vacant storefronts than anything else.

The few people he came by stared at him like he'd dropped
down from outer space. Sal glared right back at them. Naturally,
his style was too happening for the upstate squares. He walked two
more blocks and finally came upon a corner convenience store that
was open. It was a tiny joint, but among the titty mags and
tobacco products, he found a Snickers candy bar and a bag of
chips. He placed those on the counter and asked the cashier for a

carton of Camels. While the cashier was ringing him up, he asked the fella if there was a place in town where he could pick up underwear and shirts. The cashier told Sal there was a Two Guys discount store off the thruway that opened at noon and pointed out where he could catch a bus to get there for twenty-five cents.

Sal walked the five long blocks to the bus stop. Nobody was around, and Sal was getting the impression he was going to be waiting a while for the crappy bus to show up.

He scarfed down his candy bar and potato chips, went through smokes one after the other, and glanced at his watch periodically. 10:50. 11:05. Still no bus in sight. Barely any cars out on the road. By quarter to noon, Sal was still waiting around like a loser. What was with the town? Sal had seen apartments over storefronts and little houses on cross streets. Either everyone was at church or the entire population had been zapped up by a UFO. *See the sights*, Sal had told himself. Beacon was a fucking drag. He was looking like the shit and had cash in his pocket, and he was standing at a bus stop like the sole survivor of the apocalypse.

Sal noticed a pool hall that was opening up across the street. That was the first interesting thing he'd seen all day. It was your basic single-story dump with peeling paint and an OTB logo and a neon Schaefer Beer sign lit up on its single window, but Sal wouldn't have even guessed the town had that kind of establishment. He watched three local fellas traipse along to the entrance. Twangy rock music hailed from inside as they opened the door and let it close behind them.

Sal paced a bit and licked his lips. Old instincts were coursing through his veins. He couldn't say what kind of trouble he could get himself into at a pool hall in Buttfuck, USA, but part of him was eager to find out. Sal was crap at pool, but he'd worked those kinds of places. Guys came in with fat wallets, and they got friendly when they were drunk. He might get lucky and walk out with a couple hundred in his pocket from nicking unattended cash and turning a trick or two in the bathroom. He might even strike up a deal with the manager if the guy ran a dirty business. He could play a decoy to get the customers spending more money at the tables or get a cut for peddling dope around the hall.

People had to get their kicks someplace, even in the middle of nowhere, didn't they? It would make for a hell of a more interesting afternoon than taking a bus to some crummy discount store. It might turn into a better gig than mopping floors and cleaning toilets for what worked out to a dollar and fifteen cents an hour.

Sal snuck glances at the pool hall, feeling more and more inclined to ditch the bus, and then he remembered the paper bag in his hand. He'd bought a carton of smokes with money he'd earned that week. Instincts warred inside him. Working as a janitor was shit, but he'd need to work at least another week to have some traveling money to move on to a better scene. Part of him missed being in the game. He missed the rush of working a con. The kind of men who lived in Beacon had to be easy marks.

It was a damp and chilly April day, and Sal was sweating through his shirt. He'd told himself he was going straight for a while, giving the lousy racket at the motor lodge a chance. He'd made it through six days with just one little hiccup that amounted to nothing in the end. There was a sort of pride that came from getting paid for work done on the up and up.

Sal was pulling on a cigarette without remembering he'd even lit it. He could walk into the pool hall to check things out, just for an hour or so. If the scene was dry, he'd go on his way and do his shopping like he'd planned. If it wasn't dry, well, he'd limit himself to one little hustle, like working some fella who was getting soused. He could use the money to buy a new pair of jeans and work shoes. Get himself looking sharp. That would show Will he wasn't some bum. So long as the hustle didn't go sideways.

A bus lumbered down the street, and its brakes shrieked as it slowed down to the bus stop. After two hours of waiting, Sal felt like he needed to make a decision then and there. He cursed himself, and then he dug a quarter out of his pocket and boarded the bus to spend his day at a shitty discount store.

4

SAL WAS BACK in his dingy coverall mopping floors the next day, and he went through another week of working as a grunt. He'd had a long conversation with himself. Looking for action at that pool hall was a lousy idea. He barely knew the podunk town, and he needed to think smart for once in his life. Sal wasn't looking to make a career as the clean-up stiff at the motor lodge, but he'd worked his way in, and as for setting his sights on a bigger score, there could be opportunities.

If he studied the place's operations, he might find an angle for siphoning off the cash coming in. A lot of people came in and out of the motel: delivery men, vending machine stockers, meter readers. Somebody had to be open to making extra money and could use his help pulling it off.

Sal had also noticed a middle-aged suit who checked in every Wednesday for an afternoon delight. He parked his forest green Gremlin around the back, left his female companion in it, and walked around the building to the front desk. Dollars to doughnuts, the guy was married, which made him the perfect mark for a shakedown. Every guest had to sign the registry with a name, address and phone number. It could be worth a few grand to the guy to not let his wife know what was going on.

But the idea Sal liked the most was feeling out Will some more. The kid didn't seem so happy in his present situation, and he managed all the money that came into the joint. If Sal could build trust with the kid, keeping his hands to himself, he might be able to ease him into working over George's business together.

So, Sal played the perfect employee all week. The problem was, however, Will was as frosty as the North Pole. He went through the day without acknowledging Sal unless he had some project for him to do. One day, it was recaulking bathtubs. The next, Will wanted him to clear out the drain pipes around the roof. Always, he mentioned that Sal needed to finish cleaning up the graffiti in the back of the motel, which was impossible to do with just some grease and a steel brush. He'd blurred and faded 'Murray does Rush,' but he was never going to remove the paint completely from the bricks.

If Will had treated him like a human being, it might not have pissed Sal off so much. He couldn't figure the kid out. Will hadn't gotten him canned for making a move on him. Normally, that meant a person was open to the possibility and might warm up a little, especially since George was rarely around. But Will kept their conversations to no more than ten seconds and rushed off in a hurry.

These things built up in Sal's head, and by Friday morning, he was determined to catch Will alone to get some questions answered. He'd do it after the breakfast crowd cleared out of the diner and Will went to his office. Sal did his part wiping down tables while Will took orders and served customers. Then Lieutenant Hogan strolled in around nine o'clock.

Sal drifted to the far side of the diner with his washrag and turned his back to the copper. The pig might remember him and ask nosy questions. Sal didn't need to get into a conversation with him, especially with Will right there to overhear.

The cop made a beeline to the counter where Will was working. That was a walk you could hear from a hundred yards away with his utility belt clinking and his radio fizzing. "'Morning handsome."

"'Morning, Lieutenant. What can I get you?"

"I keep telling you, call me Danny."

"I keep forgetting."

"What do I got to do? Remove my badge?" Hogan chuckled. "Hey, I asked my guy on nights to swing by your backlot while he's on patrol. You have any problems with those high school punks this week?"

"This week? No."

"Look at that. Problem solved. You just let me know if the punks come back. I'll see to it personally." Sal could picture the shit-eating grin on Hogan's face.

"Right on. So, what'll it be? The pie order came in yesterday. We've got cherry, pecan, and lemon meringue."

"How 'bout another one of those grilled muffins? It hit the spot the other morning."

"Blueberry?"

"You remember! Guess I ain't so forgettable after all."

"Coffee?"

"The way you know I like it."

"Gotcha."

Sal inched toward the bathroom. Funny, he actually felt a little bad for the corny copper. Will treated him like a migraine.

"The place is looking good. I saw you took your help wanted sign down. You hire a handyman?"

"Yep."

"Somebody local?"

"An out-of-towner."

Sal gulped.

"Oh yeah? From where?"

"Don't know. The city, I think. George hired him."

"The city you think? What's he doing in our little corner of the world?"

"I didn't grill the guy. You'd have to ask George."

"None of my business anyway. Looks like he's doing a good job. That's all that counts, right? Hey, is George around? I haven't seen him in ages."

"He's taking the day off."

Hogan chuckled. "Is that Greek for *sleeping* one off? Seriously, you have to tell George we're overdue for a night out at that place up in Poughkeepsie. The chicks are wild up there. You should come along too."

"I'll let George know."

The cook's bell rang, and the conversation trailed off, presumably while Will was getting Hogan's muffin and coffee together for takeout. Sal was only a few steps away from the hallway to the john where he could hide himself for the remainder of the officer's visit, but he was curious to overhear more.

That turned out to be disastrous. He spotted Hogan glancing around the diner in his peripheral vision, and then Hogan made a quarter turn and his eyes landed squarely on Sal.

"This must be the new guy."

Sal turned himself partially around, hoping the cop might not remember him. His beard had grown out, and he was wearing his custodian's coverall. But Hogan's eyes flared in recognition.

"Jersey! You working here now?"

Sal nodded. He realized another worry was his lip from Will's nip and slap. It had scabbed over and healed a bit, but it was visible. He didn't need Hogan asking about it. Sal covered his lower mouth with his hand, playing like he was idly scratching his chin.

"Ain't that something! I thought you said you were only in town to buy a car."

Sal said nothing. Why'd the cop have to mention that lie in front of Will?

"Well, all right. Glad you're staying in town. Hey, did you end up buying that car?"

"No."

"How come?"

"Turned out the guy had another buyer. But I'm saving up to get something even better."

Will rang up the register with a loud churn and bell. Hogan's attention snapped back to him.

"Ain't that something, Will?"

Will pushed the cop's bagged muffin toward him. "What's something? We needed to hire a handyman. He needed a job. That kind of thing happens every day."

Hogan rustled out his wallet. "Happens every day. I s'pose you're right." He handed Will three dollar bills. "Now don't forget to tell George what I said. He's coming with me to that bar."

"Sure thing."

The cop took his bag and headed to the door. Along the way, he passed a long glance over Sal.

"I never caught your name, buddy."

"Sal."

Hogan smiled for some stupid reason. "Nice to see you, Sal. Sally-boy! You can call me Danny. I'll be seeing you around."

THAT WASN'T THE end of the strangeness that day. While Sal was digging into a patty melt at the counter during his lunch break, he heard George yelling at someone in the back office. Sal hadn't noticed that the bossman had come down from his room. Will was the only person who could be back there. Sal pricked up his ears. He didn't like the idea of George laying into Will. Regardless of how Will treated Sal, the kid worked hard. Though was it yelling? George could make a phone call to the gas company sound like a homicide.

All at once, George stomped into the diner with his shirt-clad belly hanging over his belted, pleated slacks. He came straight around the counter, poured himself a cup of coffee, and took a couple of moody sips, oblivious to Sal. Now Sal wished he'd made himself scarce before George walked in. After that nosy conversation with Hogan, he wasn't eager to get tripped up by the boss-man's questions and end up on George's bad side.

Inevitably, George noticed him at the counter. He brightened with a smile.

"There's our all-star janitor." He waddled over with his cup of coffee and parked himself across the counter. "How's it going?"

"Doin' great, boss. How are you?"

"I can't complain." He picked inside his ear and wiped it on his pants. "One piece of advice for you: don't get old. I got a doctor telling me I got hypertension, and I need to lose weight." He rubbed his bulging midsection. "He says I shouldn't be drinking coffee or eating salty foods. But what the hell do these doctors know?"

Sal shook his head. "Everybody's got a racket."

George fixed on him knowingly. "That's right. They've got to say something's wrong with you to keep you coming back." He waved his fleshy hand. "In the old country, people live to a hundred years without ever seeing a doctor."

Sal didn't disagree, generally. Though the bossman looked like a walking heart attack. Fat and hyper.

George looked down at Sal's pack of Camels. "S'pose I could buy one of those off you? Will's been hiding my packs. Thinks he's doing me a favor." He fished out a dollar bill from a wad of cash in his pants pocket and placed it on the counter. Sal handed his pack to George, and when he perched a cig in his lips, Sal lit him up with his Zippo.

The boss took a deep drag and exhaled, blissfully. "My doctor says I can't be smoking these either, but what can you do? Life isn't worth living without enjoying it." He frowned thoughtfully. "A smoke now and then. A drink when you feel like it. It's all about moderation. This President Carter wants us believing we're gonna get cancer from breathing the air, and meanwhile it's the inflation that's gonna kill us."

He looked at Sal for some response, but Sal had none. Sal

didn't know anything about politics. He liked George's attitude, though. George was hard not to like. He wasn't high and mighty about owning the place, and he didn't make Sal feel lesser because he mopped the floors and took out the trash. It was a strange position to be in, getting chummy with George when he was hoping to get cozy with his kept boy, if that's what Will was to him. He lit up a cigarette to join George in a smoke.

"You been doing good work," George said. "The place never looked better."

Sal tapped his cig and put on a scoff. "I just been pulling my weight, boss."

George wagged his finger at Sal. "I could tell you have a good work ethic. You come to my place of business, order food and present yourself properly for a job. That's respect. You don't see that every day from the younger generation."

"Kind of you to say."

George glanced back at the office and spoke a little quieter. "I hope Will hasn't been working you too hard."

"Oh, no sir. I don't mind the hard work. I take my marching orders 'cause I know my place."

George took a drag, puffed out a little cloud of smoke, and he glanced twice at something on Sal's face. "How'd you get that busted lip?" He grinned playfully. "Don't tell me you've been getting into trouble over at Paddy's bar down the street."

Sal had forgotten to cover his scab. He felt a blush prickling up on his cheeks. "Oh, no. I ain't the fighting type. Just took a fall when I was taking garbage bags out to the dumpster. Y'know, it's kinda dark back there."

George grimaced. "That's another thing Will's on my case about. These neighborhood delinquents broke the lamp back there. It's not cheap to replace, so I've been putting it off. I'm sorry, Sal."

"Ain't no big deal."

"How 'bout I make it up to you? You're staff now, and I consider my staff my family. How'd you like to come over for dinner?" He didn't wait for Sal to respond. "I cook on Sundays, and we can play cards after. I'll teach you pinochle. We can play a three-handed game with Will."

Sal's first thought was that was a bad idea. Sitting through a night with George and Will together? But on the other hand, it was an opportunity to scope out their relationship. Anyway, George probably wouldn't take no for an answer, so Sal said that'd be swell. George told him to come over to his room at eight, and he promised to have beer and ouzo. Then he went to the cash register, pulled out bills, and gave Sal his week's pay on the spot, two days early. Sal was liking George more and more. The bossman said he had some papers to file with his bank, and he left out.

Sal went about his routine, though that conversation had him thinking. George liked Sal. He couldn't have a clue about what happened with Will. He'd fucking invited him over for dinner. Did Will have a part in that invitation? That could be the way Will wanted to play things, making sure his old man had no suspicions before letting Sal in. Sal was even more eager to talk to the kid in private. When he finished breaking down boxes to put in the dumpster, he cleaned up in the bathroom, checked his teeth, and went to look for the kid.

Will wasn't at the front desk or in his office as Sal had hoped. Sal didn't want to ask Eddie if he'd seen him and draw attention to what he might be up to, and then Sal remembered overhearing that Loretta had taken the afternoon off because one of her kids was sick. That meant Will had no one to do the laundry. Keeping a lookout for prying eyes, Sal wandered over to the basement, where they had an industrial washer and dryer.

The basement door was open. The machines thrummed and whirred. Sal took the steps slowly and deliberately. It was a dank, dark place with bare, chipped paint walls and a concrete floor. The old wooden staircase didn't have a railing, and in the dim light, a person could break their neck coming down. The basement only had a single lightbulb strung up on the ceiling by the laundry equipment.

When he got to the bottom of the stairs, Sal spotted Will over by the machines. He was folding towels on a steel worktable with his shirt unbuttoned from the heat and not looking too happy about it. With all the noise from the washer and dryer, he hadn't noticed Sal coming down. That got Sal feeling flirty and mischievous. He watched Will's bowed head as he crept up on him, moving even slower when he reached the pool of light from the overhead fixture. The kid was crazy hot in that open shirt. His smooth, lean torso glistened with sweat down to his cute little navel.

Will didn't look up until Sal was straight across from him at the laundry table. He shuddered, threw down the towel he was folding, and glared at Sal like he was bullying away a wild animal.

Sal swallowed down his amusement. "I didn't mean to scare you."

"What do you want, Sal?"

"I heard Loretta had to leave early. Thought I'd see if you could use some help."

Will pulled the sides of his shirt together, scooped up a towel and went back to folding. "I've got it covered." He looked at Sal sharply. "You have other work to do."

"Just thought I'd see. I'm only lookin' to be helpful 'round here." Sal remembered something and eyed Will with a smirk. "I also wanted to say, I appreciate it. Y'know, you not sayin' nothin' to George."

"Maybe I haven't gotten around to it."

Sal was pretty sure Will was full of shit. He'd had a week to talk to George if he wanted to get Sal fired. Will was also being shy about exposing his body, and guys didn't act that way unless they got a little flustered in proximity to other men. Sal edged around the table. He'd finally gotten the chance try to seduce the kid again, and it was fucking irresistible.

"Maybe you got other reasons. You think 'bout what I said?"

Will looked at him funny. "To *what* you said?"

Sal gazed at the kid smolderingly and put his hand on his crotch.

Will's face darkened, and he bowed his head. "You're disgusting."

Sal stood taller and widened his shoulders. "What's the problem? That fat old Greek got you turned out for his wrinkled dick?"

Will stared back at him with some heat. "I gave you one chance to stop bothering me. You either fuck off now or you're walking out of here and never coming back."

"That's funny. 'Cause George invited me to join youse two for Sunday dinner. On account of what a good job I'm doing."

Will said nothing.

"Now I'm thinkin' you had somethin' to do with that. Seeing as you put in a good word for me before."

"You're dreaming. And I don't need George's permission to get rid of you."

That bite of his got to Sal. He clawed his fingers through his hair. "It ain't that serious, is it? We messed around a little. Nobody needs to know. I'm just tryin' to get you to give me the time of day."

Will eyed Sal mockingly. "That's what you're trying to do? How'd you end up in Beacon? You came here looking to buy a car? You didn't mention that BS story before."

"Baby, soon as I seen you behind the counter that day, I only wanted to get to know you. You think I like workin' for peanuts? I was pullin' big money in New York. I took the job because of you."

Will snorted in amusement. "I'm not stupid. You've been lying since you walked in the door. George doesn't see it, but I do."

"I had to tell Hogan somethin'. Cops ain't fans of strangers showin' up in town for no reason."

"So, what's your reason?"

Sal grimaced and stepped fully around the laundry table to try to explain.

"You don't have to come any closer."

Sal stopped in his tracks and drew a breath. He wasn't trying to frighten the kid. Why couldn't he lighten up? "Look, I got into a situation in the city. That's all. I ain't hustlin' nobody. Ain't I been puttin' in the work? I done everything you asked me to do, and that ain't 'cause I get a kick out of bein' treated like garbage."

"What kind of situation?"

Sal felt like he was taking lashes from a whip. He hesitated to say anything. If he spun a story, Will wasn't going to buy it. If he was honest, he'd be giving the kid more reason to dismiss him as a sketchy loser. In the end, Sal caved. The sad truth was, he didn't have anybody else to tell his troubles. He hadn't realized until that moment how much he needed to. So Sal told Will what happened with Joey, making himself out as best as he could.

"I made some bad decisions, but baby, don't you see? When I stepped off that train, I wasn't expectin' nothin'. Then I walked into your diner and met you. That's fate, don't you think?"

A wry gleam spread across Will's face. "And maybe if you'd made one stop further, you'd be putting it on the cashier at the New Hamburg luncheonette."

"That ain't true. You're somethin' special."

"You're something, too. How long before your mafia friends come up here looking for you?"

One thing worked from Sal laying bare the truth. Will's posture loosened some. Sal eased up closer. He was like a moth to a flame, dying for the heaven of being close to the kid.

"They ain't gonna waste their time lookin' for me. It was just some shit my old man got into."

"Aren't you a little old to have an *old man*?"

Sal's face flushed. "Ain't you?"

Will drew back from him. "You don't know anything about me."

Neither one spoke for a moment. Will skirted Sal's gaze, but he didn't look like he was going to belt Sal or make a break for the door. Sal pressed up closer. "What I got to know, Beautiful?"

Will shifted away from him. "Come off it, Sal. I don't get personal with the staff."

Sal clasped his arm. "You and George got rooms right next to each other. I ain't seen lights on at your place since I got here. People s'posed to believe youse two only got a business relationship?" He ran his hand down Will's neck and gently took his chain link necklace in his fingers like it was a delicate extension of him. "A kid who looks like he oughta be on pin-up posters living with a bachelor twice his age?"

Will forced Sal's hand away. "Pin-up posters? Where do you come up with that shit?"

"You don't know you're beautiful? Hogan knows it. George knows—"

"Cool it, Sal."

Sal was all warmed up and not capable of cooling it. He clasped Will's bottom and gazed into his eyes. Will shook him off again.

Indignantly, Sal stepped back. He gestured with his hands. "You got all this going on, and George is the only one who gets to have it?"

"It's not like that, all right?" Will glanced away, looking bothered. "If you really want to know, George adopted me."

That threw Sal off for a minute. Then he pieced things together, and it made some sense. He'd met old queens who'd adopted younger lovers. They did it to disguise their relationship so they could live together without people knowing they were queer. Back when he was tricking at Haymarket, Sal had gone home with couples like that a few times over the years. He remembered George's invitation to play cards. Was that what George was looking for? Sal hoped not. He wanted Will all to himself.

"That make George your keeper?" Sal drew close and gently brushed the side of Will's golden hair. "If you're grifting the boss-man, it ain't no kind of problem for me. I just want a chance to show I'm better for you."

Will gave him a wise look. "I'm not grifting anyone, and I don't need a janitor trying to hump my leg."

Sal grabbed Will by the jaw and got into his face. "Why you gotta be so mean to me?"

Will tried to wrest Sal's hand away and bit Sal's index finger hard. Sal yelped and shook his injured hand. His temperature spiked. In a blink, he went at Will again and wrangled him around until he got a lock around Will's arm and shoulder. Sealed against the kid's back, he dug his free hand down Will's trousers and found his delicious stuff. Sal pried open Will's belt and shoved his pants and briefs down his legs so he could get to him better.

Will fought against Sal's grip, but for all his fronting, he was as hard as a rock. Once Sal got a firm hold on him with his thumb brushing his slippery slit, the kid arched his back, leaning into Sal's embrace. Sal spat on his hand. He had the kid trapped and feverish from what he was doing to him. It was the hottest thing Sal had ever experienced. Whatever the kid's relationship with George was, he couldn't have made it with a guy he really wanted to be with in a long time.

He nuzzled against the side of Will's awestruck face. Will's lips parted, and he huffed out pressured breaths. Then he whimpered, and he let loose in hot milky jets. Sal gaped in wonder. His hips strained to feel the friction of Will's bottom, and he quickly seized up and came in his pants.

Both men breathed raggedly. Sal relaxed his hold on Will and pivoted around, angling for a kiss. Will ducked away from him. With his back turned to Sal, he pulled up his pants and straightened himself out.

"Go. We can't be doing this. And you should be upstairs helping Eddie get the place ready for dinner."

Sal spotted a hand towel in Will's laundry basket, grabbed it and wiped his hand. He couldn't believe he was getting the shove after what they'd done. "S'pose we could spend some time together? After George goes to bed, or somethin' like that?"

Will ignored him and went to the utility sink to splash some water on his face.

"I told you, I ain't lookin' to get you in trouble." Sal stepped over. "I like you, baby. I really like you. You sayin' you ain't got time for me?"

Will swung toward him. "This is never happening again. Get your ass up to the kitchen and do your job. You got me?"

Sal felt like breaking the kid's face. But he ate his pride and strolled upstairs to change his underwear in his room.

5

SAL KEPT HIS shit together for the next two days, if only barely. In the kitchen, he heaved a twenty-pound bag of ice into the sink with such force, Eddie jumped and soldered his gaze to his work at the chopping board. Refilling the toilet paper dispenser in the men's room, Sal slammed shut the side so hard, he reinjured the finger Will had bitten. Sal held down a scream, but when he found he had jammed the damn dispenser, he gave the stall wall a body slam that warped the steel. He strode over to the utility room at the far side of the motel and locked the door behind him. There, he let loose with a curse-filled holler and smashed an old wood stool to pieces.

What the fuck did he have to do for Will to show him some respect? He'd told the kid how he felt about him, and the kid still treated him like scum. Sal didn't say those things to just anybody. Who did Will think he was, acting like he was so far above him? Maybe Sal didn't have his life set up like Will did, but Sal was working on it. He'd been busting his balls for two weeks to show Will he was on the level.

In the troughs of those waves of anger, the maddening thing was, Sal was scalded by tactile memories of what they'd done. His body ached for Will. He wanted to trap him in his arms and make him come again. He'd had a taste of heaven, and now his gut was hungry for more. Sal tried to distract himself with all the grunt work he had to do around the motor lodge, but he couldn't get the kid off his brain.

Saturday night, while Will and Eddie were occupied with the dinner crowd, he skulked back to the laundry room and retrieved the hand towel he had cleaned up with from the trash bin. He huffed Will's dried spunk, dropped his pants and briefs, and rubbed the towel between his legs.

Fantasies exploded in his brain, and he nearly lost his footing. Hunched in a corner, with one hand braced against the wall, he shuttered his eyes and throttled himself relentlessly. A headrush blinded him, and Sal ejaculated into the wadded lightweight terrycloth.

He awakened cold and alone in the dank laundry room. His loneliness slashed at him like frostbite, and he was ashamed of himself. It was just something he'd had to do. Nobody had seen it, and it was Will's fault really for kissing him off after Sal had been so good to him. Sal's shame split into anger. He glanced around and hatched an idea. He found a nail and hammered the stiffened hand towel into a chink in the concrete wall. It was right at eye level between the dryer and the sink. Loretta would be off the next day, Sunday, and Will would be back down there to see it when he took the bedsheets for washing.

Sal didn't stress like this over guys. He wasn't even supposed to be stressing over the kid. Will was a ticket for grabbing George's cash, which Sal had earned as a matter of fact after working sixteen hours a day for two weeks for less than he could get on one good night at the Haymarket. It was Will's fucking cat and mouse game that had Sal going mental. Will wanted him, too. Sal's sweet talk turned him on, but Will was playing like he wasn't interested to make Sal work harder. The kid was twisted.

If Will wanted to play games, Sal could play games and show

him what twisted really was. Hell, he could tell George what they'd been up to and destroy the comfy situation Will had set up for himself. He could have the kid living on the street and see how he liked getting by on five-dollar blow jobs at trucker stops.

By Sunday, Sal cooled down some. A good night's sleep helped screw his head on straight. He was a New York hustler, and he could handle an upstate pretty boy who thought he was running the show. If Will truly didn't want anything to do with him, he would've sent him packing the first time Sal made a move on him. The kid got off from fucking with Sal, but that was going to change. Now Sal was having dinner at George's place. He was in the catbird's seat. He'd see what was really going on with Will and the bossman, and Will wouldn't be able to feed him bullshit no more. Sal would play it cool, gas up the old Greek, and get him talking.

Sal hiked over to the convenience store to pick up something nice to bring with him. That's what squares did on TV when they were invited over for dinner, though the only thing Sal could find was a plastic-wrapped box of pecan turtles left over from Easter. It would have to do. The cashier also had a little bottle of Aqua Velva aftershave behind the counter, so Sal shelled out two more dollars for that.

Back in his room, Sal washed up real good and ironed the best shirt he'd grabbed from Joey's place. It was a knit, short sleeve button down that Joey had bought Sal from a trendy shop on Bleecker Street. Sal was also lucky that in his rush, he'd packed a pair of designer jeans that fit well in all the right places. Sal pulled on his cowboy boots and went to his little bathroom mirror to study himself from all angles and get his hair looking just right. Satisfied he looked foxy, Sal left out for dinner with George and Will.

George met him at the door like they were long lost friends and ushered Sal inside. The bossman looked and smelled like he'd gotten an early start on the drinking he'd promised. He also got Sal thinking he'd overdressed. The guy was wearing a splattered kitchen apron over an undershirt, which showed off his bushy chest and shoulders. Sal held out his box of chocolates.

George lit up in delight. "You didn't have to. You're a class act, Sal." He took a close look at the box, eyeing the cartoon turtle in a top hat and tuxedo emblazoned on it. "These are the good ones," he said. "We can have them after dinner. C'mon. I'll give you the grand tour."

A pungent, strangely appetizing aroma saturated the apartment. George took Sal around, starting with the living room with its beat up foam sofa, wall cabinet with a TV and a record player, and dingy tile ceiling with a fan that whirled precariously from exposed electrical cables. The place had brown plywood paneling and forgettable landscape paintings, same as the motel rooms. Ribbed, tan wall-to-wall carpeting. George pointed out a hallway to the bathroom and bedroom.

"I'll have to show you those later. Will wanted to take a bath, and he must've fallen asleep on the bed. He says his tub has a slow drain."

Sal's heart dropped a little. Will used the guy's bath, napped on his bed, and probably slept over every night. Sal had guessed as much, but part of him had been hoping to be proven wrong.

"Hey Will," George called out. "Sal's here. How 'bout joining us?"

He waited a couple seconds, and then he waved his hand. "He'll be out." George led Sal over to a dining area with a wooden extension table set for three and four chrome and leather-padded chairs. He had the same cheap plates, silverware, and brown plastic glasses that they had in the diner.

The only things that were different were the navy placemats, blue and white striped cloth napkins, real ceramic salt and pepper shakers, and glass, stoppered jars with oil and vinegar. The big guy was proud of being Greek. He had a Greek flag hanging above family photos in ornate frames, and a china cabinet overcrowded with miniature faux marble statues, mostly featuring the male physique. His set of gold rimmed porcelain looked like it came from the old country.

George led Sal through a swinging door into a boiling hot and claustrophobic kitchen. White, metal cabinets boxed in the space, and it was cozy for two people. Four blue, enamel pots simmered on a grimy stove with a ventilation hood. Sal noticed a compact white and chrome refrigerator, and then George briskly drew him out to the dining area.

"You like lamb?"

Sal had never had it. It smelled raunchy and appealing at the same time. He gave George a nod.

"There's beans, potatoes, tzatziki, and taramasalata to go with it. Taramasalata is fish roe. You're going to love it."

Sal had never heard of fish roe, but he smiled politely. He complimented George on his "slick pad." Then George went on about shit he'd told Sal before. How he'd bought the motor lodge for a song back in 1959 and built it back up with his bare fucking hands.

George apologized about having to check on his cooking. He shouted toward the hallway, "Hey Will. How 'bout getting our guest a beer while I'm working on dinner?" About ten seconds passed, and nobody stirred. George turned to Sal with an aggravated frown. "I don't know why he's being moody. Has been all day. But he'll be out soon. Just make yourself comfortable." He pushed through the swinging door and left Sal on his own.

Sal puttered around, glancing semi-interestedly at George's family photos. He weighed the Greek figurines in his hand and eyed the porcelain set, wondering if it was really from the old country and worth something. Otherwise, the guy lived cheap for someone who owned multiple businesses. Maybe he was a lousy businessman. He didn't put much effort into his motor lodge, and Sal remembered Will saying something about that. He noticed a big glass ashtray on the coffee table in the adjoining living room. It looked like three butts were stubbed out in it.

"You mind if I have a smoke?" he called out to George.

"Sure. Make yourself at home."

Sal took out his soft pack of Camels that he'd rolled up in his shirt sleeve, pried out a cig to perch between his lips, and flicked his lighter to spark it up. He stepped around to check out George's record collection in the living room cabinet. No surprises. It was squaresville. Greek folk music and a whole lot of Perry Como. Sal glanced down the hallway. He wondered if he could get away with taking a peek into the bedroom. He felt like he needed to see Will laying on George's bed with his own eyes to truly believe it, no matter how horrible it was to see. George had started singing while he cooked. Some old-time ditty Sal didn't recognize at first. Whatever it was, the bossman was belting away like he'd sold out Carnegie Hall. Sal stepped closer to the hallway.

It was dark, but he could make out two closed doors. A bathroom and a bedroom. Sal's heartbeat quickened. If he was going to spy on Will, he had to be smooth so nobody noticed. Sal glanced back toward the kitchen and raised his voice when the old guy was between bars of his performance.

"Hey George, you mind if I use your john?"

"Of course not. The first door on the right."

George went back to singing, and Sal eased into snooping. He didn't have the nerve quite yet to open that bedroom door, so he headed to the bathroom to see if there was evidence that Will was sleeping with the bossman. The door was closed. Sal rapped lightly on it in case Will was in there. The bathroom sounded like it was still inside, though with George's awful singing, it was hard to hear.

"*When the red, red robin comes bob, bob, bobbing along…*"

Sal tried the doorknob. It turned. No lock. He pushed open the door. It was a tiny bathroom with the toilet and sink cabinet crammed together and a bathtub/shower on the other side. Empty.

He stepped inside. It didn't look or smell like anyone had taken a bath there recently. Sal shut the door behind him and peeled back the vinyl shower curtain. The tub was dry as a bone. He turned to the sink. It didn't look like it had been used recently, either. A single blue toothbrush stood in a holder next to one of the motel's cakes of soap. The towel rack had one towel, and it wasn't damp.

Sal was confused. Why had George lied about Will taking a bath? Was he lying about Will even being there? Was George's invitation a set-up to confront Sal about hitting on Will? Sal's lungs constricted. Now he really needed to know if Will was in the bedroom. He pressed his ear to the adjoining wall, straining to hear some kind of sound from that room. Heat from his cigarette nipped his finger. Sal carefully left the bathroom to ash his cig back at the coffee table. He needed to think things out.

If Will was in that bedroom, looking in on him could go sideways. But Sal had to know what was going on. Will didn't have a towel or his own toothbrush or razor in the place. That stood to reason to an extent if the two didn't want people knowing they lived together, but Sal noticed other things that got him paranoid. The brown butts in the ashtray. They were Marlboro Reds, which George smoked. Will smoked Kents, which had white filters. The old sofa cushion had a single deep indentation where George must've been sitting. Will was a neat freak. He would've fluffed that up, and he wouldn't have stood for all the dust on the TV cabinet.

It felt like the floor beneath Sal was spinning. George knew what had happened with Sal and Will. This dinner was an ambush. He turned back to the hallway. If George would give his awful singing a rest, Sal could hear any signs of life behind the bedroom door. Had George confronted Will? There'd been that heated conversation Sal overheard the other morning, and right after, George gave Sal the invitation. Was he acting like Will was in the bedroom to keep Sal there? Had he done something to Will? Sal recognized that old song all at once, and maybe he was losing it, but the words beneath the jolly melody creeped him out, like it was some kind of threat.

"Wake up, wake up, you sleepy head,
Get out, get out of bed,
Cheer up, cheer up, the sun is red.
Live, love, laugh and be happy."

The bedroom door swung open, and Sal's heart jumped out of his chest. Will traipsed out from the room. He was barefoot in a baseball shirt and a snug pair of striped racing shorts. Sal tried to hide that he'd given him a scare. His face was frozen in a grin. The kid walked right past him like Sal wasn't there and pushed through the door to the kitchen. No hello or even a look. Sal obliterated his cigarette in the ashtray with a dozen angry stubs.

Not long after, Will came out of the kitchen with three cans of Old Milwaukee, and George followed with a steaming platter of stewed meat, which he placed in the middle of the table. The two guys alternated bringing dishes to the table. Sal asked if they needed help, and George scowled and told him to take a seat. In a blink, they were all sitting down for the biggest feast Sal had seen in his life.

George was cheerfully humming a song, and Will was being Will. Thus, Sal considered he'd been freaking out for no reason. George had lied about Will taking a bath. It was as simple as that. They were just two dudes who didn't want people knowing their business. Sal really needed to loosen up. It wasn't nice that he'd had his suspicions confirmed, but meanwhile, George had put together an enormous dinner. Sal hadn't had a home-cooked meal since he was maybe five years old. His mother stopped doing that kind of thing after his pops walked out.

George pointed out this and that and heaped Sal's plate with everything. Sal waited to eat until the guys had served themselves. George scooped up big portions for himself while Will forked two potato slices onto his plate and a few green beans.

"That's all you're gonna eat?" George said.

"I'm going vegetarian. I told you that."

George shrugged. "Sal, would you like some whiskey?"

Sal raised his beer can. "I'm good with this."

George looked at Will, authoritatively. "I'll have some whiskey."

Will shoved back his chair with a screech against the floor tiles. He stood, turned around and yanked a two-liter bottle of Wild Turkey and a glass tumbler from the bottom drawer of the china cabinet.

George glanced at Sal with lighthearted humor. "A vegetarian. What'll they think of next?"

Sal watched Will slosh a good three fingers of liquor into the tumbler and plop the bottle next to George. He couldn't pry his eyes away from Will as he sat down, crossed one gorgeous leg over the other, stabbed a potato slice on his fork, and nibbled at it sideways. Even when he was being an asshole, he was goddamn adorable. Sal wished Will would look his way while George was babbling about vegetarianism. Had Will seen the hand towel in the laundry room? Was he ticked about it? Sal wanted to get the kid to crack a smile.

"It's healthy. I heard," he told George.

"Meat's healthy." George speared a big chunk of lamb with his fork and opened wide like he was proving the point. The fat old Greek chewed with his mouth open. Midchew, he turned to Sal. "It's always the fads, isn't it? If you ask me, this younger generation is too caught up with the latest thing. Next, he'll be calling himself one of them Hairy Krishnas."

"*Hare* Krishnas," Will corrected.

George swiped his mouth with his napkin. "I call 'em Hairy Krishnas, and if I wanna call 'em Hairy Krishnas, I'll call 'em Hairy Krishnas."

Will snorted. "Go ahead. You'll just sound ignorant."

"I'll tell you what ignorant is. Men wearing skirts and dancing around like Tinkerbells." He smirked to Sal. "Men should act like men, don't you think?"

"At least they've got a philosophy," Will said. "When's the last time you thought about the meaning of life?"

"The meaning of life," George grumbled. "The only people who think about that stuff are lazy bums with too much time on their hands." He fed himself another mouthful. "If *that's* the meaning of life, I'll pass. What I'm saying is all these fads are getting out of hand."

"What would you know about fads? You drive a 1967 Oldsmobile," Will said.

A tense silence passed. Sal tried to lighten the mood. "This is one hell of a spread, George. You always been a cook?"

"He takes after his mother," Will said.

"I learned a few things in the kitchen from my mother," George said. "But where I really learned to cook was my uncle's restaurant."

Will scoffed. "His greasy spoon."

George shot a frosty glance at Will. "It was a diner with a full menu of Greek specialties."

"Yeah, whatever." Will went back to nibbling at his potato.

Sal took a gulp of his beer and tried out the food, a little timidly at first. Normally, he didn't go for anything that looked too exotic, but the lamb was tasty, and the sides of potatoes, yogurt dips, and fresh tomato and cucumber salad were really good as well. Strange as the company was, Sal felt special being treated to a meal George had made himself. While they ate, George explained the makings of each dish and poured himself another generous helping of whiskey.

Will tented one leg on his seat and fired up a Kent. He wasn't a drinker like George. He was nursing his can of beer, looking bored. Sal peeked at Will's naked shin and calf. His legs had fine, curled hairs that were so light you had to look close to see them. A little triangle of his inner thigh was exposed, leading into the shadow of his shorts leg.

Sal pulled his eyes away and took a long swallow of his beer. He couldn't be leering at the kid while George was sitting a foot away. When Sal next looked across the table, Will stared back at him like he knew what Sal was up to. Then he curled his mouth ever so slightly in amusement.

George pushed more food on Sal, and after a second helping of lamb and potatoes, Sal was full to bursting and had to politely beg George off. George told Will to clear the table. A funny relationship they had. Will hopped to it, no matter whatever grudge hung between them. George was tipsy and eager to play cards. He bumbled over to the cabinet and retrieved a well-used deck from the top drawer. He tossed the deck on the table and fished out a cigar box.

"I got these Cubans from a friend up in Albany." George opened the box to offer one to Sal.

Will came back from the kitchen and dropped another chilled can of Old Milwaukee in front of Sal. "How do you even know they're Cubans?'" he said.

"'Cause he told me, and it says so right here on the box."

Will unwrapped an orange Creamsicle he had brought along from the icebox, and he plopped down in his chair. "Ten to one you paid too much."

George's face ticked, but he didn't say anything. Sal thanked George but told him cigars weren't his thing. He lit up a smoke instead and caught Will looking at him again while he munched on his two-sticked Creamsicle. Meanwhile George carved off one end of a cigar, perched it between his mustached lips, and stoked it up in a fog of cloying tobacco smoke. He set it down in a tin ashtray, and made a flashy show of shuffling the cards.

George explained the rules of pinochle to Sal. It mostly went over Sal's head. He didn't know much about cards, and he was distracted by Will's behavior. Now it was like the kid was taunting him. He folded his arms behind his chair and smirked at Sal while George wasn't looking. Sal polished off his first beer and cracked open the one Will brought him. The kid was pleased with himself, and Sal wanted to know why. He was fucking dazzling in that baseball shirt. With his arms stretched out behind him, it rode up his little tummy.

They tried out a round, and it was comical. Sal kept screwing up his play, and George collected the cards and restarted the game four times before giving up. He went to the dining cabinet and brought out a bottle of ouzo and three shot glasses. He filled them and pushed the glasses toward Will and Sal.

"Lucky you're a good handyman," he told Sal. "You're terrible at cards."

"Sorry. I ain't never played before." Sal downed the shot of liquor, which tasted awful and scalded his throat.

George waved him off and threw back his shot. He turned to Will. "How about getting Sal another beer?"

Will stood up in a huff and went to the kitchen.

"My parents brought me to America when I was three years old," George said. "They didn't have a pot to piss in, but we always had cards. This was during the Depression. We lived in a two-room apartment in Astoria with another Greek family. My brother and I shared a mattress on the floor. Some nights we only had a scoop of rice apiece and a cup of broth from chicken bones. But we didn't know from different. Every night, we got together with the kids from the neighborhood and played Go Fish or Rummy. When the grown-ups were around, my baba used to break open his big jar of pennies, and we'd all play Thirty-One. We thought we were living like kings."

Sal drew on his cigarette while George tossed back another shot of ouzo. Will shoved through the kitchen door with two more beers. He set down one for Sal and took the other to his seat. "Is George telling stories about his fascinating family history?"

"They're not for you. They're for Sal." George pulled out a handkerchief from his pants pocket and wiped his sweaty brow. "When we first came to America, the only job my baba could get was washing taxicabs. He made two dollars a week! You were lucky to even get a job like that back then. He sent me and my brother Teddy to school, and when we were old enough, a friend of the family, he owned a newspaper stand on Ditmars Boulevard, and he paid us a penny for every *Evening Sun* we could sell. That's what we did every day after school." He took a tug of his cigar and exhaled a toxic breath. "I've been working since I was eleven years old, Sal. I got a feeling you know what that's like. Eventually, my baba saved up the money to rent a cab, you know, getting fares himself, and we moved into our own two room apartment. We thought it was a palace."

Sal knew about working at a young age, though not in the same occupations the bossman was talking about. He didn't mind hearing about his past. George came from nothing, just like Sal, and sure, he was a windbag, but Sal respected that he'd made something of himself. Across the table, Will rolled his eyes.

"Like Teddy, I quit school at fourteen to bus tables at my uncle's restaurant. He had me helping out in the kitchen a few years later. Eleven o'clock at night till seven in the morning. It was a twenty-four-hour place. The cook was a big guy, fresh off the boat. He couldn't speak a lick of English, but he knew how to cook everything from a strip steak to moussaka and pastitsio and cheese blintzes. He let me work the grill for short orders. It was the best job of my life. I made cheeseburgers, omelets, pancakes, liver and onions. You name it."

George took a draw of his whiskey and set it down. "A few years later, my uncle told us he had to let us go. There was some squabble between my father and him. I'll never know what it was. Anyway, my brother Teddy was nineteen then, so he enlisted in the Navy. I was only seventeen. I got a job as a stockboy at a supermarket, thinking I'd join him when I was old enough."

Will snorted. "You? Joining the Navy? You wouldn't have passed the medical exam."

"I was in good shape back then," George said. "Every day, I unloaded trucks full of produce and crates of soda bottles." He took another big slug of liquor and fingered his cigar. "Anyway, I met a friend at that supermarket who convinced me to go with him upstate where they had work at a resort that came with room and board." He glanced at Sal. "He was an Italian fella like you."

"I ain't Italian," Sal said.

George stared at Sal and puffed out a cloud of cigar smoke. "I'm sorry. I assumed. What are you?"

"Irish and Romanian." Sal took a swig of his beer. "So far as I know. My pops named me Silviu. Silviu Minovichi. He shortened his family name to Minovich when he came over in the Forties, and people called me Sal since it's easier." He lit up another cigarette. "He never married my mom, and he took off when I was five. I heard he works in Atlantic City now, but I dunno for sure. Anyway, I quit school too to make money, so I know what you're talking about."

George glanced at Sal respectfully. "Everyone comes to America to make a better life. So, listen to this, I worked two years at that resort in the Catskills. It was one of them Jewish places that got wealthy families from the city. Hard work but good tips. One day, one of the guests, he was a stockbroker who liked me working as his caddy on the golf course, he tells me he's buying up properties upstate and turning a profit. He says if I can come up with five thousand dollars, he'll match it, and we'll go half and half on a house on Yankee Lake he's been eyeing. He says we just need to fix it up, and we can sell it for twice the price. I saved every dollar from my paycheck and tips for two summers, and by my second September, I had that five thousand dollars."

Will broke in, ungraciously. "Here we go again with the ancient history lesson."

George went on, undeterred. "I took the ten thou I got from the deal and bought a gas station in Roscoe that was going out of business. I bought new equipment, put up one of them neon signs, gave it a new coat of paint and sold it for twenty-two thou. That's America, Sal. You work hard and make good investments, and you can go from being a poor man to a rich one. I now own an apartment building in Kingston, a block of commercial businesses in Poughkeepsie, and a laundromat in Newburgh in addition to this motor lodge."

"And you're still too cheap to get a power washer," Will said.

Sal watched Will toss back his beer. The kid sure liked to ride his old man.

"You always gotta get a wisecrack in, don't you?" George said.

"It's not a wisecrack. It's the facts. You're cheap."

"I'll get that power washer once that deal goes through in Sarasota Springs." George glanced at Sal chummily. "This one's always wanting to turn the place into the Taj Mahal."

"No one's ever going to mistake this dump for the Taj Mahal," Will said.

"Who needs a Taj Mahal? What people want is an affordable stay-over on their way to Lake George or New England."

"If we had a working ice machine and the outside wasn't marked up with graffiti, they might tell their friends about the place and we'd actually bring in some business."

Sal took a gulp of beer. He'd been waiting to ask a question when the two weren't having a go at each other, but it looked like they'd be doing that all night. Frankly, it was entertaining, but while there was a lull in the action, Sal broke in. "So, how'd the two of you meet?" He glanced back and forth between his companions. Will didn't look eager to say. Eventually, George filled in.

"Will was working at a soda shop in Peekskill. I used to stop by the place when I had a property down there. Must've been 1972."

"It was a summer job," Will said. "I was eighteen years old."

George snickered. "Yes. Who could imagine *you* working as a soda jerk when it's obvious you're cut out for bigger things?" He took a puff of his cigar and glanced at Sal. "What happened was, I wanted to do a good deed after that Jewish businessman helped me out." He looked up to the ceiling. "God rest his soul." George came back to Sal. "So, I told Will, if he could show me he was serious and had a good work ethic, I'd take him on as a partner in my real estate enterprises."

Sal had a wisecrack of his own to make, but he kept it to himself.

"Your 'real estate enterprises,'" Will repeated with disdain. "You're a slumlord."

George waved him off. Then his glazed face lit up like he'd struck on a brilliant idea. "How 'bout some music? What do you like, Sal?"

Sal had seen his record collection. All he could do was frown impartially.

"I'll introduce you to some music from the old country." George stumbled over to the living room where he had a turntable in the cabinet. That walk showed he was pretty soused. After some starts and stops getting a record on the player and placing the needle, a strain of Greek guitar and ululating vocals hailed from the speakers.

Sal watched Will roll his eyes again and take a sour draw of his beer. Meanwhile, George raised his hands and took some swaying steps to the folksy beat. He looked like an overgrown hen dancing the hora.

"You dance, Sal?" George said.

"I don't know how to dance like that."

George made it over to his seat and poured himself more whiskey. "It's important for a man to know his culture. You know any of your father's Romanian traditions?"

Sal smiled to himself. "If knocking up a sixteen-year-old and running out on her and her kid is a Romanian tradition, I ain't done that one yet. Like I told you, my dad was out of my life before I could tie my shoes by myself."

"Oh. Well. You said you were Irish too." While George threw back more whiskey and shared his opinions about the Irish, Sal stretched his foot under the table to touch Will's. Will let him do it for a minute, and then he kicked Sal's foot away. That brought a goofy grin to Sal's face. Maybe he was a little tipsy. He hadn't had a drink in over two weeks. The kid was so uptight.

"The only things I learned from my ma is that beer can be a breakfast food, and there's no dishonor in giving a man a sucker punch, now and then," Sal told George.

George laughed, which turned into a loud cough. His eyes were shrinking, and he was tearing up from the booze. "I like you, Sal. You're funny." He fumbled for his cigar, which had burned out in the ashtray. He took a sloppy draw on it, to no avail, and then he fumbled around for his box of matches to relight it.

Will looked at George irascibly. "We gotta listen to this record again?"

George gestured vaguely. "Change it, if you want."

Will got up to go over to the stereo. Sal studied George. His shoulders were slumped, and his eyes were unfocused under heavy lids.

"You work hard, Sal, and there's nothing you can't have," he slurred. "It don't matter that you're a bastard. It don't matter where you come from." He waved his hand while his head bobbed drunkenly. "We live in America," he said with a hiccup. "The land of opportunity."

Sal nodded. Not that the big guy was sober enough to notice. George was propping his head up with his hand, and his elbow slipped out from under him. He briefly bowed over the table, and then he wobbled to an upright position in his seat.

Music came on again. The Eagles. The kid had good taste. *Hotel California*. Sal grinned to himself. Was the kid also making a statement?

You can check in any time you like, but you can never leave.

Will crossed his arms behind his head and swayed around to the winding refrain of electric guitar. He looked like he was in his own world, but he was giving Sal another glimpse of his bare tummy and the snugness of his shorts between his legs and around the back as he took slow rotating steps in the space between the TV cabinet and the coffee table. When Sal's glance returned to George, the big guy was tipped back in his chair with his eyelids shuttered. Will caught sight of it and stomped back to the table.

"Jesus. It's not even eleven o'clock." He raised his voice. "George. *George*. You've got a guest."

George made a fussy face and then he sloughed back in his

seat, snoring. Will collected empty cans of beer from the table and carted them into the kitchen. Sal hadn't expected the night to turn out like this. The bossman was lights out. He felt a little bad for the chump, though in his present state, he'd opened up some possibilities. Sal took another gulp of beer. He watched George closely just in case he wasn't as knocked out as he seemed.

Will came out from the kitchen, drying his hands with a kitchen towel. "That's card night. Time for you to go."

"It's early, ain't it? You said so yourself."

"In case you hadn't noticed, George drank himself to sleep. As usual."

Sal glanced at George and looked up at Will hopefully. "I can give you a hand moving him to the bedroom."

"He passes out like this all the time. I'm not his nursing aide." Will crossed his arms in front of him.

Sal put on a sexy smile. "I like this album. How 'bout you stay up with me till it finishes?"

"I've gotta clean up the kitchen." Will yawned. "Then I'm going to bed. But I can leave the stereo on if you want to listen. Knock yourself out."

He pushed into the kitchen, leaving Sal at the table with George, who was really sawing logs. Blue-balled once again by Will. If he had a shred of self-respect, he wouldn't take this shit from the kid. But the shameful truth was he was a goddamn fish on a hook, and he couldn't end the night flopping around for air. Sal got up from his chair very quietly and waved a hand in front of George's face to confirm he really was lights out. Then he snuck into the kitchen.

Will was working on a sinkful of plates and bowls, and he had a half dozen pots and pans lined up on the counter to scrub. He didn't even look over to Sal at first. Sal's heart hovered in his throat. Did the kid really hate him? Was he *that* bad?

Finally, Will glanced at him. "You know George is right outside that swinging door."

"I just came in to talk to you."

"Oh yeah?"

Sal's gaze fixed on the kid's beautiful behind in his running shorts. He was speechless.

"I saw what you left for me in the laundry room."

Sal raised his eyes to him.

"It was fucking perverted." Will rinsed a plate, set it in the drying rack with a clang, and picked up another to scrub. "You wanna lose your job? George catches you doing that kind of shit, you're out on your ass."

Sal sidled over to him. "'S'pose I don't care? George is sleepin' through Christmas anyway." He looked up and down Will's body.

"I thought you just wanted to talk."

"I do. But it ain't so easy to make conversation when you're wearing those shorts."

He reached to grab Will's ass, but Will swung away too fast. Sal caught him by the arm. "Just tell me, why you with the old buzzard?"

Will ripped his arm away. "'Cause I don't have anything better."

"*I'm* better," Sal snarled. "You like George bossing you 'round and putting his greasy hands all over you?"

Will faced Sal, angrily. "What do you think? Would you like it?" He turned back to the dishes. "Don't worry. I'm not sticking around for long."

Sal pushed into the space in front of Will. "Then what 'bout me?" He clasped Will's shoulder, and he slid his hand along his shoulder blades. The kid's body was steamy from working in the overheated kitchen. "You got me crazy for you, beautiful."

"Yeah. You told me that before." Will elbowed Sal away. "Go home, Sal. I've got work to do here."

His attitude had softened, just a little. Sal pounced on that opportunity, getting both hands around the kid and pressing their mouths together in a hot, wet kiss. He nuzzled against Will's neck, tasting his sweat and kissing him there.

"Sal, we can't be doing this."

Sal didn't answer.

"George is right next door."

Sal locked his arms around Will to bring him even closer. "I got a room downstairs. All to ourselves. George ain't gonna know the difference."

Will held his hand up to Sal's chest. "Somebody could see. Besides, I've gotta clean up George's mess."

He wasn't pushing Sal away. In fact, there was something a little sensual about the way the kid's big warm palm lingered on his chest, right around his nipple. Sal wriggled his eyebrows, and then he dug his hand into Will's shorts and found him between the legs. *Christ*, he'd been dreaming about being in this position again since Friday. He couldn't even wait to get Will to his room. Sal maneuvered him against the sink and got down on his knees. He tugged down Will's shorts and briefs and took him in his mouth.

Will gasped in disbelief and fumbled to prop his hands on the counter. The sink overflowed with sudsy water. Sal was kneeling in a puddle, but he didn't notice until it soaked through the knees of his jeans. That got Sal working harder, punch-drunk on the thrill of having his way with the kid when at any minute the bossman could throw open the door and see what was going on. Will's hips writhed, and he breathed out an anguished curse. Sal held him captive and strangled out a second, third, and fourth tortured spew from Will. When he was satisfied the kid was drained, he wiped his mouth and stood.

"I bet George ain't that good to you."

Will said nothing while he caught his breath. Then he pulled up his shorts and briefs, turned off the sink, and thrust his hand into the water to clear the drain. When the water level went down, he took up washing the dishes again. Sal hovered behind him.

"You got nothing to say?"

Will kept doing what he was doing.

"Look. I'll help you clean up if that's what's got you all pissy."

Will set down his plate and faced Sal. "Why?"

"Why what?"

"Why are you trying to get with me so bad?"

Sal was briefly amused. "You that thick I gotta spell it out? You're primo. I can't stop thinking 'bout you." Will scoffed, which pissed Sal off. "You ain't never felt that way about a person?"

Will pushed past Sal to click on the noisy stove fan and pulled him over to the fridge, which was farthest from the door. "It's not going to work, Sal. Whatever it is you want. If we keep doing this, George is going to find out, and it's not going to be pretty for you and it's not going to be pretty for me."

Sal held his side. "I'll handle George. He gotta understand he ain't right for you. It's you and me, baby."

Will mildly shook his head. He looked like he was struggling with something. "I've got some say in that, don't I?"

"What you worried 'bout? Baby, you want out of here? So do I. George is passed out. We can leave right now. We grab some cash and go wherever we want."

"Right. I get it now." Will broke away from Sal.

"Get what?"

"You just want my help to rob George."

Sal raised his voice. "I didn't say that." He realized he'd spoken too loud. He tried to smooth things over, quietly. "All's I'm saying is, if you wanna cut loose from this guy, I'll help you."

"Yeah, I bet you're good at cutting people loose. Like your 'old man' in the city. Soon as you get George's cash, you gonna cut me loose too?"

Sal gripped Will by the shoulders. "What I gotta do to get through your head I ain't playin' you?" He snorted. "I'm fuckin' pouring my heart out, and you act like I'm some piece of shit."

Will shrugged Sal's hands away. "Take it easy." He rubbed his face. The kid looked like he was breaking down, which was miserable to see.

Sal drew up close to him again. "Baby, listen. I only wanna take care of you."

Will bowed his head. Sal took him in his arms, gently, and

then Will gripped the back of Sal's shirt. He was trembling, on the verge of tears.

Sal held him tight. "C'mon, baby. You ain't gotta be scared."

"I don't know what I'm supposed to do."

Sal crushed Will's body against his. The kid was making his heart bleed. Sal knew what it was like being trapped in a bad relationship, feeling like you had no place to go. He stroked the nape of Will's neck. "We gonna figure it out together. That's what I been tryin' to tell you. I ain't never gonna let nothin' bad happen to you."

6

THAT NIGHT, SAL helped Will clean the kitchen, and later, they shouldered the bossman to his bed, took off his shoes, and left him to sleep. After that, Will begged Sal to go home. He said he just wanted to take a bath and crash on the couch. He needed to sleep over to make sure George got up in the morning. George had a meeting with his lawyer that was really important. Something to do with buying a property up north, Will said.

Sal didn't push the issue. He could see Will was stressed out, and Sal was pretty exhausted himself. As Will was walking him to the door, Sal coaxed him into his arms once more, and they made out like teenagers against the living room wall before they said goodnight. Then Sal went down to his room. That Sunday dinner had been a whole lot more than he'd expected, but in the end, it hadn't been bad at all. Sal passed out for five glorious hours until his alarm went off, and he had to get the diner ready for opening.

Will was finally letting him in, and it was goddamn wonderful. Sal knew the score now. Will wanted out from under George. He was skittish about making that move and maybe too straightlaced to do his old man dirty. Sal didn't like the idea of stealing from the bossman, either. George had been nothing but good to him, but Will just needed to understand it was nothing personal. Everybody was on the make when it came down to it. You had to look out for yourself to get ahead. Otherwise, you were playing someone else's patsy. They wouldn't have to clean George out. They could just take a little nest egg for themselves, and with all his businesses, George would make up for that loss in no time. Sal needed to play things cool and wait for the right time to nudge Will in that direction.

When Will came down to the diner that morning, Sal acted like nothing had happened and everything was normal. Nobody paid much attention to a janitor anyway, which allowed Sal to study the place a little closer. If he and Will were going to pull one over on George, they had to get ahead of any complications.

Glancing around the diner, Sal wondered if other people knew about George and Will's relationship. They had some regular customers, old-timers mostly, but it was hard to figure any of those squares would have a clue. Lieutenant Hogan might. He didn't come by that morning, but he dropped in once or twice a week, and he was always asking about George. Then there was Eddie, the Portuguese cook.

Eddie had been working at the diner a lot longer than Sal had. His English was bad, but he wasn't blind. He'd probably picked up something funny going on with George and Will. With the language barrier and Eddie's straight-to-business work style, Sal could only take guesses at what was going on in the cook's head. George had mentioned Eddie had a wife and three kids. Maybe Eddie didn't care particularly about his employer's private life so long as he had a job. Work didn't come easy for guys who didn't speak English, especially in a small town.

George knew some Portuguese and chatted with Eddie whenever he passed by the kitchen. Their conversations always sounded friendly and playful. The bossman was like that with everyone, but now Sal was thinking he should be careful around the cook. Could be he felt some loyalty to George, and if he caught a whiff of Sal and Will being in cahoots, he'd go straight to the bossman.

Later that day, when Sal was fixing the number plate on one of the back rooms, he noticed George's sedan was gone. The bossman must've made it to his appointment with that lawyer. It was always good to know when the guy was off the premises. Anyway, Sal had plenty to do to keep himself out of trouble. He had to finish the flower beds and give cleaning off the graffiti in the back another try. The sun was out, and it had warmed up so it wasn't a bad day to do that outdoor work. Then Sal spotted Loretta just down the walk.

She was wearing a polka dot scarf over her big blond hair, and she was having a smoke outside a room she was cleaning. Sal had been working at the place for going on three weeks, and they saw each other every day, but they'd barely spoken. Sal gave her a wave, thinking he should break the ice and start feeling her out, too. Loretta was a quiet one like Eddie, but unlike the cook, she had a keen eye on goings-on.

To Sal's surprise, Loretta called out to him. Sal strolled over, curious to see what he could find out from her.

Loretta had school-aged kids, which meant she must've been in her thirties, but hard living, cheap make-up, and hair treatments had aged her. "How you making out 'round here?" she said in a smoker's gravelly voice. She offered Sal one of her Parliaments. Sal thanked her but said he had his own and pulled out a Camel from his shirt pocket. Loretta lit him up with a novelty lighter that had a picture of Niagara Falls. She noticed Sal glancing at it, and a quiet grin passed over her face. "People leave all kinds of things behind. You probably noticed yourself."

Sal shrugged impartially. He'd been a Boy Scout all month, taking any item a guest had left to the lost and found box under the front desk. Not that he had a problem with playing finders keepers generally.

Loretta put a hand on her hip. "You ain't gonna tell Will, are you?"

"It ain't my business."

"Good. 'Cause I share and share alike." She dug her hand into the deep pocket of her apron and came out with a fistful of gift shop lighters. The Pocono Mountains. Statue of Liberty. Carlsbad Caverns. Loretta looked at Sal expectantly. "Go on. I ain't gonna use 'em all, and I ain't startin' a collection."

The smart thing to do was to take one to gain her trust. Sal chose Carlsbad Caverns since he'd never been there. He gave Loretta a big smile, though he was already feeling wary of her. Some mischief was brewing in her shrewd, crow's feet-lined eyes.

"So, how you like working at the Ritz?" she said.

Sal snickered mildly and rolled back on his heels. "I done worse."

"Yeah. Sure. We all have." She exhaled a puff of smoke and studied Sal. "How you like working for Will?"

Sal blanked his face. Loretta cackled. Then she took a glance around and lowered her voice. "He's a prick, ain't he? I seen the way he treats you. Same way he treats all of us, so don't take it personal. Nothing worse than having a twenty-four-year-old as your boss, y'know what I mean? He thinks he knows everything, and God forbid he'd admit when he's wrong."

Sal nodded along.

"I heard you're from New York City," Loretta said. She had that glimmer of awe on her face that small town folks tended to get. "I had a girlfriend who moved down there. She got a job working at a cafeteria at Hunter College. You heard of it?"

"No. But I didn't spend much time at colleges."

Loretta clucked. "Tell me 'bout it. Who needs college? Y'know, they've got one of 'em across the river in Newburgh. Mount Saint Mary's. A bunch of spoiled brats. And listen to this. A couple weeks ago, one of them students got a room here and snuck in a dozen of his friends. They left beer cans and cigarette butts and puked all over the place, and you know who had to clean it up? Me." She took an angry pull on her cig. "So's I tell Will, he gotta be more careful 'bout who he's lettin' rent rooms. You know what Mr. Know-It-All says? He says, so long as they paid, I ain't got a right to complain." She looked at Sal. "You tell me, what kinda way is that to treat the people who keep you in business?"

Sal kept his face impartial. He could picture Will reacting like that, and he didn't disagree that it was a prick thing for him to say. But he was also feeling protective of Will and wasn't going to jump on the bandwagon badmouthing him.

"That's Skippy for you," she grumbled. "I call him that, but you'll keep it between the two of us, right?"

"Mm-hmm."

"I been working here since '71, and Pretty Boy comes along two years ago and says my annual raise is too steep. I got a family just like Eddie, and he can't afford an extra twenty cents an hour?"

Sal shook his head and glanced at her sympathetically. "You talk to George 'bout it?"

She snorted. "'Course I did. He said he's 'looking into it,' but he ain't gonna do nothin'. Will's got him wrapped around his finger." She took another quick glance at their surroundings. The motel's back lot was deserted. As far as Sal knew, they'd had two guests who checked out that morning and no new guests so far that day. Loretta's face turned mirthful. "I'll tell you something 'bout Will and George if you can keep a secret." She made a limp wrist and cackled.

Sal played stupid, waiting to be let in on the joke.

"You don't know 'bout fairies?"

"Fairies? I know 'bout fairies, but…" He put on an incredulous expression. "You sayin' George and Will…?"

"I'll tell you this. Skippy's room is always neat as a pin. Like it ain't never been used. And I seen Skippy coming out of George's room in the early morning, and I know it's only got one bed. So you tell me what's goin' on?"

"I'da never suspected," Sal said. "You sure? I mean, Will could get a girl, don't you think? Why would he be messin' 'round with George?"

Loretta looked at Sal like he was dense. "He's trying to turn George into one of them. That's how them queers reproduce since they can't make children of their own." She curled her lip in disgust. "It grosses me out working for a man like that. I bet it grosses you out too."

Sal hammed up a laugh. "You serious? Will and George?"

Loretta nodded. "I says to my girlfriend Kim, it's a crying shame what that kid done to George. He used to be respectable, but now he's boozin' and slackin' off with his businesses. All 'cause Skippy got him under his spell." She pointed her cigarette at Sal. "I think he's skimmin' the fat from the register, right under George's nose."

"Skimmin' the fat from the register?" Sal repeated, a little too loudly, making Loretta tense up and shush him.

"I ain't seen it, but I ain't stupid neither." Loretta tapped her forehead. "He wants George thinking the place ain't turning a profit so's he can say he can't afford my twenty-cent raise."

Sal looked her in the eyes just long enough to convey she might've said too much to him. She took one last pull on her cigarette, bent down to crush it on the walk, and threw the stub in the trash bin of her cart. "Just thought you should know. Watch yourself 'round Will."

"Thanks for the advice. You're a real lifesaver. Say, you been workin' here a while. What's the story with Lieutenant Hogan?"

That flipped a switch in Loretta. "I don't know nothin' 'bout him."

Sal smiled absurdly. "The local 5-0? He stops by here all the time. Seems to like talking to Will."

Loretta shrugged. "Guess he likes the coffee. I gotta get back to work. The shower rod in 114 is coming off the hinges if you got time to check it out."

Sal told her he would, and she pushed her cleaning cart down the walk.

THAT CONVERSATION HAD Sal thinking about a number of things while he went through the rest of his day. He'd been worrying about Eddie, but who he really needed to watch himself around was Loretta. She liked to gossip, and she had a chip on her shoulder. If she found out what was going on with him and Will, she could make trouble spreading the news. She was also wary about sharing her opinions about Hogan. She had no problem saying Will was trying to turn George queer, but she didn't have nothing to say about him flirting with Will right in front of her face? Like she didn't want to be involved. Or was she scared of Hogan? It was weird.

She'd also implied Will and George were fucking on a regular basis, and that had Sal sprouting horns. Now he'd figured that George had set Will up with a job to get down his pants, but after hearing that they'd been together for six years and seeing George drinking himself into a stupor, well, maybe Sal had been living in fantasy land, but he'd left George's place thinking that they probably didn't screw around anymore. Will never slept in his own bed, according to Loretta. Was she exaggerating because she had a problem with fags and had it out for Will? None of Will's stuff was in George's apartment, but they could've scrubbed the place before Sal came over. Maybe the sex hadn't fizzled between them. Last night, Will had sent Sal out of George's apartment, saying he was taking a bath and sleeping on the couch. Had he crawled into bed with George?

Later that day, between lunch and dinner, when the place was empty, Sal couldn't stop himself from looking for Will. George hadn't returned from his lawyer. Loretta had clocked out at three. Eddie took his break around the same time, and he'd driven off in his rusted Volkswagen bug, presumably to visit his wife and kids for a while. Sal found Will in the storage room off the kitchen, taking inventory with a clipboard. The kid was occupied with what he was doing and didn't take notice of Sal. Sal hung his hands from the top of the doorframe, studying the kid for a moment before getting his attention with a whistle. *When the red, red robin comes bob, bob bobbing along.*

Will looked Sal's way and glanced beyond him.

"Relax. Eddie's cleared out, and George ain't come back."

The kid still looked jumpy. Something was off with him. Sal came over and tried to get his arms around him, but Will turned away.

"I'm not doing that, Sal."

A grin split Sal's face, though he wasn't feeling happy. "It's a hug, baby. I ain't looking for nothin' more."

"Sure, you're not." Will stepped around him. Sal caught his arm, and Will pulled away.

"What's your problem?" Sal demanded.

"What's my problem? How about this? I think George knows about last night."

Will's face was seriously stressed. But he had to be worrying over nothing. "How you mean? He was passed out hard. He say something to you this morning?" *Or while you were in bed with him after I left?*

"No. But I know him. He barely said a word before he left out this morning." Will raked through his hair.

"He had to be good and hung over."

"Could you please close the door?"

Sal peeked out to the kitchen and shut the storage room door behind him. When he turned back to Will, the kid was staring at him with wide, frightened eyes. Sal was stricken. "Baby. C'mon. It ain't that bad, is it?"

"You can't be fucking with me."

Sal scowled at him, wounded.

"Did you mean what you said last night? Or are you just looking for someone to mess around with?"

"I ain't never tried this hard with nobody just to mess around." Sal held up his hand. "Yeah, it's true, you got everything I like. That gets me worked up sometimes." He adjusted himself between the legs. "But that don't mean I ain't got genuine feelings."

Will stared at him like he had X-ray vision. It was working Sal's nerves.

Will stretched out his arms sideways. "This is who I am, Sal. I'm a fuck-up who ran away with the first person who treated me nice. And now I'm trapped. I've got no savings. I'm not even pulling a salary from this sinking motel that's probably going broke by the end of the year 'cause George couldn't qualify for a fifty-dollar bank loan. And I'm not getting work anyplace else when the only reference I've got is a guy who's gonna ruin me if I leave him." He rubbed his forehead and fixed on Sal. "So, is that the kind of person you've got 'genuine feelings' for?"

Sal shifted his weight, reached for Will's arm, and stopped short of the motion. "You ever consider I might understand what you're going through? Before I met you, I was sleeping with a guy who was taking care of me. 'Cause I didn't think I could do better. I know what it's like to be trapped, and I also know what better is now. 'Cause of you."

Will's face turned haggard. He turned his head and raked and raked his hand through his hair.

"The point I'm making is we like each other, don't we?" Sal said. "That's the only thing that matters."

"You sound like a corny script from the movies. We're not living in Hollywood."

"Why you always gotta make me feel dumb? I never felt this way about nobody."

"I'm not trying to make you feel dumb, Sal. It's just not easy trusting people when everyone you've known has let you down."

"It ain't easy for me neither. Did George fuck you last night?"

Will recoiled. "What? No."

Sal fixed on him. "I ain't lookin' to be nobody's patsy. If the two of us gonna be something, I gotta know what's going on with you and George."

"You saw what's going on with me and George. He drinks himself to sleep every night."

"When's the last time he touched you?"

Will's face reddened. Then he balled up his fists and shouted, "You think I like it?"

Sal's anger fell away. He hadn't meant to hurt the kid. "All's I'm saying is you ain't gotta do it no more. You got me now." Sal took

Will in his arms. He'd never been good at saying how he felt. He was better at showing it. Sal dug his fingers into Will's hair and breathed him in.

"What do you want from me, Sal?"

"You let me be your man?" Sal kissed Will's neck, making him squirm and smile.

"Does that mean I gotta be your woman?"

"You like playin' like that, it ain't a problem for me." Sal got both his hands on Will's bottom and pressed his fingers into the sultry warmth between Will's cheeks. "I'll take such good care of you, Beautiful. Just want you all to myself."

Will forced Sal's hands away. "I'm not doing that."

"Why you gettin' me all heated up then?" Will didn't look like he was taking that so well. "You get me carried away. That ain't a bad thing, is it?"

The kid snorted, though a quiet smile was on his reddened face. "You're always on the make, aren't you?"

"I ain't on the make. I'm asking to be your man. That's a big deal where I come from."

Will dropped his gaze with an amused expression on his face.

"What? I'm too low class for you?" Sal said.

"No. I just never had anybody ask me that before." He peeked up at Sal. Sal gave him a questioning shrug.

Will smiled a little. "Where'd you really come from? Outer space?" He laid his hand on Sal's arm. "You want to know the truth, you're not so bad yourself." He touched Sal's ear lobe. "How come you don't wear an earring anymore? I bet it looks good on you."

Sal's face blossomed. "I'll start wearing it again. For you." He hooked his hands inside Will's belted pants. "So, that a yes 'bout the two of us?"

Will sighed. "I don't know how this is supposed to work."

"Maybe you're thinking too hard about it."

"One of us needs to be thinking." Will looked Sal in the eye, and in a heartbeat, they were making out hot and heavy. It was blissful for a moment, and then Will slowed things down. "How're we gonna break out of here, Sal? We've got nothing."

"Baby, we got everything." Sal grabbed Will's mouth with his again and backed him up against a shelf. Cans and boxes toppled, and they kept going at each other. Sal wrestled off Will's belt and slacks, dropped his own, spit on his hand, and bound the two of them together. Wrenching, stroking, straining. Will's hot breaths against his lips. They came together, gasping from how good it felt. Sal collapsed against Will while sweat rolled down his face, and his body shuddered in tender aftershocks.

7

SAL NEVER WOULD'VE expected to find himself chasing after a pretty boy in Nowheresville, begging to be his man. But there he was. Will had turned him softer than an ice cream cone on a New York sidewalk in the middle of July.

The kid brought out realizations that Sal had locked down for a long time. Sal needed to belong to somebody. He didn't want to be a loner for the rest of his life. He'd been lonely, so goddamn lonely for as far back as he could remember, and with Will, he didn't feel lonely any more.

He wanted to do right by Will and even got to thinking they didn't have to steal George's money to run off together. Sal already had a warrant following him around. If he was going to be taking care of the kid, he shouldn't be adding potential problems with the law. Sal could work hard, scrimp and save, and even find a second job to put together the money they needed to quit the motor lodge. Then, they could go someplace far away like California and start a life together, doing things legit.

That was all a nice daydream for a while. But after a month, saving almost every dollar he'd earned, Sal had all of four hundred bucks. He figured he needed at least a G to impress Will. With that, they could get cross-country bus tickets and rent a little apartment somewhere while looking for jobs. As Sal thought about it, he started getting itchy. Would Will laugh at him about running away with a measly one thou? Maybe not with two thou, or five thou.

At the rate he was getting paid, he'd need to work three, four months to get that kind of money, and that felt like an eternity while they were sleeping in separate beds. Sal thought about scouting for extra work in town, but that was going to be difficult when he only had his Sundays off. The situation was giving Sal a migraine. He had one day a week to scope around for some business that only needed a guy to clean the place on a Sunday, maybe for an extra twenty dollars a week. Sal considered hocking Joey's gold watch, his diamond earring, and even his suede jacket. Another two hundred bucks or so, maybe? It still wasn't enough. Sal was mentally exhausted. He couldn't figure things out. So, he set aside the problem for a while and tried to make the best of a complicated situation.

The motor lodge had a lot of places where he and Will could be alone if they were smart about it. On a good day, they had guests in ten of the motel's forty rooms and small batches of customers coming to the diner. It was scarce in the late morning and in the middle of the afternoon. George was rarely a worry. He had business to do at his other properties most days. Eddie wasn't much of a problem either since he kept to the kitchen. Loretta was trickier. She moved around the lodge to do her work. But once Sal got a hang of her routine, he could stay a step ahead of her.

One morning, when Loretta had an appointment with one of her kids, Sal coaxed Will into the janitor's closet for some sweet talk and messing around. He was dying to really make love to Will and told him so while he had his hands down the back of his pants. Will got huffy again. He wasn't doing that until they had some real privacy and time on their hands. Sal didn't know how to arrange that. The motel had plenty of vacant rooms, but each one faced out to either the front or back lot. Without any cover, they could be seen going in or coming out, from many angles.

They stole moments together while they worked, and days turned to weeks. Sneaking down to the cellar below the kitchen when Eddie drove home for his break. Waiting for Loretta to clock out and skulking over to the utility room one at a time. They always had to be quick about it, but that created a sense of urgency, which made it hot. As soon as they were alone, they were kissing and grinding and getting each other off.

It was exciting, sneaking around to have those secret rendezvous, but at times, Sal felt like it wasn't enough. Every night, he went to bed alone, and his body was heated and too restless to sleep. He tossed and turned while thoughts of George fucking Will ate away at his heart. Will had said it didn't happen very often, that George was always too drunk to have an interest, but they were still sleeping in the same damn apartment. Some nights, the situation got Sal so crazy, he went outside to look up at the place.

George always played his Greek music till midnight, and not long after it cut out, lights went off and Sal couldn't hear a thing. April had turned to June, and George had never invited Sal for Sunday dinner a second time. It occurred to Sal, there could be a lot of reasons for that. Maybe the bossman was a phony, telling him he considered his employees like family. George could've been embarrassed about having gotten so drunk the last time. But the worst of all reasons got Sal worked up at night. George was fucking Will, and the two of them didn't want Sal knowing about it.

One afternoon, when the place was dead, Sal persuaded Will to come with him to the diner bathroom, and he took him into a stall. He got his hands and mouth all over him to warm him up, and then he showed Will a bottle of lube he'd picked up from the convenience store. His cock throbbed for him, and he dug his hand inside Will's briefs to feel his bottom.

Will moved Sal's hand away. Sal pressed his chest into him, pinned his legs with his, and ground his achy boner against Will. He couldn't stop himself from grabbing another feel of the kid's behind.

"You got me crazy, baby. I'll make it nice for you." He wrung

Will's taut cheeks and searched for the steamy heaven of his opening.

Will pushed back his shoulders. "Knock it off. A customer could come in."

Sal came back at him with a lopsided smile. "The door's locked. I got the Out of Order sign on it."

Will snorted and fought Sal's grip. "You know I don't have time. I've got to get back to the front desk."

"Just let me feel you a little. For a minute is all I'm askin'."

Will shoved him hard. "What's wrong with you? I told you I'm not doing that till we've got some privacy."

Sal's pent-up frustration had his horns twisted. "When's that happening? I been asking you to come to my room when George goes to sleep, and you always got some excuse."

Will wrestled his way out of the stall, cranked on the sink and splashed water on his face. Sal followed him out.

"Are you fucking George?"

Will glared at Sal's reflection in the bathroom mirror. "Keep your voice down."

Sal turned and shook his head. "Y'know, a person could get tired of waiting for you."

"Figure it out, Sal. You keep saying you're going to put together the money so we can get out of here." Will cranked off the sink and grabbed paper towels to dry his face. "You think I like having to worry every minute that someone saw us coming out of the janitor's closet or some other stinking place?"

Heat rose up Sal's neck. "I'm trying to get the money. It ain't easy when I'm busting my ass day and night."

"*You're* busting your ass," Will said with a sneer. "At least you've got something to show for it. Thanks to genius George who won't shell out a dime to improve the place, this shithole's in the red for the fourth straight month. You tell me, who's renting a room here when they've got a brand new Super 8 off the thruway for sixteen dollars a night?"

Sal faced him. "Get out with me."

"How Sal?"

"I don't care. I don't want you sleeping with George no more."

"I'm not sleeping with George."

Sal crowded up on the kid aggressively, but when he spoke, he was surprised by the desperation of his own voice. "You're in his bed every night. You oughta be in my bed."

"I'm not in his bed. I'm keeping an eye on him so he gets up in the morning to manage his properties. So we all have a roof over our heads. You know that. Until we've got some money and a place to go, you've gotta live with it."

"I don't give a fuck. I'll talk to George myself. I'll tell him everythin', and if he don't want people knowin' he's a fruit, he gotta give us the money to get settled somewhere."

Will grinned madly. "You think he's gonna just give you a wad of cash to walk out of here with me? Men like George don't do that, Sal."

"I told you not to talk to me like I'm stupid." Sal's anger burned in his throat. He nearly took a swing at Will, but instead, he slapped the hand dryer inches from Will's head. It muffled the noise when he kicked the stall door and sent it slamming into the divider. Sal paced around and ended up in front of Will, gazing at him pleadingly.

"Are you fucking nuts?" Will said in a hushed voice.

Sal hid his face. "I'm sorry. I just got a little worked up, all right?"

"You can't be doing that. What's to get worked up about? You want me to say it again? I'm not sleeping with George. Why do you gotta act like an animal? Are you trying to turn what we've got to shit?"

Sal sealed his lips and shook his head.

Will sighed. "Jesus, you're a piece of work. Now you look like a little kid."

"I'm sorry," Sal repeated.

Will gently took him in his arms. "Easy, baby." Will rubbed his back. "I'm not two-timing you, Sal. You've gotta keep your cool."

Sal winced to try to stop tears bleeding from his eyes. He belonged to Will, and Will belonged to him. Why couldn't they run off and be together all the time?

"Listen," Will said. "I'm working on an idea for getting the money, too." He patted Sal's back and broke off their hug. "Just keep it together for a little while longer, okay?"

He left Sal in the bathroom. This affair with Will was making him a wreck, and Sal didn't know how much longer he could deal with it.

THE FOLLOWING FRIDAY, while Sal was watering the flower beds in the front lot, a delivery truck drove in and pulled up by the diner. Two stiffs in brown, polyester uniforms hopped out from the cab, hauled a jukebox out of the back door, and laid it on a dolly. George strode out of the diner to greet them. Sal hadn't seen the bossman for a couple of days. He'd been counting that as a blessing, though the truth was, George's absence hadn't changed anything. Will was still being moody, and Sal was no closer to having the cash so they could break out on their own. Sal looked away to act like he was minding his own business. He heard the bossman chatting with the guys in his usual loud and excitable way. Then George called Sal to come over and help out.

It was a heavy piece of equipment, but the delivery men rolled it inside, and all Sal needed to do was clear out some space in a corner of the diner where they could install it. The guys plugged it into an outlet, and George gave them two five-dollar bills and sent them off with a friendly smile. The bossman was real pleased with himself. Will was behind the counter, glancing every now and then at the new contraption. He had two old geezers over there eating breakfast.

"What did I tell you?" George shouted to Will. "You got your jukebox." He turned to Sal. "How 'bout giving it a Windex?"

Sal grabbed a rag and his spray bottle and got to wiping down the Wurlitzer. It wasn't brand new, but it was in pretty good shape. Just had a few scratches on the glass and by the coin slot.

"Go on. Check it out," George told Will.

Will came around, and Sal stepped aside. Will's reaction was muted. Then George handed him a dime, and Will put it in the slot and selected a track.

The Beach Boys. *Wouldn't It Be Nice?* The sound was amazing. The pair from the counter looked over approvingly, and even Will got a little grin on his face.

George came up next to him. "I bought it on contract. Every month, they replace old records with new ones. Top Forty. Rock. Motown. Whatever you like." He turned to the customers to brag to them. "Two hundred forty-fives this thing can hold."

Will took a closer look at the playlist in the glass-enclosed console. Sal could tell he was impressed. Sal had to admit he was impressed, too. The jukebox sure livened up the place. Maybe they'd get more locals coming in on Friday and Saturday nights. He watched George standing by Will, all hero-like.

George patted Will's shoulder. "I've gotta head down to the city for my cousin's wedding. I'll be back on Monday. But you'll have fun with this in the meantime." He glanced at Sal. "Tomorrow, why don't you close up after breakfast and show Sal around town? He's been working so hard, I bet he hasn't had a chance to see the sights."

He looked at Sal expectantly. Sal played it cool. "Sounds great. So long as it's all right with Will."

"Will won't mind." George turned to him. "It'll do you both some good to take the afternoon off. Take the truck. You can show Sal the state park and Bannerman Castle."

He wandered off to the back office, humming the Beach Boys along the way. Will's eyes passed over Sal for a half second, and then he spotted some dishes to clear from one of the tables and went about his business. Sal stood there for a moment, wondering if George was genuinely clueless or testing out a theory about what was going on. The situation was almost too good to be true.

8

GEORGE DROVE OFF that day, and Sal was anxious to have a conversation with Will. But Will was tied up working at the diner all through the day and into the evening. That jukebox was a hit. Somehow, word spread quickly. They had steady customers from five o'clock to ten. Like an old time diner, the place was rocking with Martha and the Vandellas, Creedence Clearwater Revival, and the Supremes. They even got groups of high school kids coming in to order fries and milkshakes and play the Top 40 tracks.

Later, Sal helped Eddie close up the kitchen. Eddie took off, and Sal finally found Will behind the diner counter. Will looked tense, clearing out the register. Without a word, he took the cash over to the office safe. Sal followed him into the office.

Will sat down at his desk to count the night's take. "The sooner you take out the trash, the sooner I can lock up the place."

It was quite a haul of bills he was handling. More than the place had made on a single night since Sal had been there, but that hadn't lightened Will's mood. Sal stepped up to the desk. "What's goin' on with George?"

"He's got a wedding in the city."

"I heard that. He's also actin' like we should spend some time together. What's *going on* with him?"

"Don't know."

Sal waited for him to elaborate, but he didn't. He was absorbed in counting out twenties and wrapping them up with rubber bands.

"How 'bout I take a shower, and you come over to my place?"

Will shook his head.

"Why not?"

"I'm trying to count here."

Sal wanted to swat the money out from under him. He drew a breath. "We ain't gotta hide with George cleared outta here for the weekend."

Will looked up at him, blank-faced. "Oh yeah? You think George didn't ask somebody to keep an eye on me while he's out of town?" He went back to counting bills. "Happens every time he takes trips. He probably has one of his Greek pals parked out front already."

Sal wasn't sure he believed that at first. He'd never noticed anybody on the premises who looked like one of George's "Greek pals."

"Take a look for yourself," Will told him.

Sal did just that. He left the lights off in the diner and found a shadowy route to the side of the big window where a pale glow from the neon sign shone through. Nobody was out there, were they? He swept a gaze from one side of the lot to the other, and then his lungs froze over. A sedan was parked at the curb, right by the entrance. Sal could just make out the familiar silhouette in the murky lake of darkness. He couldn't tell the make or model. He couldn't even say if anyone was in it, but he was spooked.

Quietly, he stepped back to Will's office and told Will what he'd seen.

"Figures," Will said with a yawn.

"It's one of George's pals?" Sal scratched his ear. "What's he gonna do? Watch the place all night?"

Will got up and put stacks of money into the safe. "Could be. Or he could get bored. Drive off and come back in an hour."

Sal's throat was dry, and his hands were ice cold. "You sayin' George suspects somethin'? It don't make sense. Why's he pushin' you to take me out on the town tomorrow?"

"I don't know, Sal. But you see, it's not the time for me to be sleeping over in your room." He glanced at his watch. "Tommy's gonna be here any minute. Finish with the trash, and we'll see each other in the morning."

Tommy was a kid who worked at the front desk overnights. Sal understood what Will was saying, but he didn't like it. They finally had George out of their hair for three nights and two full days, and they couldn't even enjoy it?

"How 'bout I come up to you? I'll wait till you turn the lights off. Be real quiet about it."

Will shut the safe and faced Sal. "Get some sleep, all right? I've got a plan for tomorrow."

Sal eased up close. Will huffed, wearily. Nonetheless, Sal held his hips and reached for a kiss. Will turned his face too quickly, and then he pushed Sal back with his hand.

"You ain't sweet for me no more?" Sal said.

"I'm tired, Sal. It's been a long day."

Sal had been working since early in the morning, too. It was all the more reason that they should toss back a beer and have some smokes. They didn't have to mess around if Will was too tired. They could just cuddle up together.

Will met Sal's gaze. "Don't look so disappointed. I've got a surprise for you tomorrow."

Sal hooked two fingers in the waistband of Will's slacks. "What kinda surprise?"

Will grinned slightly. "Just pack a swimsuit and a towel, stud. Meet me out front by the truck at noon."

Sal was mighty curious and wanted to ask more about that. Then a familiar jangle of bells traveled from outside.

"That's Tommy," Will said. Sal smothered Will's mouth with his, and Will broke things off much too soon. He hustled Sal out of the office and went to get Tommy set up for the night.

. . .

SAL SPENT MOST of that night peeking out of the curtain of his window and chain smoking. Will was real sure George had asked someone to keep an eye on the place, and Sal wanted to see for himself. By one o'clock, nobody had driven around to the back lot. Around one-thirty, a station wagon pulled into a space a few doors down, but it was just some out-of-towners moving into a room and arguing along the way. Sal's eyes were crossing. Five straight days of working from six o'clock in the morning until eleven at night, and now he had to stay up to lookout for whatever shenanigans George had planned for that weekend. It was stupid.

Somewhere around two o'clock, he heard a familiar mewl and spotted his old friend pacing in front of his door. Sal got his can opener and a can of tuna. He opened his door, set the can out for the pushy tomcat and gave him a rub between the ears as he chowed down. The tiger-striped boy looked well-fed. Sal might've been the second or third chump he'd suckered in to give him some food that night, but Sal didn't hold it against him. He was a good hustler. Why go through the trouble of hunting mice when you can get somebody to feed you fish cut up in nice flaked pieces. Sal could take lessons from the brassy stray. He purred like a real flirt while Sal stroked his fur.

The tom wandered off after a while. Sal shut himself in his room and flopped down on his bed. He really was exhausted. His eyelids were like twenty-pound weights and soon he drifted off to sleep.

SAL WOKE UP at eleven thirty the next morning. His empty stomach ached, but he curled back under the covers, savoring the lazy comfort until the fog cleared from his head, and he remembered he had plans with Will. He shot up and staggered into the bathroom for a quick shower.

He dried off and stepped into a fresh pair of briefs. Will had been real mysterious, saying he had a surprise for Sal. He said to bring a towel and a swimsuit. Sal rolled up one of his room's towels and packed it in his rucksack. He didn't have a swimsuit, but he had a pair of cut-off shorts, and where Sal came from, that had always been sufficient for the beach or wherever they were going to swim. It was a sunny day, and the weather had been mild. He pulled on the short sleeve button down he'd worn to George's dinner. He hadn't had time to hand wash it in the sink, but he'd only worn it once before. Then Sal ventured out of his room to look for Will.

When he came around the front of the motor lodge, he saw George's truck parked near the diner. It was a beat-up Chevy that had some miles on it. George must've used it for construction work in the past. Sal headed in that direction, and then Will came out the door off the kitchen carrying a hand-held cooler. Sal walked over with some extra pep in his step.

Will had on a striped polo shirt that had shrunk in the wash, a pair of corduroy shorts over a swimsuit, and flip flops. He could've passed for a preppy college kid, and a smoking hot one at that. Will loaded the cooler into the truck bed. When Sal came over, Will pointed his eyes at the cab, and they both got in. Sal was liking the big utility vehicle with its raised cab and comfy vinyl booth. Will sparked up the ignition, got on the road, and didn't say a word until they were southbound on the country highway out of town.

"Thought you overslept, and I was going on my own."

Sal gazed across the endless great outdoors ahead of them. Sun was shining down over a lush, forested landscape. Sal hadn't had a chance to see the scenery beyond Beacon. Busy as he'd been, he'd practically forgotten that he was living so far from the city.

He squeezed Will's thigh. "I got you stressed, baby?" Will made a face and didn't answer. "Just wanted to get myself looking good for you." Sal leaned back in his seat and spread out his body. "What you think?"

Moody Will just shook his head.

"So, where you takin' me?"

"You'll find out when we get there."

Sal eyed him playfully. "Why you ain't sayin'?"

"I told you, it's a surprise."

"Is it a surprise I'm gonna like?"

Will bulged his lip equivocally.

"Just tell me, why don't you?" Sal said.

"What's the problem, Sal? You don't like surprises?"

"Not particularly."

"Tough shit."

Sal frowned and looked out the passenger side window. Along the shoulder, he saw a numbered sign for the country road. 9D. If he had his bearings right, south was toward the city, not that it meant much to him. He knew nothing about the area, and that got Sal apprehensive. He lit up a smoke.

"You ain't worried 'bout one of George's friends trailin' us?"

"Nope. So long as you behave yourself."

Sal went back to checking out the scenery. He hadn't been out in the country since he was a little kid. He remembered a day trip to the Pocono Mountains with his mom and her boyfriend Lou. It was one of his few happy memories from his childhood. Lou was a tattooed big hulk of a guy, but he was really just a teddy bear. He was the only man his mom had brought home who didn't treat Sal like a rival for his mom's attention. From the backseat of Lou's beat up Pontiac, Sal had seen pine forests and wooded lakes and deer. They got a cabin on Lake Wallenpaupack, and Lou had shown Sal how to fish off a dock while his mom was suntanning on a little beach. It had been a great weekend, and then a week later, Lou and his mom got into some kind of scrap, and Lou stormed out of her apartment, never to return.

Gazing out his window, Sal spotted a sign for a state park. He remembered that was one of the "sights" George had suggested. Just before the turnoff, a cop car was parked on the shoulder of the road. Will waved to the guy in the driver's seat and took the inclined road into forested hills.

A quarter mile up the road, they came to a turnstile station. Will pulled up and paid the attendant the fifty-cent admission fee. They passed signs about camping rules and littering and warnings about bears. Not far down the park road, Will turned into a visitor's lot. He pulled into a parking space and cut out the ignition.

Will drew Sal's glance to one side of the lot. "See that trailer?"

Sal nodded. A gravel driveway off the lot led to a prefab outbuilding partially hidden by the woods. It looked like a station for park rangers.

"Wait ten minutes and meet me around the back. Bring the cooler with you." Will climbed out of the truck, shut the door behind him, and headed to the trailer.

Sal had zero idea what was going on. More hiding places to mess around? He watched Will walk up the driveway and disappear behind the trailer. Sal looked at the clock on the dashboard. Wait ten minutes, Will said. Why? There were a few cars in the lot, but no one was around. The kid was being cautious about something. Maybe coppers patrolled the place.

When ten minutes was up, Sal got out of the truck and grabbed the cooler from the bed. It had a single handle, but it was heavy, loaded with ice. Sal hauled it along to the gravel driveway, keeping an eye on things. He passed by an entrance to a wood-chipped hiking trail and saw a picnic area in the distance. A couple families were over there, but they were at least fifty yards away. A sign by the trailer's driveway read: *Employees only. No trespassing.* Well, that's where Will had told Sal to go, so he pushed along to the trailer.

Everything was quiet. The trailer looked like it was locked up, actually. Sal grew more curious about what Will was up to, and along with that, a wary feeling crept in. Tall pine woods surrounded him. He lightened his step and slowed down his pace. Sal didn't like going into situations blindly. He wasn't crazy about being so far from civilization either. It made him think about a horror flick. Madmen with axes hung out in the woods.

He slowly came around the trailer and set his eyes on Will. It had occurred to him that the kid might've ditched him, so that was a relief. Will had found a tool kit and was fastening a luggage rack to a Kawasaki motorcycle. He was acting as routine as could be. Gradually, an answer occurred to Sal, though it was so incredible, he almost didn't trust it.

Sal set down the cooler. "This the surprise?"

Will asked him to hold the rack while he wrenched a bolt into the fender. "Part of it."

The bike was boss. A deep purple fuel tank with a flaming orange stripe. Leather seats. Chrome mufflers. Sal didn't know much about motorcycles, but it looked like a little beast. Clean-cut Will owned a bike? Sal was impressed.

"Guess we're switchin' up wheels."

Will finished bolting in the rack and returned the wrench to the steel toolkit. "It's my brother's. He lets me borrow it some-times." Will lugged the toolkit over to a shed behind the trailer. Sal spotted a motorcycle cover thrown in there before Will closed the shed door and wrapped a padlock chain around the door bar. When he was done, he came back and looked at Sal expectantly.

"Where's the cooler?"

Sal went to bring it over. Will directed him to set it on the rack and got it secured in place with bungee cords.

"Your brother work here?"

"Ding, ding, ding, Einstein." He scooped up a helmet from the driveway and thrust it at Sal. "There's only one of these. You should wear it."

It sounded like a put-down, the way he said it. The kid was enjoying having one over on Sal. That never played well with him, but meanwhile, the inevitability of what was happening next had Sal's heart doing skips. He'd never been on a bike.

"George know 'bout this?"

"No. Which is why we're taking it."

"Where?"

"That's the surprise." Will straddled the bike. "Put on the helmet."

Sal looked at the space behind where Will was sitting. It was the width of a piano bench, with nothing to hold on to. He turned over the helmet in his hands.

"Why d'ya say, *I* should wear it?"

Will glanced back at him, impatiently. "'Cause you've never been on a bike, have you?" Sal said nothing. "Thought so. It's not legal to ride without a helmet, but I'm going to stay off the highways, mostly."

Sal got next to the bike and threw a leg around the seat. Sneaking off on a Kawasaki with the possibility of getting pulled over by the pigs. The day was turning out to be one hell of an adrenaline rush. He eased up behind Will and snuck his hand inside the kid's shorts leg, digging for the heat of his crotch.

Will wrestled Sal's arm away. Sal snickered. "You went to a lot of trouble just to take us somewhere to fuck."

"In your dreams."

Sal slid his hands inside Will's shirt, feeling his bare skin and the fine hairs on his stomach. He leaned over his shoulder, inhaling his washed and shampooed body. "You gonna make it worth the wait?"

Will shrugged him off, but only so much. "I can't be driving George's truck to the place we're going. No funny business back there, all right?"

Sal put the helmet on, and Will kicked on the ignition. The bike's engine growled and knocked, sending birds flying away from the trees. Sal couldn't help himself from howling like a rowdy teenager. Will wheeled forward to a dirt service road that wound and declined steeply through the woods.

At the bottom, they came to a gate, and Will drove them through and closed it behind them. Sal spotted that they'd ended up back on Route 9D. Will pulled onto the two-lane highway and churned up some speed.

Sal hugged Will around the waist. His stomach had jumped up to his throat, and flashes of disaster ran havoc in his head. It was better than a rollercoaster ride. It was almost better than sex. The forested countryside whirred by, and Sal's only security was holding on to the crazy kid who had turned into a daredevil now that he was free of the motor lodge.

The road opened up to the yawning Hudson River on one side, and then they took a bridge across. Will gunned the bike when they had open road, and slowed down when they passed through little towns. They had to have traveled for an hour, and then he turned off to a two lane highway, heading west, into the mountains.

A hot rod sedan gained up on them, gunned into the incoming traffic lane, and swerved in front of them. The car was blaring Aerosmith and packed with long-haired local kids. Sal glared at the punks. That shit was dangerous. The road carved along a forested hill with sharp bends and a narrow shoulder with just a shallow guard rail to stop vehicles from plummeting down a near vertical drop. Sal cursed the fuckwads. One of them stuck his arm out the window, flipped Sal the bird, and then they accelerated away and disappeared far ahead.

A few miles later, Will pulled into a hidden lot off the road. It was hedged in by trees and had a dozen cars parked on the grass, along with bicycles chained to an old fence. Will found a shaded spot to park the bike and hopped off. Wobbily, Sal dismounted as well. It didn't look like a very impressive place for the end of their journey. Some kind of rest area? There was no beach or lake in sight. Sal's shirt was drenched from the ride, and now he could feel the heat and the humidity from the sultry summer day. He pulled the helmet off his sweaty head. Will went about locking the bike and unfastening the cooler.

"Now you gonna tell me where the hell we goin'?"

Will grabbed the helmet from Sal and stowed it in the under-seat compartment. Then he looked at the cooler as a cue for Sal to carry it. "Follow me."

He headed to a narrow, rocky trail that disappeared into the woods and declined steeply. The sweet scent of maple leaves filled Sal's sinuses. The trail was a little treacherous and too far from civilization and quiet for Sal's taste. Just the chirps and cricketing of creatures in the trees and brush. Will plodded down the trail for a good ten minutes until hints of their destination finally came into view. Faint, echoing voices. A steady flush of water. In spaces between lush maple and oak trees, Sal saw a ravine and glimpses of water. Then they came to the rocky shore of the ravine, and their surroundings opened up to a thirty- or so-foot waterfall that teemed down a jagged shelf to a creek that was twenty yards across.

Sal scoped around and saw they weren't alone. A dozen or more people had taken up spots on either side of the gorge. While Will judged a place to set themselves up, Sal slyly took account. It was all men, and some of them were fully undressed. Some lay out on flat boulders, sunbathing in the nude. Others were drinking beers or passing joints. A young queeny pair squawked back and forth in that familiar, affected way. An older mustached man, propped up on his elbows, stared boldly at Sal, telepathing his desire. It was a gay hideaway, out in the middle of nowhere. Sal wouldn't have believed it unless he'd seen it with his own eyes.

Will hiked up to a sunny ledge that looked like it had room for the two of them to spread out a bit. Sal lumbered his way up and around jutting rocks to follow him, and Will took the cooler off his hands so he could manage the final big step. Sal climbed up and told Will, "They got places like this in the city." He was thinking of the West Side piers where queens sunbathed in the summer, and it was cruisy at night year-round. "Not like this, exactly. Just, y'know, the same kind of crowd."

Will pulled off his shirt, and Sal did the same. It was a little cooler by the waterfall, and the sun felt amazing against his shoulders. He was coursing with the thrill of freedom. It had been a long time since Sal had been around his own kind. A group of queens across the creek had a transistor radio that was playing Donna Summer. Sal dug her catchy disco hits.

"You come here a lot?" he asked Will.

"Yeah, with all my free time." Will grubbed out two cans of beer from the cooler, peeled off the tabs, and handed one to Sal.

He kicked off his flip flops and sat down with his legs and bare feet hanging off the shelf. They were maybe ten feet above the eddying creek.

Sal pried off his sneakers and socks and sat down next to him, shoulder to shoulder. "How'd you find the place?"

"From a guy I used to know."

Sal gazed at him crookedly. "Somebody you were gettin' down with?"

"Maybe. It's none of your business."

Sal watched Will slug down some beer. "You ain't gotta be so uptight. We got the day to ourselves." He swept a glance around. The sun sparkled on the water and dappled the green-leaved tree limbs draping the gorge. It smelled fresh and earthy and wonderful. "I know you brought me to your special spot to impress me."

"Maybe it was a bad idea."

Sal set down his beer can and swiped Will's.

"What the hell?"

"You wanna yank my chain, I can yank yours too."

Will went to grab his beer back, but Sal was too quick. He switched hands and placed the can out of reach. Will fought to get it, and Sal caught his hands. They wrangled fiercely. Sal smiled the whole time, and the tight-ass kid actually laughed.

"Why do you gotta be such a douche?" Will said.

"*I'm* a douche? You're the one who's been a moody bitch all day."

"Fuck off."

Will tried to pull his hands away, but Sal wouldn't let him. Sal leaned into his face with a playful spirit he hadn't possessed since he was a teenager. "It's all right. I know you got it bad for me."

Will jabbed his elbow into Sal's side and ripped his hands free. "Sure. I got it *bad* for you."

"You brought me here. Showed off with your Kawasaki. Packed a picnic lunch." He picked up Will's beer to give it back to him. Will ripped it from his hand, stared away from him, and took a swig.

"I don't get you," Sal said. "We're gettin' to know each other, ain't we? We been messing around for two months."

"Yeah? That mean something to you?"

"'Course it means something to me." Sal rustled up closer to Will so they were shoulder-to-shoulder again. Will was giving off an icy draft. Sal could've tried warming him up like he usually did, but the kid's attitude ticked him off. Instead, Sal glanced around the gorge. A pair of butch queens were splashing around in the creek. Guys were cruising each other from their various perches. It made Sal happy, and soon enough he gave it a try with Will again.

"This where you trick when you wanna get away from George?"

"Trick? I told you, I haven't been here in years."

Sal studied Will, sidelong. He had the clearest skin, and freckles had spread across his shoulders in the sun. "So, tell me something 'bout yourself."

"What do you want to know?"

"You grow up 'round here? You got a family?"

Will brought his knees into his chest and crossed his arms over them. He looked away from Sal, hesitating. "I grew up in Tarry-town. That's more toward the city."

Sal scrounged out his cigarette pack from his shorts pocket. He offered one to Will, but he shook his head. Sal perched a cig between his lips and glanced at Will before he hit it with a flame. "You like it there?"

"Yeah, it was paradise." Will scratched the side of his head. "So. listen to this. Something I didn't even tell George. I had a scholar-ship to Cornell University. They've got the best hotel management program in the country. It was one of those things that's kind of a big deal, y'know? So, the night I got the letter in the mail, when we're all having dinner, my mom, my dad, and my older brother, I decide to tell them the news, thinking, y'know, they'll all say 'good job' or something like that. What happens is my dad sets down his fork and knife, sits up a bit, and he punches me in the face, so hard, it's like whiplash. He says to me, he says, 'You ain't ever doing any better than me and your brother, which is working at the water treatment plant. What you think? You gonna go to college and become some fag manager at a fancy hotel?'" Will's upper lip twitched, and he took another draw of beer. "Oh, and here's the clincher, Sal. He'd been fucking me since I was eleven years old."

Will's face was hard. Sal had figured the kid had a tough time at home. He'd never come across a queer who hadn't, and every hustler he'd known had been molested by some man in his family. Sal had his own story. His mother's ex-boyfriend Donny used to beat him up and fuck him when he was a thirteen-year-old weakling. Sal felt for the kid. He gently clasped the side of Will's neck.

Will pulled away. "You don't have to act all sympathetic."

Sal took a drag of his cigarette and minded himself for the moment. "So, what did you do after that?"

Will broke out a cigarette for himself and took the lighter from Sal. "I left home the day after I graduated high school." He exhaled a plume of smoke. "I couldn't go to college. Even with the scholarship, I'd have needed a couple grand a year for the dorms and books and food. I had a friend, this girl from Peekskill. Her hippie mom let all kinds of people crash at her place, so I went there. I got a job at a soda shop, and I gave her mom twenty-five bucks a week to sleep on her couch." Will gazed off thoughtfully, tugged on his cig and wriggled his toes. "Maybe I should've stuck around. Something better might've come along, but weeks seemed like years back then. It felt like time was slipping away. I didn't want to end up like my pops in a dead-end job for the rest of my life. I'd been working at the soda shop for three months when I met George, and you know the rest of the story."

The kid bowed his head, and when he blinked, his long eyelashes flecked a tear from his eyes. Sal eased up closer and took Will's hand in his. "I'm gonna take care of you now. Never let nobody hurt you."

"How, Sal?"

"I'm savin' money." Sal pulled out a swaggering grin. "There's a situation in town I'm workin' on, but y'know, it takes some time."

Will cocked his head and gave Sal a piercing gaze. "I don't think you even like me."

"What're you sayin'? Baby, I'm crazy 'bout you."

"Don't hustle me, Sal."

"Jesus, here we go. I'm *hustlin'* you. Just workin' my ass off day and night, waiting on you, while you're upstairs with George every night."

"You know the reason for that."

"I'm tryin' to get us set up so we can be together. If anybody's gettin' hustled, it's me."

Will looked down at his feet. Then his face shrank up, and he tried to hide it from Sal.

Sal hadn't meant to make him cry. He was just tired of having the same argument over and over again. "Your problem is you got no faith in me." He snorted. "There's only so much of that I can take. I got my pride." He took a long pull on his cigarette. "Why you gotta be like that?"

"I want to believe you. It's just not easy for me, okay?"

Sal brought both of his arms around Will and nuzzled against his bare shoulder. "I ain't never gonna lie to you. I want you. All the time." Will's face relaxed, and he held Sal's forearm. He sank into Sal's embrace, back-to-chest. Will's bare body was warm and delicious. Sal kissed his neck with some playful nibbles. Will clutched Sal's forearm, brushing his hairs, sliding his palm along the tender underside. Their surroundings faded away, and Sal only knew the lusciousness of their intermingled bodies. He rustled around to join their mouths, but Will held him back.

"How'd you get so much style?"

"What do you mean?"

Will fingered Sal's diamond stud. "I dig your look. That suede jacket is hot. You really used to make half a thou a week managing that nightclub in the city?"

"Yeah, and I was livin' rent free. Things was flush for a while. I bought clothes and shoes at all the best shops in the Village." Will's eyes were wide, like he was imagining it himself. Sal held the side of Will's face. "Once we get settled someplace, I'm gonna take you shopping, baby. Buy you anything you want."

Will nuzzled against Sal's hand for a moment. "If you're serious about us, we've got to find a way out soon. George is going to put two and two together, and when that day comes, he's going to destroy both me and you."

Sal thought Will was being a little dramatic, or maybe paranoid. George didn't seem like he had a clue, and the whole thing about George keeping tabs on Will while he was away felt farfetched too. Sal gave him a little squeeze. "I been tellin' you all along, I'm ready to get out with you. We can take off right now while he's out of town."

"You've got words, Sal, but what're they worth? We've got no plan, no money, no car. I know, you've scraped by before. I have too. But for once, I want to come out on top."

Sal swiped his face. If he could, he'd give Will the world, but at the same time, he wished he'd say he'd run off with him even if they had to get by a little lean at first. He was about to say something about that, but Will cut in again.

"I've been thinking, and the only answer I can come up with is we've got to get George out of the way."

Sal looked at Will funny. "How you mean? Get him a one-way ticket on a cruise to Greece?"

Will lowered his voice. "You remember that day after George's card night when I told you he was going to see a lawyer? It wasn't about an investment. He put my name on the papers for his corporation. So, if he goes, I get control of everything."

A shiver ran down Sal's spine.

Will took Sal's hand, massaging his knuckles and rolling the pad of his thumb down the length of his fingers. "We get George out of the way, and we'll be set up to be together all the time like you said." He looked up at Sal's bugged out face and scowled. "What? You been holding out on telling me a better plan?"

Sal huffed. "I been thinkin' twenty-four seven, but I ain't come up with somethin' like that."

"It's not so crazy. We sell his properties, it's a quarter mil in the bank."

Sal shifted his weight. The kid was serious. Or was he? "The guy's got a family. How you cutting them out?"

"His parents are gone, and his brother got killed in Korea. He has some relatives in the city, but he only sees them once or twice a year. They've never come up to visit him so I'm thinking they're not going to be a problem. Besides, legally, I'm his son."

Sal still doubted how well Will had thought things out. Murder for money? That was big league. The feds got involved in that kinda shit. "He's got friends, don't he? You said he's got people lookin' out for him."

"He's got people looking out for *me*."

"Which says he told people he's suspicious. He's worried 'bout you two-timing him. Dont'cha think they're gonna get more suspicious when George croaks and you're sittin' pretty?"

"When *we're* sittin' pretty. I'm not talking about doing it just for me. But if that's not important to you, forget I mentioned it." Will set Sal's hand aside and sat up, away from him.

"Baby, all's I'm sayin' is there's gotta be other options."

"Like what?"

Sal sat up, too, and rubbed the stubble on his chin. "What we need, you figure? Five thou?"

Will coughed out a bitter chuckle. "I'm telling you there's a way to get a quarter mil, and you're talking about five thou?"

"Your way is like tryin' to walk out of the auction house with the Hope Diamond."

"Nice. Glad you've got confidence in me." Will flicked his butt out to the water and stared blankly into the woods on the other side of the gorge.

"It ain't that I don't got confidence, but you done a job like that before?"

"Have you?"

"No. But I got a warrant and a record. You think 'bout that? What 'bout Hogan? He's sniffin' 'round the motel every week."

"Hogan can't figure out how to stop a teenager from marking walls with graffiti. He's not gonna be a problem."

"He can look up a crime registry, can't he? George turns up dead, I'm the first guy he's gonna wanna see."

Will snuck his hand under Sal's thigh. "You gonna let me explain? I didn't just get this idea from watching *Columbo*." Despite the fact that Sal was stressing, he sure liked what the kid's hand was doing. Will didn't touch him like that too often.

"With George's medical history, he's already living on borrowed time. I've seen his doctors' reports. He's got a coronary artery that's seventy-five percent blocked, and he's too stubborn to go for surgery. Meanwhile, he's on three prescriptions, and he's not supposed to be drinking or smoking." Sal watched him, transfixed. "What I'm thinking is, we make it look like an accident. One slip in the bathtub, and he's a goner. It doesn't even have to knock him out. With his heart, soon as he panics, he'll go into cardiac arrest. I've been looking into it. Falls are one of the most common causes of death for people with coronary disease. All we need to do is get him liquored up like you've seen him before. We do things right, when the paramedics find him, there won't be any questions. Then, as the executor of his properties, all I've gotta do is sell them off, and we can buy a place to make our own. I've been eyeing a lodge with cabins up in the Thousand Islands. It needs some work, but the location is prime. We can get it for forty grand and really turn it into something."

Sal licked his lips. Partly, he still couldn't believe they were having this conversation, but partly, he was flattered and impressed. Will was thinking about them running a business together? "How'd you find out about the place?"

"George's business newspapers. One of them has North Country real estate listings. I've been watching that lodge for weeks. I gave the agent a call the other day to ask some questions. It's a good deal, but it's not going to stay on the market forever."

Sal held Will's shoulder. "Baby, that's beautiful. But wouldn't it be safer to boost the money outta George?"

"'He's not liquid like that. I've been telling you, the motor lodge is gonna put him in bankruptcy in a couple months." Will brought up his knee and knit his hands over it. "The only way out for him is dumping his assets, and he's too bull-headed to do that."

"He been braggin' 'bout some big deal upstate."

"George is always bragging. Believe me, I've been with him for six years, and he hasn't come up with jack shit."

Sal tried to think things out. He was feeling antsy and short of breath.

Will clasped the hand Sal had put on his shoulder. "It's a nice place, Sal. The lodge is one of those log cabins. All exposed wood. Classical rustic, y'know? It's got four guest rooms, and a separate apartment for the owner. A big fireplace in the lobby, and it's got space for a cozy sitting area, a dining room overlooking the river, and a full-service kitchen. The property's got a little beach and a dock for renting canoes and fishing boats. Twelve cottages over five acres of wooded land. It's got a badminton and a shuffleboard court and a little playground for kids. I was thinking, we get a liquor license and bring in a band to perform on weekends, we could get business year round."

Will pulled Sal's arm around him tight. It was a pretty picture the kid was painting. Sal maneuvered so they were snuggled up together sleigh-style. Will slid his hand around the outside of Sal's calf.

"Maybe we'll both go to hell doing it," Will said. "But the thing is, I don't know if I care anymore. We deserve it, don't we? From all the shit we've had to put up with."

Sal smiled to himself. "I got experience with nightclubs. You know motels. We could make the place hot." He slipped his hand inside Will's shirt, found his nipple, and brushed it with his finger. "I'd have you in my bed every night."

Will reached his hand to the place between Sal's legs and

squeezed his hard-on through his denim shorts. "I know what you'd want to do."

Hunger wound up in Sal's gut. It was nearly stupefying. He played it off with some macho talk. "You want that? How much you want it, baby?"

"We take care of George, and you can be giving it to me every night."

Sal throbbed against his zippered fly. He heaved a breath. "George gotta be dead for me to give it to you? We could get a room right now at that thruway motel we passed by."

Will removed his hand. "I shouldn't have gotten you worked up. I was talking about the future."

Sal bowed his head and shrank into himself. "Yeah, it's true, you got me worked up, but what you never understand is I don't want to be with you like that just 'cause you turn me on. I'm tryin' to be your man. Y'know, take care of you, all the time."

Will held Sal's arm and caressed him. "I know, Sal. But we can't be taking chances being seen together at an economy motel. George knows people from Yonkers to Albany, especially in those kinds of places. But once he's out of the picture and we're up in the Thousand Islands, we can do whatever we want."

Sal didn't want to try wrapping his brain around what it meant to get George out of the picture. All he knew was they'd finally gotten away somewhere nice and private and ought to be able to show each other how much they felt. He rustled around, grabbed Will's mouth for a kiss, and leaned in to get on top of him. They made out, bare chest to bare chest, and Sal crept his hand toward Will's goods.

Will stilled Sal's hand. "If you want to do it, we gotta do it here." He glanced to one side, farther down the bank where it looked like there was a trail into the forest. He ran his fingers over Sal's hand. "Then we gotta head back to pick up George's truck so it doesn't look like we've been together till dark."

Sal didn't like the implication that their time together was going to end when they got back to the motor lodge. But he nodded, and the two stood up. Will sorted out a route to that trail, and Sal hiked behind him with his hard-on leading the way.

9

SAL'S HEAD WAS happily in the clouds while they rode back to the park, exchanged wheels, and drove on to the motor lodge. It was more from the fact he had made it with Will versus the actual making. The whole thing had been street, if he was being honest, like tricking in Central Park, and not the way he'd pictured their first time. He wanted to make love to Will the classy way, with a bottle of wine, a dim lit bedroom, and plenty of time to take things slow and easy. Still, it had happened, bringing him and Will even closer, and it was hot enough to linger in Sal's head.

The spot Will led them to was behind a concave boulder in the forest. Somebody had painted the words *Gay Love* on the face of it, and the ground was strewn with used rubbers, empty popper bottles, and cigarette butts. They had the place to themselves, and when Sal turned back to Will, he was kicking his shorts and briefs off his ankles. Sal closed in on him, crushed their mouths together, and took his bare ass in his hands.

Sal brought out the bottle of lube from his pocket and dropped his cut-off shorts. He started with the intention of making it sweet, but soon, he needed more of the delicious friction from Will's tight hole. He held Will fast and thrusted harder, gnawing on his neck, desperate for release. It was full-on fucking, outdoors in the daylight for any passerby to see.

When they arrived back at the motor lodge, that happy memory evaporated. Hogan's squad car was parked outside the diner. Will muttered to Sal to play along and pulled the truck into a spot in the front.

As they hopped out, Hogan strode over from his dickmobile with a big, dopey grin. Will retrieved the cooler from the back, and Sal stood around, trying to look chill.

"Howdy, boys," Hogan said. He raised his eyebrows at the sight of Sal.

Will lifted his hand in something of a wave. "What brings you here, Lieutenant?"

"Just doing my rounds. Hey, I told you, call me Danny."

"Diner's closed. You've got nothing better to do on a Sunday than hang out in the parking lot?"

In spite of Will's cold tone, Hogan smiled. "The thing is, my officer who works weekends called out sick. Food poisoning, he says. We're bare bones with the city's 'austerity budget,' so I gotta cover. I thought, might as well drive by George's place since you're having that problem with the high school punks."

"You'd have better luck checking out the other side of the building."

Sal noticed Hogan's face tick. He'd seen that look before on guys who were barely containing their shit. But Hogan was real good at containing it, at least with Will. He perked up with another dopey grin.

"You're right about that. I been back there, and you're squeaky clean."

"Thanks a million." Will started toward the kitchen door.

Hogan glanced at the cooler Will was holding. "Say, you guys coming back from the park?"

"Yep."

"Which one?"

"Hudson Highlands."

"No kidding. That's my favorite. You make it over to Lake Surprise?"

Will halted and looked at Hogan, impatiently.

"What time would you say you left out? I'm just curious."

"Is this an interrogation?"

Hogan chuckled. "No. You don't have to say. I'm just curious. I bet they get a good crowd over there on a sunny day like today." He glanced at Sal. "And this out-of-towner here, it must've been your first time. How'd you like the scenery?"

"It was swell."

"Youse two go fishing?"

Sal shook his head.

"That's too bad. Nothing better than fishing on a summer day. I should take you over to Wappinger Falls. It's the best place to catch trout. Whaddaya say, Sally-boy?"

"I ain't got many days free. 'Sides, I ain't got no fishin' gear."

"I'll take care of that. You just say what day, what time."

Will cut in. "If you don't mind, Lieutenant, we've got to unpack and check in with Tommy." He eyed the service door.

"Sure. I ain't gonna hold you up. Say, too bad George couldn't go with youse. He away for the weekend?"

"He's down in the city for his cousin's wedding."

"Ah, I see." Hogan looked back and forth between Will and Sal. His eyes twinkled in amusement. "Funny, ain't it? You two having a picnic lunch together."

Will looked at Hogan, dully.

"I mean, just a couple weeks ago, you was saying you barely knew Sally-boy, and now you're spending your day off together. Guess you hit it off, after all."

Will rolled his eyes.

Hogan went on. "When the cat's away, the mice will play. Ain't that the expression?" He winked at Sal.

"We did a quick run of the park, and now it's back to work," Will said. "You planning on hanging out? 'Cause it's not exactly great for business having a cop car in the lot like we've got a criminal investigation going on."

"Don't you worry. I've got to do my rounds. But make sure you let George know I've been looking for him."

"Sure thing."

"Hey, nice runnin' into you. You too, Sal. Them flower beds are something else. What do you call them spotted ones? Peonies?"

"They're pansies."

Hogan let out a stupid chuckle. "Pansies," he repeated. "Ain't that something?"

Will shoved off to the kitchen, and Sal took it slow in following him. He didn't want to look like they were too buddy-buddy. He heard Hogan whistling as he stepped back to his car. The melody was familiar. Sal went through the service door and stopped in his tracks.

It was that frickin' red robin song he was whistling.

SAL HAD HOPED to convince Will to sleep in his bed that night. But he didn't need Will to say that was a bad idea. The prick lieutenant had been sizing them up and making a point. He had eyes on them. The infuriating thing was that Will didn't even want to talk about it while they had some privacy in the kitchen.

"He's a crooked cop trying to throw his weight around," Will told Sal.

"What's his angle?" Sal peeked through the order counter toward the diner window. Hogan's car was long gone, but he still wanted to check. "He get somethin' outta tellin' George 'bout us?"

"It's not that serious, Sal. George greases his palm every now and then. That's how you do business in this town. It's another reason why I want to get the hell out of here."

Sal hadn't considered Hogan was putting the squeeze on George. The boys in blue did that to club owners. Sal didn't realize it happened in the boondocks, too.

Will finished getting the menu board ready for breakfast. "Take a shower and watch TV or something," he said. "I'm gonna see if Tommy needs anything, then I'm going up. I'll see you tomorrow."

Sal gained up on him as he headed toward the front desk. He pulled Will close and kissed him with some heat, tangling his fingers in the kid's thick hair. Afterward, he brushed his lips against Will's ear. "I don't like you running off on me."

Will's face colored, and he snuck his hand down Sal's shorts, holding him there. "You really got the hots for me, don't you? Wanna make it all the time."

Sal's body steamed. He reached for another kiss.

"You've gotta be patient, Sal." Will removed his hand. "George'll be back in the morning, but he'll probably go straight to bed to sleep off all the booze he drank at the wedding. When Loretta clocks out tomorrow, we can pick up on what we discussed."

Will went on his way to the front desk, and Sal drifted out the back door to his room. He threw off his clothes and took a long soak in the shower to cool his body. Every instinct was telling him he and Will should run off that night. He felt like screws were tightening around them. Maybe Sal was going paranoid, but things weren't adding up.

Will said Hogan was only interested in getting bribe money from George, but he sure was keeping a close eye on him and Will. He'd been whistling that same red robin song George was singing the other night!

Why that fucking song? It wasn't exactly popular. It was corny and old-fashioned, and it got Sal thinking Hogan had picked it up from George and was giving Sal a signal. *I know what you're up to.* Maybe Hogan knew Sal had a warrant. Sal's head was spinning. That night they'd played cards, Sal had told George his full legal name Silviu Minovichi. Had George given his name to Hogan so he could look him up? Was Hogan fronting like he hadn't seen George in ages, and the two guys had been talking all along? What was Hogan's game? Threatening to send him to the pen unless he coughed up some cash? Or had George asked Hogan to keep an eye on him? Sal remembered the sedan that had been parked across the street Friday night after closing. It could have been Hogan's squad car. Sal had barely made out the shape of it in the dark.

Keep it together, Sal told himself. He cut off the shower, stepped out, and toweled off. He was probably jumping to conclusions. Sure, it was a corny song, but George and Hogan were corny too. Tomorrow, Sal would ask Will if George and Hogan had gotten together in the past few weeks. The copper would've confronted Sal by now if he knew about his warrant. Sal snorted out a chuckle. He was finally getting to a good place with his life, and now his head was going screwy. Self-sabotage, they called it.

Sal sat down on his bed facing away from the window. His knee was bouncing. One thing he knew for sure is he wanted to get the hell out of the creepy town. It was playing with his head. He'd been thinking he and Will should get out with no muss or fuss, but now Will had this plan to ice George for a quarter mil. It was a big-time hustle. Enough bread for him and Sal to set up long-term. Will had put a lot of thought into the plan. He had his name on George's papers. He'd been keeping tabs on the old man's medical history. Sal fired up a cigarette and paced around the room.

Did he have the guts to kill George? He'd never done something so serious. It was a huge payoff, but could they really get away with it?

10

AROUND NOON THE next day, while Sal was sweeping out the breezeway by the ice machine, George's Oldsmobile rolled into the lot. Sal decided to play things friendly to get a read on the big guy. George parked by the diner and stepped out of the car. He noticed Sal waving hello, and he waved back. But he didn't come over. He shuffled into the diner.

Strange, it was. George usually shot the shit with anyone who crossed his path. And Will had mentioned, George would probably go straight to bed after living it up all weekend in New York. It would've made more sense for him to park in the back, near his apartment, to take his travel bag upstairs and relax a little. But something had the bossman eager to show face with his staff and most likely Will.

Sal kept sweeping for a minute or so, and then he couldn't contain his need to check things out. If he was slick about it, he could snoop on what George was up to. So, Sal put down his outdoor broom and strolled over to the diner. He would make like he was getting some cleaning gear out of the janitor's closet.

A pair of mechanics from the auto shop down the road were sitting at the counter, finishing their meal, and Sal heard Eddie spraying dishes in the kitchen. George and Will were nowhere to be found, which meant they were either in the office or by the front desk. Sal measured his steps to linger around. Voices carried from Will's office though they were low and indistinct. The janitor's closet was closer to that room, so Sal took his time over there filling up his cleaning tray. Then all hell broke loose in the office.

Shouting. Sal missed some words at first, but as he honed in, he caught pieces of the conversation.

"*Because I'm telling you, it's not due till the first of the month...*"

"*You want to see me lose my shit, I'll show you...*"

A metallic clang, like a hand slamming against a file cabinet.

"*Speak to me like that again, and you're gonna regret it...*"

"*How I spend my money is none of your concern...Yes, as a matter of fact, I bought myself a good time last night. 'CAUSE I DESERVE IT, having to put up with your shit day and night. You're the one who makes me do it.*"

That was all George. Sal wouldn't have been able to move if there'd been flames circling him.

"*I'll call Mohammed myself, and you can pick up the air conditioner units. You want to be a ball-breaker, try growing your own set of balls...What's that? WHEN I FUCKING FEEL LIKE IT. I been back for all of fifteen minutes and I ain't even had a cup of coffee.*"

George came storming out of the office. Sal quickly stooped inside the janitor's closet like he was going about his business. George stomped past him and went into the diner. Bells jangled, and Sal caught something interesting. Loretta was making an exit out the front door. Sal had a feeling she'd been listening to the commotion as well.

Sal waited for a count of ten, and he wandered over to the diner. The mechanics must've already settled their bill and cleared out. The bossman was alone, behind the counter. He was hunched over a little, breathing hard, and holding a handkerchief to his forehead.

Maybe another ten seconds passed, and then the bossman straightened up, and his glance landed on Sal. George wiped his sweaty brow, and he smiled at Sal like he was delighted to see him.

"How you doing, Sal?" He made a show of fanning himself with his handkerchief. "Can you believe this heat? We're only halfway through June! It's gonna be a hot one this summer."

Sal stood straight. "Good to see you, boss. How'd the city treat you?"

"It's not like it used to be. You know them panhandlers have gotten so uppity, they spit on your windshield at traffic lights so they can wash it with a dirty rag and expect you to give them money?"

George grabbed a mug and poured himself some coffee. "That Mayor Koch has got his work cut out from him. Transit worker strikes. Criminals and freeloaders taking over the city. All the good people are moving out, and who can blame 'em? Who wants to be harassed by bums just walking down the street?"

Sal scowled woefully. George took a sip of his coffee and fixed on him again. "I gotta ask you for a favor, Sal. Will needs some help picking up a pair of air conditioner units. The ones in 111 and 203 conked out. You think you could take a ride with him over to Newburgh?"

"Oh yeah. Sure. No problem." Sal lifted his tray of cleaning supplies. "I was just gonna give the vending machines a once over. Soon as I finish up, I'll give Will a hand."

"You're a prince, Sally-boy." George grabbed his mug. "I'm gonna take this up to my room. Gotta take a shower and change, and I'll be back to watch the place while youse two get those units. I got a good price for 'em from a friend who manages condos." He belched and winced like he had an upset stomach, or maybe he was out of breath.

"You got it."

George dabbed his brow with his handkerchief again. His complexion was the color of rotten meat, but he managed to collect himself and give Sal a wink. Then his glance strayed. "How 'bout giving the jukebox a polish? It's a beaut, ain't it?"

Sal nodded, and George bustled out the back door.

· · ·

SAL HAD A small window of time to go over to Will's office and find out what was going on. But he also could use that window to check out something else. He hadn't been the only one trying to nose in on George and Will's conversation. Sal watched the clock while he was wiping down the jukebox, and when five minutes passed, he figured it was safe to look for Loretta.

He'd noticed a family checking out of one of the front rooms that morning, so he swung over to the walkway along that wing. Sure enough, Loretta's laundry cart was parked at the open door where the family had been staying. She came out of the room as Sal was strolling along. Sal perched a cig between his lips and gave her a friendly glance.

Loretta took a sly account of their surroundings. Even in the street-facing lot, in the middle of the day, they had some privacy. The motel only had two guests in rooms around the back, and George and Will were far away in their respective places. Loretta picked out a cigarette from her apron, lit it up, and hung around as Sal approached.

"Nice weather we havin', ain't it?" he said.

Loretta got a sour look on her face and exhaled a puff of smoke. "Maybe for you. I gotta strip beds and vacuum in this heat. Half the rooms ain't got air conditioners that work, and Skippy says I can't use 'em anyway 'cause it's running up the electric bill."

Sal pulled out a friendly grin. "Say, you come across anything good lately?" He glanced at her apron pocket.

"No. Have you?"

Sal glanced here and there and sidled closer to her. "Nope." He set down his tray and sparked up his cigarette to join her. "But I think you was in the diner earlier. You hear them fireworks coming from the office?"

"You was there, too." Loretta studied Sal.

"I was getting my supplies outta the closet." He picked a fleck of tobacco from his tongue. "Didn't hear much, but it sounded kinda heated."

"Them two's always bickering. It ain't breaking news."

"Bickering, was it? The bossman…" Sal shook his head and grinned. "Sounded like he was losing his shit."

Loretta leaned over a little, confidentially, though her voice wasn't so low. "The way Skippy winds him up, wouldn't you be losing your shit too?"

Sal narrowed his brow.

"He was laying into George the minute he come back from the city. A lover's squabble." She made her stupid limp wrist gesture and took a drag on her Parliament. "I stay out of it. But I'll tell you this. One of these days the kid's gonna get what he deserves."

Sal faked a gleeful look. "How you mean he was winding George up?"

"He ain't got no respect. He's swindlin' George. Saying George ain't paid his bills when he's cookin' the books."

"That so?" Sal leaned closer to her himself. "I heard George say something 'bout paying for a good time last night." Sal watched Loretta carefully. She glanced to the side and ashed her cig.

"I don't know nothin' 'bout that."

"You think George is two-timing Will?"

Loretta shrugged. "I don't write the soaps. Got enough drama in my own life, if you know what I mean. But I wouldn't blame George if he was. The way the kid talks to him! How'd you like being called a useless, fat fuck?"

Sal skipped a beat. Did Will really say that? It was in the kid's vocabulary, but why would Will have a go at George when he was planning a double-cross, quiet-like? Sal wondered if Loretta was spinning things on account of her personal gripe with Will. He didn't like her attitude.

"You really think the two of 'em are queer?"

Loretta blew out smoke. "It's like I told you. Skippy's a snake, and he got George into that lifestyle. Probably blackmailing him or something."

Sal put on a chuckle. "You sayin' Will's forcing George to get down with him? That's far out. Say, you think a queer like him could turn somebody like me?" Loretta looked at him, blankly. Sal went on with some humor. "You think he could turn someone like you? With his queer voodoo or whatever you call it."

Loretta's face paled. "I ain't that kinda person."

"But you're sayin' George is?"

"No. That's not what I'm sayin'."

"So what're you sayin' 'bout the bossman?"

Her mouth hung open, though she didn't produce a word.

Sal burst out laughing. "I'm just fuckin' with you. Jesus, you should see your face."

Loretta gave him a chastising glare. It made her look even more ridiculous, and maybe Sal had taken things too far, but he sure enjoyed popping her hot air balloon. In his experience, people who judged other people's sex lives were hung up on their own. Meanwhile he remembered something else he wanted to ask her. "Hey, Hogan's been lookin' for George again. What you think that's about?"

Loretta took a final hard pull on her cig and crushed it under her grayed tennis shoe. "I think persons like me and you are better off stayin' out of that." She glanced at Sal knowingly and grabbed her gloves from her cart. "You oughta finish cleaning the graffiti around the corner. It ain't looking so good." With that, she went back into the room.

THAT LAST COMMENT of Loretta's bugged Sal. *Persons like me and you.* She seemed to be getting at something with that parting glance. What did she know about Sal to say something like that? Did she just mean shit workers like the two of them ought to know their place and stay out of whatever was going on with George and Hogan? Or had she clocked Sal as a guy who'd had trouble with the law, and she also had a criminal history? Either way, Sal didn't appreciate the warning and whatever implication she was making.

He was also miffed about the graffiti she mentioned. Sal had been doing a little work on that every couple of days, the best he

could. He took a walk over to that wall, and as he was coming
along, it didn't look so bad at first. Maybe the spray paint hadn't
vanished completely, but like George said himself, he wasn't
running the Taj Mahal.

He came up to the spot and looked at it from different angles,
and then he stepped back to look at it squarely. You couldn't see
the original writing: "Murphy Does Rush," could you? It was early
afternoon, and the sun hit that wall so hard, it glowed. Sal
squinted. Like a flaming message from the devil, words blared out.

Mur D e R

Sal nearly shit himself. Had he just not noticed that he'd made
more progress with certain letters and less with others? Had
someone touched it up? He couldn't have been so oblivious, could
he? It looked like it could be seen from a mile away. He stepped
quickly to the utility room to get the steel brush and the WD-40,
and he tried to scrub away those six letters until his fingers were
bleeding.

11

SAL FOUGHT OUT of the sinking feeling somebody was fucking with him. It was just graffiti. People marked up walls with all kinds of shit. Maybe it was just the way the light hit that wall at that time of day, accenting the letters, which formed that word.

After scouring the spot, he stepped back and studied it from every angle. It didn't look much different from the muddy blur it had been the last time he did some work on it, three days ago. Sal got to thinking the word might never have even been there in the first place. Could be Loretta had put it in his head something serious was going on with that spot, and he'd imagined it. He'd been stressing bad that day.

Sal didn't have a lot of time to think about it. As he was putting away his cleaning gear, Will came around the front of the diner in George's truck, honking for Sal to get in. He looked pretty steady, but he was also giving off the vibe he wasn't in the mood to talk. Sal wasn't crazy about that. He wasn't crazy about a lot of things. When they made it over the bridge to Newburgh, Sal brought up what was on his mind.

"Couldn't help hearing George shoutin' in the office."

Will kept his gaze pinned straight ahead.

Sal picked some dirt from his fingernails. "Eddie and the

customers in the diner must've heard it too. So, you gonna tell me what happened?"

"George is a fucking prick."

Sal glanced at him, waiting for more.

"He's two months overdue on the gas bill. So, what am I supposed to do? Just pretend like it's not a problem 'cause he doesn't want to hear it?" He stretched and balled up his hands a couple times, working out some tension. "George gets like that. Thinks he can use me as his punching bag."

"He ain't like hearin' 'bout his debts or he ain't like hearin' you accuse him of sleepin' 'round?"

Will scowled. "Why would I give a shit if he's sleeping around?"

Sal gave him a sidelong glance.

"He talks about it like he's bragging, but it's pathetic. The only way he's getting any is paying some street kid to let him suck his dick in his car. You think I care?"

"Just sounded kinda serious."

They sat in silence for a while. Then Will pulled into the lot for an apartment building, parked the car, and turned to Sal.

"We gotta do this soon. George is pissing away money left and right. The way things are going, he won't be able to make payroll next week." Will glanced around. "This Sunday, I'll get George to invite you over to play cards. We'll make sure he's good and drunk and get this over with."

Sal froze up for a moment. He hadn't expected Will to come back to that topic so soon.

"What?" Will said.

Sal shifted in his seat. "Youse two just had a blow up over money that people probably heard across the river. You think it's a good time to do that kind of thing?"

Will stared grimly out the windshield with his hands still curled around the wheel. "You like him treating me like shit?"

"No."

"Then what's your problem?"

"Baby, I'm with you. I'm just talkin' things out. We don't need nothin' callin' attention to what we're doin'."

"That's fucking hysterical coming from you. You're all over me any chance you get, but I'm the one who's 'calling attention.'"

Sal clasped his arm. "That's only 'cause I can't get enough of you." Not a muscle moved on Will's face, and his entire body was tensed.

"So, what's your point?"

"We gotta look out for complications, don't we? It ain't gonna work if people are suspicious."

"Nobody's going to be suspicious about George having a heart attack."

Sal remembered the way George looked earlier that day. He wasn't well. Anybody could see that. But they still ought to be concerned about Hogan and Loretta, shouldn't they?

"George talk to Hogan lately?"

Will gave Sal a surly look. "No. Why would you ask that? You know he's always bitching about George not being around."

"I just been thinkin', how would you know?" Sal watched Will closely.

"George's got no reason to be talking to Hogan. He knows Hogan's looking for money. That's why he makes himself scarce. I thought you understood that."

Again, Will's snotty tone got under Sal's skin. He wasn't a goddamn idiot. "So, what you're sayin' is, Hogan already has a reason to be suspicious. 'Cause George is avoiding him."

"Hogan's a small-time bully. You don't need to be afraid of him."

"I ain't afraid of him." Sal drew into himself. Something wasn't feeling kosher. Or was he just getting cold feet?

"Then what're you worried about?" Will said.

Sal pushed back his hair. "It ain't a little job to get away with, is it? You thought about Loretta? I seen her after you and George had that fight."

Will looked at him like he was way off the mark. "Loretta?"

"Yeah. She's nosy, and she's no fan of yours. Somethin' 'bout a raise she says you owe her."

"Loretta's lucky she's still got a job. I would've gotten rid of her if it weren't for George."

"That's my point. She's got beef with you. She's already sayin' you're scammin' George so what you think she's gonna say when the cops start askin' questions?"

"Loretta's saying I'm scamming George?"

Sal nodded.

Will smiled bitterly. "She's the fucking scam artist. Let me tell you something about Loretta. She got canned from her last job for running up charges on stolen credit cards. She spent time in prison. Had her kids taken away. The whole nine yards." Will lit up a cigarette. "The only reason George hired her is 'cause he can't resist hard luck cases. But I'm telling you, you're freakin' out over nothing. Even if Loretta was dumb enough to try to make trouble, nobody's gonna believe her. She's a felon with a shitty work record. I got it documented. I caught her trying to lift bathroom supplies."

That filled out a picture for Sal, but he still wasn't feeling good about Loretta. It was true, cops took the testimony of a con with a grain of salt, but they also liked pressuring them for information.

"Hogan know 'bout her?"

"Maybe. Probably. Which means he's not gonna waste his time on her opinions."

Sal looked Will in the eyes. "You say he's a dirty cop."

Will huffed. "You're overthinking things, Sal. George has a ticker that could go anytime. It's the easiest job in the world."

"Easy for you, maybe. I got a warrant."

Will's gaze softened. He switched out hands on his cigarette so he could place his right hand on Sal's knee. "I know. But listen, I got a plan. After he goes, we'll get you out of town. I'll shut down the motor lodge. Lay off the staff. We'll get you a place to stay up north while I sort things out. You see? You won't be around for anyone to question you."

Sal hadn't thought much about how they were going to handle things after they did it. "You gonna send me away?"

Will squeezed Sal's knee. "It's for your protection. So nobody can say you're involved."

"I ain't leavin' you on your own. 'Sides, ain't it gonna look worse, me skippin' town?"

"Sal, what you've got to understand is we do this right, there's not going to be an investigation. George drops dead. He's got coronary disease. There's no other cause of death. People don't know about you and me. I lay you off like everybody else, and nobody's gonna raise an eyebrow about you leaving town. Meanwhile, I go about my business closing George's estate and buying that property in the Thousand Islands. All you've got to do is wait up there until it's safe for me to come up."

It made sense, but it sank in to Sal, he could be waiting a long time. "How long you figure?"

Will shrugged. "I have to sell off George's properties. Wait for the money to come through, and then I've got to buy that lodge. It'll be better nobody sees us together for a while anyway. Figure three, four months."

Sal eyed Will, cooly. "S'pose I don't want to be away from you that long?"

"I'm not gonna like it either, but you're going to have to, Sal." Will tossed his cig out the window.

"You says we're doin' this so we can be together."

"We are. You're the one who's freaking out about your record. That's why we get you out of town so nobody's looking at you."

Sal shifted in his seat. "If we're doin' this to be together, I'm sayin' there's other ways."

Will stared at him. "You're shitting me."

"Baby, at the end of the week, I'll have close to a thou saved up. That's enough to get us settled up north."

Will looked at Sal in disbelief. "Why are you backpedaling all of the sudden?"

"What I'm saying is we ain't gotta do this job to be together. I got some funds to get us started, and we can save up money to buy that place in the Thousand Islands."

Will laughed. "You've got a thousand dollars. We need four times that to put a deposit on the place, and then we've gotta pay for a mortgage. You're fucking dreaming, Sal."

Sal laid his hand on Will's leg. "It's enough to rent an apartment. We get jobs for a while. Between the two of us, the money'll stack up fast."

Will removed Sal's hand from his leg. "I can't fucking believe you're backing out now. Guess I was wrong. You don't give a shit about anyone but yourself."

"Take it easy. I'm tryin' to look out for you."

"I didn't spend six years with George bossing me around to end up with nothing. It's a quarter mil, Sal. I'm not washing dishes or bussing tables on the chance I'll have that kind of money by the time I'm sixty years old. But if you want to bail, go set yourself up somewhere with the money you got from working at the motel. I don't have shit, but I guess that's the breaks, right?"

Sal couldn't put words together to make Will see he was only looking out for their future. Will climbed out of the truck to see the manager about the air conditioner units, and Sal followed him.

12

SAL DIDN'T GET much sleep that night, and when his clock alarm went off, it didn't take long for his stomach to sink again from the predicament he was in. He couldn't get Will to understand there were easier options for them to get out together. He hated Will questioned his loyalty. It was getting Sal thinking that maybe he was being a pussy. Will had a plan. He knew the motel's whole cast of characters better than Sal. Sal was having trouble trusting his own instincts. Was he going a little mental? He'd been freaking out about weird shit like that graffiti turning into the word *Murder*, and that red robin song that kept coming up.

Sal fought through his gloom and came down to the diner to get it cleaned up for opening. Eddie came along a little after seven. They got the place ready for business, and Tommy was popping his head in the diner every five minutes, looking for Will to relieve him from his night shift at the front desk. But Will didn't show up at seven like he usually did, and by eight o'clock, he still hadn't come down from his room. A pair of motel guests were waiting outside the diner, and Tommy had his hands full checking out a family. Sal wandered over to the kitchen to see what Eddie wanted to do.

He and the cook had figured out how to communicate in

broken English, and Eddie was anxious to get some business going that morning. So, Sal decided to open the front door and get the two motel guests seated at a table. He brought the couple mugs and poured their coffees, and a little later, he scratched down their orders on one of Will's pads. It wasn't hard to do, but if neither Will or George showed up that morning, things were going to get hairy when it came time to settle the bills. The cash register was locked.

Just as Sal was bringing the couple's order to their table, he spotted Will ducking into the place wearing sunglasses. He went straight to his office. Sal got the customers settled with their breakfast and glanced out front. He saw Tommy skipping along to his car. Otherwise, the parking lot was empty. Loretta wasn't due to show up until nine. Sal casually drifted off to see what was up with Will.

He was getting cash from the safe to stock the register. Why was he wearing sunglasses indoors? Will had never been late to open up the place, and his bearing was kind of timid, like he didn't want Sal looking at him.

Sal shut the office door behind him and stepped over to Will. On closer inspection, his nose was swollen. His movements were jerky. The sight of that halted Sal, and then Will grabbed the money wallet for the cash register and tried to step by him.

"You gonna get out of the way?"

Sal held Will's arm. "You gonna tell me what's going on?"

Will pushed the money wallet on Sal, removed his sunglasses, and faced Sal squarely. His right eye was half shut and bloodshot, and a blue bruise was blooming under it. Sal cringed like he'd been socked in the face himself. Soon after, his anger flared.

"George do that to you?"

Will replaced his sunglasses and said nothing.

"Tell me. I'll fucking kill him."

"I'm fine, Sal." Will grabbed back the money purse.

Sal stood in his way. "He hit you before?"

Will looked down at the floor and said nothing.

"You never tol' me."

"Sometimes. When he's drinking." Will raised his head. "It's my problem to deal with. You made it clear you're not getting involved." He turned to the side. "It'll look pretty gruesome for a couple of days, and then it goes away."

Sal pushed back his hair and rounded himself. He wanted to break something, or kick Will's metal trash can hard, but he managed to hold it down.

"I'll make him pay for what he done." Sal swallowed a lump in his throat. "Baby, I'm sorry. I didn't know."

Will's face was hard. "What didn't you know, Sal? You didn't know George humiliates me, and I've gotta take it 'cause I've got nowhere else to go?"

Sal's voice trembled. "He ain't gonna do that to you never again."

"Really? 'Cause you been acting like you couldn't be bothered."

"Baby, listen. I promise, I'll do whatever it takes."

"Yeah. Sure." Will bumped past Sal with the money purse. "C'mon. We've got a place to run."

SAL WAS SEETHING that morning and feeling shitty about himself. He'd known Will and George had heated arguments. He'd heard them fighting just the day before. Sal also knew George drank, which made him liable to get out of hand when he was alone with Will. Yesterday, instead of showing concern, Sal had grilled Will about the fight and given him shit. He should've stepped in to protect the kid. He left Will on his own with his drunk old man that night, and George had hit Will hard to give him that shiner. Sal wanted to march straight up to George's apartment and break the fucker's face to let him know how things were going to be.

First thing was, though, he ought to beg for Will's forgiveness. He'd fucked up, and he had to make Will understand he'd never, ever do that again. Sal could barely focus on his work. Should he go to Will right away? Or give him a little time? Sal couldn't decide. Will shouldn't have to be alone after what he went through, but he still had a business to run and wouldn't want anything calling attention to what happened with George.

The diner was empty after the two guests settled their bill, and then Will set himself up at the front desk for a trickle of customers checking out or checking in. Sal settled on giving him some breathing room, but he didn't wander far. He took his time spraying down wall tiles in the hallway to the john. Then, he heard George come down to the diner. He was chatting up Eddie in Portuguese like the scumbag phony he was. Sal snuck over to take a peek.

George got himself a mug of coffee, and Eddie passed him a plate of eggs, corned beef hash, and toast through the order window. George sat down at the counter to feed his face. He had some big legal envelope with him, but he didn't look different than any other day. Acid rose in Sal's throat. Someone who done what he did ought to at least look guilty.

George finished his breakfast, threw down his napkin, and picked his teeth with his finger. Then he headed to the front door, near where Sal was spying on him. Sal slunk deeper in the hall, and the bossman didn't look his way while he was bustling along. Once George was out the door, Sal snuck up to the front to see where George was going. The big guy got into his Oldsmobile and drove off.

The diner was dead, and with George cleared out, it was the perfect time to see how Will was doing and reassure him that he had his back. But out of nowhere, Sal was crawling with nerves. He wasn't good with words, and if Will told him off again for what he'd done, Sal felt like he'd break into pieces. He decided to do some shit that needed to be done. He had those air conditioner units he'd picked up with Will, and they needed to be installed. There were some cracks in the parking lot that he'd been meaning to seal. Sal kept busy with those tasks, thinking it meant something that he was taking care of things Will wanted him to do. Later in the afternoon, Sal had a second wave of self-recrimination. He ought to be a man and tell Will he'd fucked up. Sal didn't have experience with that kind of situation, but with Will, he was trying to be a better person.

Sal put away his supplies, and he skulked over to the front desk where Will was working.

Will's eyes were hidden behind his sunglasses. He looked up briefly and went back to opening letters from the mail. Sal stared at him with all his repentance pouring from his face. Eventually, Will stood, caught Sal's gaze, and went into the back office. Sal followed him and closed the door behind them.

"What is it, Sal?" Will said.

Sal pressed up on him and lightly touched his shoulder. "Just wanna make sure you're okay."

"I'm fine."

Sal clasped Will's neck. "How's your head?"

"I took a couple aspirins."

Sal hugged him gently and kissed the side of his face.

"Sal, it's not the time."

"I'm sorry, baby." Sal's eyes burned. "I shoulda looked out for you." He didn't know how to say anything more about what he was feeling. The only language he knew was physical. Sal nuzzled at the crook of Will's neck, and he grasped Will's belt and unbuckled it.

Will held Sal's hand still. Sal pushed Will's hand aside and captured him through his briefs. "I wanna take care of you, baby," he croaked. A hungry pang ached from Sal's gut, and simultaneously he felt fragile. "Just wanna make you feel good again."

"You're fucking crazy," Will cursed lightly.

"Crazy for you." Sal dug inside Will's briefs.

Will gasped and gripped Sal's arm hard. "Jesus. Me getting beat up makes you horny?"

"I wanna take you away from all this." He kissed Will's neck while he caressed him tenderly between the legs. Will slowed Sal down.

"This is as far as it goes."

Sal nuzzled against Will's neck. "Lemme get you off. You want my mouth? My ass?"

"I want to get back to the front desk. I've got things to do, and George'll be back soon."

"We do him tonight, and we ain't gotta be careful no more."

Will gasped again when Sal hit a sweet spot. "We can't do it tonight. I told you, Sunday. I've got it planned out. You've got to promise you'll behave till then."

Will's cockhead was dewy with precum. Sal used it to lubricate his motions, watching Will's body tense, his lips part with a labored breath, and then he choked out Will's spunk. Mostly, it volcanoed on Sal's hand, but a few spurts globbed Will's shirt tails.

Will broke away, got a box of tissues from the shelf and ripped out a couple to clean up. He looked down at himself. "Great. Now I've got a busted face *and* a nice big stain on my shirt."

Sal took a look. It didn't seem so bad. Will tucked his shirt into his pants, anyway. He grabbed some tissues for himself.

Will patted his shirt with his tissues. "This your way of saying you're not going to bail on me? Or did you just want to fuck with me again?"

Sal figured he deserved some licks. "I ain't bailing on you."

"If you're serious, we've got to cool it for a few days." Will redressed himself while carefully holding his wad of tissues. He looked up at Sal who also had a gluey mess of tissues in his hand. Will pushed his tissues on Sal. "Take 'em with you. Make sure no one sees you, and flush 'em down the toilet."

Sal understood that precaution. He didn't like the kid's dismissive tone. "I ain't leaving you alone with George."

"You've got to leave me alone with George."

Sal pressed up on him again. "I ain't letting you get hurt again." His chest was heaving.

"You my big protector now?"

Sal clasped Will's shoulder blades and bowed his head.

Will gently took Sal's hands and held them at his sides. "I

appreciate it, but Sal, you understand we've got to let things play out? It only works if George doesn't know it's coming."

Sal snorted and shifted his weight. "What am I supposed to do? Sit outside his apartment all night?" He shrugged. "I'll do it, and if he so much as raises his voice to you, I'm breakin' down the door."

Will wrapped his arms around Sal's shoulders. "Come here. You know you can't do that. It's not about me. It's about us. And a quarter mil. You've got to trust me on this, okay?"

That fragile feeling was sneaking up on Sal again. He sucked in a breath, but his voice still came out tremoring. "If he touches you again, I'm killing him."

Will hugged Sal's head against him. "Baby, take it easy. He's not going to do it again. Thursday night, he has a trip to Saratoga Springs. He says it's to see about a property, but I think he met some kid up there he's fucking. He won't be back till Sunday. So, it's just two nights I've got to play along, and when he comes back from his trip, we'll get him out of the way for good."

Sal was a little bit encouraged by that, though Sunday was five days away.

ANOTHER SLEEPLESS NIGHT bled into another hazy, grouchy day for Sal. It was useless trying to sleep when Will was upstairs with George, possibly getting pushed around, or worse. Sal sat by his open window in his underwear, chain-smoking cigarettes and listening for clues of what was happening. He heard George's boisterous voice, his awful singing, and then his Greek music came on.

Sal couldn't say it sounded argumentative. At one point, he thought he heard laughter. Were they drunk and laughing? It was driving Sal crazy not knowing what was going on. At midnight on the dot, the music cut out, and Sal didn't hear a peep from up there.

Everybody went about their business the next day, and it was the same thing Wednesday night. All Sal could figure was the two were getting along. He hoped they weren't getting along *too* well. It was a goddamn nightmare he was living. Too many things were fucking with his head.

He knew schemes required patience. You had to make a mark feel comfortable 'cause if you struck too soon, things could go left. But the thought of George touching Will, whether hurtfully or intimately, had Sal losing his mind. It didn't help that the early summer heat wave didn't let up, and his room didn't have an air conditioner. There was barely a breeze at night, and Sal was sweating through his bed sheet under a useless ceiling fan. At one point, he did push-ups on the floor to try to wear out his body. Then he went to his bathroom to splash some water on his face, and at the sight of his reflection, he launched his fist into the mirror, shattering the glass and sending his hand screaming to high heaven.

Like a fucking mook, Sal came down to the diner Thursday morning with an Ace bandage wrapped around his hand. It was so sore, he couldn't use it to hold a toothbrush, let alone a mop or broom, and he'd have to spin a story about jamming it in a door if anybody asked. Nobody did, but it slowed down his routine that morning while he was favoring his left hand. Eddie came in at seven fifteen. Will took over the counter a little after that. They had some customers while Sal was grunting through his daily clean-up of the bathrooms and mopping the floors. Then to his surprise, he heard George's whistling and the bossman waddled in behind the counter in an upbeat mood.

Sal pushed his mop and bucket over to the bathroom hallway and listened to George converse with Eddie while Will tended the booths. They were all acting like nothing special was going on. Then Sal caught a glance of Hogan's squad car pulling up outside. He slipped into the men's room and listened at the door.

He heard Hogan give George a big, friendly greeting, and then the conversation was too low for Sal to make out. He carefully stepped out of the bathroom to overhear.

"It's my lucky day," Hogan said. "I been telling Will I been looking for you for weeks. Business good up in Kingston? That the reason you ain't been slumming it down here?"

"Not at all. I've just been doing some traveling here and there."

"Sure you have. That's the life of a big shot real estate developer, ain't it? I don't know how you do it, George, with all the hustle and bustle. Makes it hard to keep up with people, now don't it? I says to Will, when am I gonna hang out with George again? We had a good time at that place up in Poughkeepsie, didn't we?"

"Sure we did. But you forget I'm an old man. It's not easy keeping up with you."

"Keeping up with *me*?" Hogan balked. "I'd be lucky to keep up with *you*."

George pshawed. "I'm driving up to Sarasota Springs tonight. It's a big deal I'm working on, but we'll see about that place in Poughkeepsie real soon."

"A big deal you're workin' on? No kiddin'! What you got going on now?"

"I can't say just yet. The party involved prefers to keep things private, but you'll be hearing about it soon enough. Now what can I get you, Lieutenant?"

Sal took a peek around the wall of the bathroom hallway. Hogan was parked in front of the counter with his back turned to Sal. George's attention was on Hogan. Will drifted behind the counter with his order pad looking less confident than usual.

"This guy here knows what I like," Hogan said, fixing on Will. "Holy Moses. What happened to you? That a shiner behind those sunglasses?"

George chuckled, maybe a little nervously. "It was an accident, and he won't let me forget it. Will keeps telling me we need to replace the lamp out back. He fell flat on his face taking the garbage out to the dumpster the other night." George pantomimed and whistled the motion.

"Get out. And here I thought you was gonna tell me I oughta see the other fella." Hogan turned around, and Sal ducked his head just in time. "Say, what're you doing taking the trash out in the middle of the night? Ain't you got Sally-boy to take care of that?"

"I told him the same thing," George cut in. "Will says he likes to set a good example for the employees."

Sal took another peek into the room. Will was facing Hogan with his order pad.

"One coffee. One blueberry muffin. That it?"

"You know it, handsome."

Will went to give the order slip to Eddie and fetch Hogan's coffee. Hogan pepped up in his typical cocky way.

"Hey George, I don't think he likes me calling him handsome, but you don't mind, do you? You gotta admit, he's got a million-dollar face. Like that teen idol." Hogan snapped his fingers. "Leif Garrett. That's the one, ain't it?"

George smiled. "I don't know anything about teen idols."

"Look 'im up," Hogan said. "He's all over the magazines at the supermarket. I saw 'im the other day on the cover of *TV Guide*, which is when it hit me. That's Will. The babyface, I mean. Y'know, without all that fairy feathered hair."

Neither George nor Will said anything. Soon enough, the kitchen bell rang, and Will bagged Hogan's muffin and coffee and brought them over. Hogan took out his big wallet, but George waved him off.

"It's on the house."

"You sure? I got three singles here."

"You've been keeping the riffraff away," George said.

Hogan put his wallet back into his pocket. "Ain't that some-thing? The celebrity treatment." He pointed his finger at George. "But don't think that gets you off the hook. You're coming with me to Poughkeepsie. What's it they say in that song? Take a break and smell the roses?"

"You've gotta stop and smell the roses," Will corrected him.

"That's it. By that country singer Gordon Lightfoot."

"Mac Davis."

"Mac Davis?" Hogan repeated. "Mac Davis! That's right. Listen to this kid. He's got looks *and* brains. Well fellas, I gotta be on my way."

Sal slipped back into the bathroom. He listened as Hogan strutted out of the diner, and he waited to hear the engine of his car vroom to life and the squeak of its wheels rolling away. Then a bustle of steps gained up on the door. Sal didn't have time to hide in the stall. He backed away, and then the door flew open, nearly giving him a heart attack.

George looked as surprised as Sal was. "Sal. What you doing hiding in here?"

Quick on his feet, Sal told him. "I ain't hiding, boss. Just been a little queasy." He glanced at the stall. "I think I'm feeling better now. Hope you don't mind."

George put two and two together, looking a little queasy himself as he peeked at the stall, imagining things. "Of course not. You just gave me a scare." He walked past Sal to the urinal, unfastened his belt and zipper, and let out a stream. He called over his shoulder. "Take it easy today if you're not feeling well. Will'll understand."

Sal wanted to get the hell out of there, but running off too quickly felt disrespectful and possibly suspicious. He remembered to hide his bandaged hand behind him. "I think it's out of my system, if you know what I mean. I'll be fine."

George zipped up and stepped over to the sink to wash his hands. He smiled at Sal in the mirror. "I like your attitude. If you want to make money, there's no time to be sick. When I was younger, I never let a fever or a stomach ache hold me back. The work still needs to get done, doesn't it? It's just going to be waiting for you the next day, right?"

"Right."

George grabbed some paper towels to dry his hands. "Say Sal, I'm glad I ran into you. I'm going upstate for the next three days, but I been meaning to ask you, how'd you like to come over for dinner and cards this Sunday?"

"This Sunday?"

George tossed his towels into the trash and looked at Sal chummily. "Will's been after me to invite you. I know the card game didn't go so well last time, but I think you liked my cooking." He wriggled his eyebrows. "And my beer."

"That's real nice of you."

"We can say 'round eight. Like last time."

"All right."

"Good. I'm leaving Will in charge while I'm gone." George halted, as though he had struck on a brilliant idea. "Youse can knock off early Saturday and take one of your excursions together. I'll ask Tommy to come in at seven, and between him and Eddie, they can handle the late dinner crowd. You'll still have daylight to take a walk 'round the dock park or whatever youse want to do."

Sal dropped his gaze and nodded along.

"Eight on Sunday," George repeated. "And don't be spending your money on candies, Sal. Just bring yourself."

With that, George exited the bathroom.

13

SAL WAS REELING while he headed out to spread some black top around the rear parking lot. These upstate people were acting loony. First, it was Hogan. Will said the lieutenant was only interested in shaking George down for money, but the guy kept sticking it on Will. He either had a thing for him or he was harassing the kid the way some straight guys tried to bully queers. Sal didn't think it was the latter. Will held his own with the cop.

The weird shit Hogan came up with! It was always some oddball phrase, and it always got a reaction out of Will. Almost like they had some kind of code for talking in front of other people. The idea of the two having a secret relationship slashed at Sal.

Then there was George. He lied to Hogan about how Will had gotten his shiner. That showed the prick he was, and then he was acting all smug about inviting Sal to dinner and pushing him to spend more time with Will while he was away. The guy couldn't be that clueless. Was he throwing it in Sal's face that he knew they'd been messing around? *Take one of your excursions together.* He and Will had only gone out once. It was a screwy thing to say, wasn't it?

George had to be trying to mess with his head. He was playing the big kahuna, like Sal ought to be so honored he was inviting him over for dinner again. Or like he wanted Sal to know he was far above being threatened by someone like him. Throwing it in Sal's face that Sal could fuck Will as much as he liked, but the kid belonged to him.

George left for his trip to Saratoga Springs, and Saturday night, when Tommy showed up to take over from Will at the diner, Will told Sal to meet him out back in twenty minutes. He was going to take a shower, and they'd take the truck to a drive-in movie theater. Sal gave Will a two-minute head start and fast tracked to his room to quickly shower and change.

Earlier in the day, he'd run over to the liquor store and bought a bottle of bubbly to surprise Will. He got himself looking sexy in a sleeveless T-shirt and a tight pair of jeans, and he grabbed the bottle from the ice bucket and sized up the back lot. They only had one guest in a room back there, and his car was gone. With nobody around, Sal stepped upstairs, sweeping a glance here and there along the way. Will's room was dark. There was a light on in George's place. Sal took another look around, confirming that nobody had seen him, and he rapped on George's door.

He had to do it twice, and then steps gained up from inside, and Sal heard the clink of the eyehole on the other side of the door.

"What're you doing here, Sal?"

Sal drew a breath and didn't answer.

The door cracked open, and Will peeked out. Without Will's sunglasses, Sal could see that the swelling around his eye had lessened, but it was purple under the lid with a yellow semi-circle. He had just gotten out of the shower with a towel wrapped around his waist, and he had a mixture of terror and irritation on his face. Will mouthed in a whisper, "I told you to give me twenty minutes and meet me by the truck."

Sal showed him the bottle of bubbly. "I thought we'd stay in instead."

Will's gaze sharpened forbiddingly. Sal put his hand on the

door. "Ain't nobody 'round to see. You keep me waitin' out here, it might be a different story."

Will gradually took in the dilemma, stood back, and Sal pushed in. Will shut the door and locked it. He started saying some bullshit, and Sal set down the champagne on a table and shut him up with a forceful kiss. He hoisted him into his arms and powered through carrying Will to the bedroom. Sal threw him down on the queen-size bed and pounced on top of him.

Will tried to slow Sal down and cursed him out at first. But by the time Sal had Will's knees on his shoulders and his mouth all over his peach, Will lay still with his hands gripping the sheets. Sal wrestled out of his shirt, shrugged off his jeans, knelt between the kid's legs and palmed himself with lube. Then he raised the kid's knees, slapped his bottom, and forced his cock inside him.

Sal's brain whited out from how good it felt. The kid bellowed on the cusp of agony and ecstasy, and he punched Sal's chest and dug his short-clipped fingernails into the back of Sal's shoulders. The smell of George, saturated in the bedding, got Sal working harder, wanting to obliterate the smug fucker. They grinded and grasped for each other, and Sal jacked out Will's spew while he lost it inside him.

Sal lay down on the bed and entwined their sweaty bodies. He shut his eyes. His heartbeat pounded against Will's back.

Will played with Sal's hand, which was attached to his hip. "We could've done it in the truck. You couldn't wait or does it get you off sticking it to George?"

Sal kissed the damp nape of his neck. Will smelled so damn good after sex. He craned over him to nuzzle against his cheek. "Want you all the time, baby."

Will flinched. Sal drew back, realizing he must've come too close to his sore eye.

"Yeah, I must be a real looker," Will said.

Sal gripped Will's thigh between his and gently kissed the back of his head. "You always beautiful. This way or any way."

They were quiet for a while, just touching here and there. It was luxurious, finally having a bed to lay down in together. Then, Will found Sal's bandaged hand.

"What did you do to yourself?"

Sal drew his hand away. "It's nothin'. I got pissed. Needed to let off some steam."

Will turned over to face him. "You don't need to do that. Two days from now, we won't have to worry about George."

Sal propped himself up on his elbow and studied Will. Every aspect of his face was perfection. Sal's heart soared, and then it dropped from the reservations that still fluttered in his gut.

Will fingered Sal's hair, which had grown below his ears. "You need a haircut." He got up from the bed. "C'mon. We'll wash up, and I'll cut your hair."

Sal followed him to the bathroom with a lopsided smile on his face. He didn't mind having new experiences. Will cranked on the water in the bathtub shower and held his hand under the faucet until it was the temperature he liked. He shut the stopper to get it spraying through the handheld showerhead and waved Sal inside.

Will stepped in behind him, and Sal was already feeling frisky again. He faced Will and grabbed his bottom. Will swatted him away and took the showerhead in his hand.

"Control yourself." Will sprayed Sal in the face, which got Sal scowling and thinking about yanking the showerhead away from him. Then Will focused on his shoulder and spread the water down his arm with his hand. That was sweet. He raised Sal's arm to rinse his armpit and sprayed him down top to bottom with his warm hand touching him all over to direct the flow over his skin.

Sal was tense and ticklish at first. He'd been naked with hundreds of men before and let strangers touch his body, but what Will was doing had him feeling strangely shy. Like it was the first time somebody had discovered how tightly strung his body was. His hands were magic, and soon enough, Sal shut his eyes and relaxed while Will washed away all that tension.

Will lathered Sal with soap from front to back and rinsed him off with the showerhead and his guiding hand. No one had ever done that to Sal before. It felt more intimate than anything he'd done sexually and raised emotions in Sal. He chased them away by making a wisecrack.

"I took a shower 'fore I came here. You just like feeling me up?"

Will doused Sal's head and worked a handful of shampoo into his hair. "I'm only doing this to get you ready to cut your hair. So you don't look like Captain Caveman." He raked Sal's scalp with his fingers, releasing the tension there. Will rinsed Sal and shuffled him out of the shower, and then he scrubbed up and rinsed himself.

Sal dried off with the single towel in the bathroom, and when Will turned off the shower and came out, he grabbed the towel from him to dry off too. He rolled back the shower curtain, sat Sal down on the rim of the tub, and told him to stay put. He came back to the bathroom with a transistor radio, set it on the sink, and clicked on an AM station that was playing *Dr. Love Coast to Coast.*

Sal smirked while Will dug through the sink cabinet drawer. "You like this show?"

"I used to listen to it when I was a kid. Every Saturday night."

"I wouldn't have guessed you'd go for love songs. I'm still learnin' things about you, baby."

"I only listen for the dedications. It's funny, the shit people come up with."

Sal listened to Dr. Love do his corny bit.

How you doing, Love-Junkies? This next song goes out to Joe from Mandy. Mandy says, Joe, I knew you were the one for me the day you walked me home from school in junior high. We've had some tough times since then, but ten years later, you're still the love of my life. This song will always remind me of our first date and how I feel about you. So, from Mandy to Joe, here's a sweet track taking us back to 1968.

I Cry Like a Baby by The Box Tops. A grin spread across Sal's face. He and Will finally had some alone time together, and the romantic music was a nice vibe. It got Sal thinking they could be having nights like this all the time. Then Will shut the drawer and turned to Sal with a comb and a pair of black-handled shears.

"You done this before?"

"Why? You scared?" Will pushed Sal's forehead down and combed his hair over his brow.

Sal was a little scared, but the situation was also pretty hot. Will was standing over him, buck naked, with the golden fuzz beneath his navel at eye level. Sal peeked up at him. "I just don't wanna be your guinea pig."

"I used to cut people's hair when I lived with that hippie family I told you about. You know, people hear you're gay, and they assume being a hairdresser is in your genes."

"It ain't in *my* genes. You sure you know what you're doing?"

Will pressed Sal's head down again so he was looking at his feet. "Don't be such a baby. You're worse than George." He drew up a portion of Sal's hair with his comb and snipped. An inch, or more?

"Just a trim, all right? I like it long."

"Maybe I like it short." Will took another snip, which landed on Sal's knee. "Some guys look better when you can see the shape of their face."

Sal's eyes shot up to him again. "You ain't gonna make me look like a square?"

Will smoothed out one side of Sal's hair with his comb. "Relax. I'm not gonna mess with your *macho* style. I'm just cleaning you up."

He seemed to know what he was doing, so Sal shut his mouth. Then Sal remembered him mentioning George.

"You cut George's hair, too?"

"From time to time."

Sal rubbed his nose. He thought about holding back, but he couldn't do it. "Like this?"

"Yeah, like this. How else?"

"After takin' a shower together?"

Will tugged two fingers of Sal's hair up from the roots and scissored. "You still jealous of George? I keep telling you, I can't wait to be rid of him."

That was reassuring to an extent. He was always being cute, never answering Sal's questions directly.

"He knows 'bout us. Don't you think?"

Will stepped into the bathtub to work on the back of Sal's head. Again, no answer. Sal told him about his strange conversation with George earlier that day.

"George gasses up everybody 'cause he thinks it makes him look good. Believe me, he's totally oblivious."

Sal wanted to believe that. He didn't want to bring down the mood when they finally had some time to themselves. He'd promised to help get rid of Will's old man, and the guy deserved it for hurting Will. But Sal's brain couldn't stop calculating risks.

"Some people gotta know 'bout you and George, though?"

Will was still behind Sal, raking hair with his comb and fingers and clipping the tips with his squeaking shears. "You ever notice, people don't ask questions about things they don't want to know about? Even when it's right in front of their face?" His hand closed on Sal's bare shoulder as he stooped to trim around the nape of his neck. "Besides, most people are idiots. They're not all savvy like you, Sal."

"His family know he adopted you?"

"What do *you* think? George is a total closet case."

"They're gonna find out, ain't they?"

"Yeah. And they're gonna stay in denial. You know, the average person would rather have a dead son than a queer one."

Sal knew that was the case with most families. Still, he was antsy. "The average person likes money too, don't they?"

Will stopped working on his hair. "You having a go at me?"

Sal turned sideways to cock a glance at him. "I'm askin' a question."

Will wrenched Sal's head to face forward again and roughly combed his hair. "So, here's your answer. George has two-hundred fifty dollars in his personal bank account. His business is surviving on credit. He's got equity in his properties, but nobody's going to be interested in inheriting that mess. It's not worth the time or the money they'd have to pay somebody to figure out how to get his ledger in the black. His financial statements are a disaster. He's been undervaluing his assets to save money on his taxes."

Most of what he said went over Sal's head, but it left him with impressions. "So, what makes it worth it to us?"

Will backed away. "You serious, Sal? We're going back to this bullshit?"

"It's just sounding complicated."

"Yeah, it's complicated. That's why I've been poring over his books the past two weeks and working things out."

Sal brought one leg over the bathtub rim and looked Will in the eyes. "What if it don't have to be complicated? Say you don't stick around after we ice him?" Will's jaw clenched. He was getting angry. "Baby, I'm just lookin' out for you. What you're talking about, if it don't go right, you could be doing life in maximum security."

"You think we've got better odds as fugitives from murder?"

"Say we take his body somewhere. Up here, you got forests and lakes all over the place and nobody for miles."

"I can't fucking believe you're doing me like this. The day before. What about the lodge in the Thousand Islands? You said you wanted that too."

Sal didn't know what to say or what to feel. Running that lodge with Will would be a dream come true, but Will was dreaming too much, wasn't he?

"I gave you a second chance not to bail on me," Will said. "Why'd you even come up here? This your plan all along to sabotage my life?"

"I'm just running an idea by you." Sal reached for Will's hip, but he sidestepped him. "I wanna get rid of George. We just gotta be smart about it, don't we?"

"You're telling *me* to be smart? I thought this all out, Sal."

"What 'bout Hogan? He just been by here, and I heard him asking how you got that shiner."

Will's gaze drifted. "Yeah, he did. He's always poking into shit. But we make it look like an accident, and he's not gonna be any trouble."

"You think he bought George's story?"

"I don't know. Probably not. But what I'm saying is it doesn't matter. Hogan's got no reason to open an investigation. That would involve bringing in a detective from the county sheriff's office, and he's not going to want that kind of attention. Use your brain, Sal. You think Hogan wants people looking into the death of a guy he's been extorting money from?"

Sal didn't like Will insinuating he was stupid. He'd thought about that angle before, but he'd also been thinking about Hogan's creepy behavior. "Guess you know him better than me. How well you know him, anyway?"

"Jesus. I'm not fucking him, Sal. Is that what this is about? I'm trying to get us set up for the future, and it doesn't help you going mental at the eleventh hour."

Sal stood and swaggered up close to Will. "All right. We do it your way. It make you feel better calling the shots?" He had Will backed against the shower wall, and the smart look was wiped clean from his face. Sal shrugged. "I let you handle it. This time."

Will placed his free hand on the outside of Sal's arm. "I know you like doing it your way." Will traced the hardened contours of Sal's upper arm and shoulder. "It turns me on, but you've got to trust me on this, okay?"

Sal was driving for a make-up smooch and the places that could lead. But Will nudged him back to the rim of the tub. "Let's get this done. Before you get all heated again."

He took up with the comb and scissors, and Sal resigned himself to let Will finish. He was heated for sure, but he didn't want to be walking around with his hair short on one side and long on the other.

"I'll let you in on a little story. How I know 'bout dirty cops like Hogan," Will said. "You remember George talking about that rich guy who helped him flip his first property? Al Shapiro was his name. George and him were real friendly when we met. This was before he bought the motor lodge. We were living in an apartment on the other side of the river. Al stayed over sometimes when he came up from the city to do business. He was a good guy. George always said he'd never guess about the two of us, but Al knew. It was a one bedroom apartment. Anyway, Al always treated me with respect, like it was no big thing."

Will carefully scissored along Sal's ear. "Al was the real deal. He wasn't just buying rundown gas stations to flip them for a few thousand dollars like George. The guy had funds, and he knew what he was doing. He found a twenty acre lot in Highland Falls that was under foreclosure. Just south of Newburgh. The original owner was some dude who inherited it from his pops, and he'd lost his shit in 'Nam and couldn't keep up with it. Al bought it for a song. It was a prime location off 9W, with views of the river. Al was going to turn it into a nice little housing development. Parcel it out in one-acre plots and sell 'em to rich suits working at the chemical companies, wanting to impress their wives. Al knew a lot of people, and he already had some buyers in mind. The entire twenty-acre lot was undeveloped with the exception of six crappy cottages. The first owner had put them up on the cheap in the 40s for guys coming back from the war."

Sal liked a good story. As Will had stepped out of the tub to stand in front of him, he placed his hand on Will's hip, just idly touching him there and feeling his behind while he told it.

"Al just needed to get that row of cottages demolished, and he had pristine, wooded land from 9W to the shore of the river. It was going to be exclusive, quiet, and the perfect place to raise kids. There was a Jewish school right down the road, and it was thirty minutes from Union Carbide's headquarters in Tarrytown. You'd have to be an idiot to lose money on the deal. Al was going to sell each plot for twice the price he paid for the entire thing. It was a four hundred times return on his investment! He had a construction contractor lined up for the buyers and everything."

Will turned a little to trim around Sal's other ear. "The problem was, Al didn't know the local PD was letting some guys from the city use the abandoned cottages to run coke upstate. A bunch of thugs showed up at Al's house in Bronxville, trying to intimidate him into leaving the deal. Meanwhile, he's got patrol cars trailing him whenever he's in town, and one day, a pair of officers show up while he's got a surveyor looking at the property. They tell him he ought to think twice about what he's doing. Al offered them some money to cool off, but whatever racket they were running must've been worth more to them. The drug gang did Al in, and the cops looked the other way."

Will stepped around to work at the other side of Sal's head. "George was pretty sure it was this day when Al was over at the property by himself. He didn't hear from Al for two weeks, and then we found out watching the news. Some kid went canoeing on the river and found a body washed up by some boathouse. The guy's facial features are unrecognizable and his kneecaps are broken, but the police chief rules it as an accident. Al's family even got a big shot lawyer to try to pressure him into looking into foul play, but a few months later, the whole thing blows away."

Will stepped back to study his work and did a little trim of the hairs above Sal's brow. "So, that's how I know about corrupt cops. That police chief in Highland Falls is pallsy with Hogan. He probably told him George and Al were friends. That's why he's always leaning on George for money. Dirty cops stick together. That's also how I know Hogan's not gonna make a big deal about George kicking the bucket. There's nothing in it for him, and if he does, his higher-ups could get wise to all the bribes he's been taking. It could even catch the interest of that drug gang down in the city if they get worried about George's death leading to questions about Al's. Then Hogan's got himself some real trouble."

Sal glanced up at Will and held the back of his leg. "How'd you get so smart?"

"I'm not smart. I never even went to college. I've just been in a position to observe things, y'know?"

Sal ran his hand up to Will's bottom. "So, what you been observing 'bout me?"

Will pushed Sal's hand away. "I'm working here." He smirked. "With you, I don't have to do a lot of observing to figure you out."

Sal's eyes sparked. "That ain't a nice thing to say."

"What do you want me to say, Sal? If you're fishing for compliments, yeah, you're a good-looking guy."

"Probably not the type you normally dig, right?"

Will looked over Sal's head and did a final snip here and there. "Maybe. You're a little mental, but you make up for it in other ways."

Sal grasped the kid's bottom. "Oh yeah? What kinds of ways? You just keepin' me 'round 'cause you like the way I screw you?"

Will's face reddened, but he came back with a smart face. "Guess it helps when you've had a lot of practice."

That poked Sal like a dental probe hitting a cavity. "You always gotta put me down, don't you?"

"I'm kidding around. You take things too seriously." Will brushed some hairs off Sal's shoulders. "You're done. You want to take a look in the mirror?"

The only thing Sal hated more than being called trash was being told he was a pussy who couldn't take a joke. He didn't move. Will leaned over with his hand on his arm. "Really, Sal? You're *that* sensitive?"

Sal tucked into himself. All of a sudden, he was hurting. He'd never cared about what other people thought of him, but with Will, it cut him deep.

"You called me a moody bitch, and I didn't get bent out of shape," Will reminded him.

Sal flicked away a tear drop from his eye. "Don't call me mental."

"All right. I won't call you mental."

Sal's chin quivered. "If you knew how hard I been tryin' to clean up my act for you, you wouldn't talk to me like that."

"I know you've been working hard–"

"What I got to do for you to be a little kind to me?" Sal sniffed. "I ain't proud of what I done, but I can't change the past."

"Come here." Sal didn't move, but when Will pulled him up into his arms, he didn't resist. "I didn't mean to put you down. We both been stressed." He squeezed Sal tight. "In forty-eight hours, we're gonna have a quarter mil. We'll get out of this place and never look back."

Sal didn't care about the money. He just liked being close to Will. He shut his eyes and nestled into his embrace. He loved Will, and Will was going to love him back. If there was any justice in the world, he'd finally found someone to love him. Nothing could get in their way.

14

SAL WAS FEELING steadier after that night, but show time crept up real fast. Around noon the next day while he was resting in bed inside his room, he heard George's Oldsmobile pull up behind the motel. The big guy had come back from his trip, and before the sun rose the next day, he and Will had to kill him. Sal's jitters returned like he was coming down with a tropical disease.

He turned on his alarm clock radio. He didn't want to hear George unloading his stuff from his car and yapping along the way like he always did. Sal had never murdered anybody before. He felt like he ought to be struck by lightning just for thinking about it.

Sal wasn't sure he had it in him to do it. Particularly when he was going to have to make it through dinner with George, keeping his cool like nothing was going on. Sal did his laundry in the basement to occupy himself and later, he cleaned his room and bathroom until they were spotless. After, he took a long, cold shower to cool down from the heat and force himself to toughen up. George was an uppity old troll who lured Will into letting him fuck him because the kid needed a place to stay. He was beating Will to boot. He deserved to be dead. If Sal and Will didn't do it, he'd get away with what he'd done. No authorities would ever be interested in punishing him. Justice didn't work that way for queers.

By the time he dried off from his shower, it was eight o'clock. Sal grabbed the shirt he'd ironed and a pair of jeans. Naturally, it had to be a hot, sticky night. When he finished dressing, he was sweating all over the place again. Sal splashed water on his face, sprayed on some more deodorant and changed clothes. After that, he stood in front of his bedroom mirror, airing out his shirt and trying to put himself together. He had to admit, Will had done a good job giving his hair a trim. It looked nice shorter on the sides like guys were wearing it those days. He stepped out to go up to George's apartment.

George let him in with his usual blowhard charm. The apartment was sweltry and thick with a savory odor. George had made moussaka, he explained, which was some kind of Greek casserole. His air conditioner had conked out, he said. The bossman's face had a ruddy sheen. He reeked of aftershave and whiskey and was sweating in the heat. Sal pulled out some compliments and thanked him for having him over for dinner.

Will came out of the bedroom to help George get things to the table, and the three of them sat down. The kid was wearing a tank top and running shorts and glistening with sweat as much as Sal and George.

"This is real Greek cooking," George boasted while he loaded up Sal's plate. Sal's stomach was sewn up tight. He wasn't sure if he could eat with the apartment being so hot and all the nerves coursing through him. Air circulated a little from the wobbly living room fan, but the only window over there was covered by the broken air conditioner unit. He took a slow draw on his can of beer while George served himself and Will.

"On the hottest day of the year, *he* decides to use the oven," Will complained.

"How was I supposed to know the air conditioner was on the fritz?" George turned to Sal. "It'll cool down now that I turned off the oven." He stopped heaping Will's plate. "I forgot you're not eating meat. You'll have to make do with the salad."

"I can make an exception for tonight."

George gave him a second glance, and then he shook his head. "How do you like this one, Sal? I guess he's finally come to his senses." He shrugged. "Maybe the heat got more oxygen circulating to his brain so that he realizes human beings eat meat."

"I'm still a vegetarian. I said I can make an exception for tonight." Will poured George a good three fingers of whiskey.

They dug into the meal–George robustly, Will more moderately, and Sal just eating little forkfuls here and there. He was hoping George got drunk quickly, and they could get things over with. He was feeling so restless, he could barely stay in his seat.

"What's wrong, Sal? You don't like my moussaka?"

Sal grinned nervously. "Oh no. It's super. My stomach's just been off, y'know?" Before George could give his opinion about that, he added, "How was your trip?"

"Yeah George. Tell us about your trip to Saratoga Springs," Will said.

George wiped his face with his napkin. "It's beautiful up there. Especially this time of year. Saratoga Springs is at the foot of the Adirondack Mountains. They have a track up there for some of the biggest horse races in the country."

"No kiddin'." Sal lit up a smoke. "I don't know nothin' 'bout horses. Are you a bettin' man?"

"Now and then. When I was a kid, my brother and I used to sneak into Belmont Park." George belched. "We'd skip school and take the bus to Woodside, hop on the Long Island Railroad, and we'd duck the conductor all the way to the racetrack." He smiled, remembering. "Teddy was always getting us in trouble. He'd put on papa's fedora, hoping it made him look older, and try to place bets at the counter. But the bookies always shooed us away."

Sal took a generous sip of his beer, hoping it might encourage George to do some work on his whiskey. George tossed back his tumbler. Will lit up a Kent.

"So, how much money did you lose this time?" Will said.

"There weren't no race."

"Aw. That's too bad. You see anybody interesting up there?"

"I was meeting buyers for the property. You knew about that."

Will pulled a leg up to his seat and smirked. "Sure. But a big deal businessman like you must've lined up some recreation for himself on a three-night trip."

George waved him off. "I got in Thursday night. I had meetings straight through Saturday and drove back this morning. You think I had time for recreation?"

"I don't know. Did you?" Will gave George another heavy pour of whiskey.

George looked down at his full tumbler. Sal was thinking Will was getting too confrontational and being too obvious about getting George drunk. For a dicey moment, George's expression was hard to read. Then he laughed.

"I'll take you with me next time." George looked at Sal chummily. "Will's got a jealous streak. I can't go nowhere without him acting like this."

"That's 'cause you've got me chained to this shithole," Will said. "I don't get a day off to go anywhere, let alone three."

George's face darkened, and he took a slug of whiskey. Sal picked up then that Will's strategy was to tick the guy off to get him drinking more. It looked like it was working, though it seemed a little risky. It was hot enough in the apartment already.

"That's business," George said. "You pay your dues." He eyed Sal like he might back him up. "I didn't take a day off from work till I turned forty. And since then, it's only been a weekend here and there. Unless you're related to John Paul Getty, you can't afford to take time off from work."

Sal nodded, generally. Will crushed out his cig and collected dishes to take into the kitchen. Sal stood up and offered to help, but George told him to stay put.

"Will can do it. Pick out some music to put on the record player while I get the cards."

Sal glanced at Will. The kid didn't look back and took the dishes into the kitchen. Sal stepped over to the living room and flipped through the record collection. He was hoping to find Will's

Eagles album. There had to be a couple hundred records on the shelves, and after a minute or two of searching, Sal was too antsy to keep looking for what he wanted. He came upon a Bobby Lewis record he could tolerate. Sal set it up on the turntable and came back to his seat.

George was slumped a little, shuffling the cards. Sal noted the time on the wood-carved wall clock in the dining room. Quarter to nine. It was still light out. They had some time to bide before they could pull off Will's plan.

"I bought this record when I was thirty years old," George said. "Bobby Lewis was all the rage. You probably like the new rock 'n' roll, do you Sal?"

Sal took a seat and lit up another cigarette. "I like all kinds of music."

George downed his whiskey. "There's nothing like the originals though, is there? Them hippies took over the music industry with all their commie peace-and-love BS. If it weren't for them, we would've won the war in Vietnam, don't you think?"

Sal's opinions on hippies were generally favorable, so he said nothing at first. He wanted to make George comfortable, though. "You got a nice set up here. Couldn't ask for more, could you?"

George refilled his tumbler. "I think I done pretty well for myself. And it's a big deal I'm working on in Sarasota Springs. When that goes through, I can make some improvements to the motor lodge. Turn this place into something special like Will's always wanted."

Sal watched George down his whiskey. "That jukebox is ace. You got other big ideas?"

"I do." George picked out a cigar from his box, clipped off the end and stoked it up. "I'm going to give the diner a makeover. Put some classic Greek dishes on the menu and update the dining area. Turn it into a classy place. Not just for travelers but for the locals too."

Will came through the swinging door. "You've been talking about making improvements since you moved into the place five years ago." He picked up the last plates and utensils from the table and carted them into the kitchen.

"I've been waiting on this deal to do it," George called after him. He gave Sal a beleaguered frown.

Sal puffed on his cig. An idea occurred to him, and before he thought it out, it came out of his mouth. "If I had a business partner like that…" He made a fist and pantomimed a right hook.

George chuckled. Then he saw Sal's hand. "What happened to you?"

Sal had taken off the bandage, but he had some gory scabs across his knuckles. Reflexively, he brought his hand under the table. "Nothin'. I just jammed it in a door while I was fixin' one of the rooms."

"Good grief. Between you and Will, I ought to consider putting in a nursing unit." George called out to the kitchen. "Before you bust my chops, I called that electrician. He's coming to fix the lamp out back first thing in the morning." George turned back to Sal. "I understand it happens sometimes, but make sure you take out the trash at the end of the night. If Will trips and falls again, I'll never hear the end of it."

Thunder boomed like it was tearing through the very fabric of the atmosphere. It sent Sal jumping out of his seat. He felt like an ass doing that in front of George, but he was wound up like a spring. As he settled back in his seat, he was confused. Was George just covering up what he'd done to Will? He hadn't needed to bring up the subject, and he seemed so sincere about it being an accident.

Will came back in. "Storm started. It's supposed to be bad. Now I've gotta shut all the windows, and it'll be a furnace in here." He trudged off to the bedroom.

Rain drummed on the roof. George brought out his handkerchief to wipe his brow. "I saw on the evening news, it's gonna be a big one. That's a good thing. We might finally get some relief from this humidity."

Sal glanced at the living room window. It looked like night had fallen out of the blue. Wind shrieked and rattled the window pane. Will went around turning on lamps throughout the apartment.

"I got a game for you, Sal," George said, shuffling the cards. "Crazy Eights."

Will walked past them into the kitchen. All at once, Sal had a dreadful feeling. George was acting too normal. Not that he shouldn't be acting normal. Sal couldn't say what was off, but his gut was telling him it wasn't the right time to do the job. He couldn't think straight in the heat, and now the thunderstorm had him on edge. Sal needed to talk to Will, but there wasn't any way to do that without George thinking that something funny was going on.

Will came back to the dining room with a pair of beers. "We can make it a drinking game." He set one beer in front of Sal and sat down with the other. "Every time you gotta pick from the pile, you also gotta take a drink."

George scowled. "What's the point of that? We're all drinking anyway."

"It's for fun, George. That's the point."

"If I want to take a drink, I'll take a drink."

"Nobody's saying you can't do that. It's just an added rule."

"I don't get it. How does having to take a drink when you pick from the pile make it more fun?"

"If you don't like it, we can play strip poker. It might be the only way to cool down."

George's face flushed, and he burst out in a chuckle. "You've got a screw loose." He glanced at Sal. "You're the guest, Sally-boy. What do you think about Will's idea of making it a drinking game?"

Sal shifted in his seat. "Sure. Sounds like fun."

Will drifted over to the living room and deep-sixed Bobby Lewis. Soon after, the twangy groove of the Steve Miller Band blared from the speakers. Sal winced. He didn't mind the choice, but the loud music wasn't helping his nerves.

"Turn it down," George barked. "We ain't gonna be able to hear ourselves think."

Will dialed down the volume a little, came back to the table, and topped off George's tumbler. He threw himself down in his seat and grumbled, "You'd think we're living in a retirement community."

George dealt out the cards. Sal peeked at Will, but he wouldn't look Sal's way. Sal supposed he was being careful. He tried to compute all the strangeness that was going on. Will was definitely trying to get George blitzed. Maybe his bull-in-a-china-shop routine was meant to distract George from that.

They played a round, and Will took delight every time George couldn't follow suit and had to take a drink. The big guy was looking glazed and got a little messy with his play. But he was still sitting upright in his chair with his cards fanned out in his fat, hairy hands. The old Greek had to have a hollow leg. He must've drank a liter of whiskey. Then Will made a smug display of going out with his last card.

"Drink up, losers."

George shouted in disbelief. "I gotta have a hundred points."

Will collected the cards. "We're not playing for points."

"You always count points. How else do you keep track of who's winning?"

Will got up to grab more beers from the kitchen. "We're just playing rounds. It's a drinking game."

George waved him off with a hiccup. "You two play."

"Don't be an old lady. It's better with three." Will pushed into the kitchen.

George shrugged weakly. He looked like gravity was bearing down on him.

"You ain't played drinkin' games 'fore?" Sal said.

George fumbled for his smoldering cigar. He took a drag, shrank up his face, and lost his hold on it. Sal picked up the cigar from the table and held it out for George to take. The big guy was not registering much. Sal set the cigar in the ashtray where it burnt out.

Will returned with the beers, sat down, shuffled the cards and dealt them. He seemed plenty sober. Sal had downed three beers and was feeling a little tipsy. He decided to slow down with his fourth.

The next round was a joke. George kept forgetting when it was his turn and asked each time what suit they were playing. He dropped cards out of his hand, and Will laid into him about taking a drink each time he had to pull from the deck. When Will went out again, George's head tipped down like he was falling asleep.

"That's the round, George," Will said loudly. "You gotta set down your cards."

George jerked awake and lost hold of his cards. Then he collapsed face first on the table, and drowsy breaths sawed from his nostrils.

"You gotta drink, George," Will shouted.

The big guy didn't budge.

Will glanced at Sal, and then he enunciated plainly to George. "You got too drunk. Guess we'll have to quit early, *again*." George didn't react. Will stood up from his seat. "It's pathetic, but what are you gonna do? I'll clean up in the kitchen."

He walked out, leaving Sal with the bossman who was passing gas while he was visiting Sleepy Town. Sal gave his arm a light jostle, and George kept snoring. The guy was pissed to the hilt. Sal quietly got out of his chair and slipped into the kitchen.

Will stood at a sudsy sink, scouring a casserole dish with a steel sponge. Sal came over and didn't say anything at first. His brain was still tangled up.

Will grinned. "He's knocked out, right?"

Lightning flashed, and rain rushed against the kitchen's single window like a hurricane was passing through. Sal stretched his hands behind his head.

"Yeah. But maybe this ain't the best time."

"What do you mean? It's going perfect."

"I dunno. Something's up with him."

"He's fucking soused. We just need to get him to the bathroom."

Sal fanned out his shirt. "Why's it so goddamn hot in here?"

Will smiled cleverly. "I threw the fuse for the air conditioner."

Sal followed along. An extra touch to explain why George was taking a shower so late at night. Sal was still feeling like he needed to claw out of his skin.

"You sure 'bout this? Feels like it's going too easy."

"That's 'cause we planned it to go easy. We just give him another few minutes to be sure, and we'll get it done."

Sal paced around. "Why'd George say you hurt yourself taking the garbage to the dumpster?"

Will jetted on the spray from the sink to rinse the big dish. "'Cause that's what he's telling people."

Sal studied him. Will was acting as regular as could be. Sal didn't know what to think. It could be George was slyer than he'd given him credit for. Did he know Sal had been listening to his conversation with Hogan? *Maybe.* Sal couldn't shake the feeling that something was off.

"What happens if he wakes up in the middle?"

Will turned and placed a warm hand on Sal's chest. "He's not gonna wake up. I put four of his tranquilizers in his bottle."

Sal's temperature spiked. "What's that gonna do?"

"It's not gonna kill him. They make him drowsy. It's a little extra insurance."

"Ain't that risky? They do blood work on dead people, don't they?"

"They're *his* prescription. Relax Sal." Will finished drying the casserole dish and set it on the counter. "Nobody's gonna be interested in an autopsy, and even if they were, a middle-aged man with that drug in his system isn't going to raise questions. The doctor gave him the pills to chill out 'cause he's always hyper." Will shrugged. "Maybe he double dosed by mistake."

Sal really wasn't feeling good about what they were about to do, and then Will opened the cabinet under the sink and brought out a cast-iron pipe wrench.

"What's that for?"

"In case the fall doesn't crack his skull."

The violence of what Will was implying flashed before Sal's eyes. Will pushed the wrench on him.

"C'mon. Let's get it over with."

"*I* gotta hit him?"

"If it's necessary."

"Why me?"

Will gave Sal a square look. "I thought you'd want to. You were ready to kill him the other day." Sal tried not to look frightened, but it must've shown. "What's with the cold feet? That fucker is the only thing that stands between us and our freedom."

Freedom. That resonated with Sal, though he had expected the moment to feel different. He tried remembering the good reasons that had led to this. Will would finally be his, one hundred percent. They'd have a big nest egg and redo their lives with a clean slate. Get that lodge in the Thousand Islands, make it a rocking business. George deserved it for how he treated Will, didn't he?

"Stay here for a sec. I'm gonna give him one last look-over. I'll give you a knock on the table to come out and help me get him to the bathroom."

Will stepped out of the kitchen. Alone, the wrench felt twice as heavy in Sal's hand. He grabbed the kitchen towel draped on the oven door and wiped the sweat from his face. Everything felt surreal. Rain was coming down horizontal against the window, and the overhead light flickered. It was like living in *Looney Tunes.* Then the knock came from the other room. Twice.

Sal opened the kitchen's swinging door. Will was crouched on one side of George, readying to lift him up under his arm. Sal switched up his hands on the wrench and got under George on his other side. He was dead weight, but they raised him pretty easily. Sal was suddenly shocked sober and focused on the task. Together, they carted George along, toppling his chair in the process, but otherwise, it went smoothly through the living room. George was definitely knocked out. His head hung from his neck, and he didn't move one iota. He had to weigh two hundred and fifty pounds or more. God, he stunk of body odor and booze.

They made it into the bathroom, and Will told Sal to pass him the wrench and get under both of George's arms.

"Hold him up while I take off his clothes."

Sal hadn't considered that was part of the plan. But of course, it made sense. They had to make it look like George was taking a shower. It was a struggle holding him up. Sal was crushed against the door while Will took off George's shoes, socks, belt, and slacks. Then Sal had to get his arms around George's middle so Will could peel his undershirt over his arms and head and strip off his boxer shorts. Sal was pressed against the old Greek's sweaty, hairy, stinking flesh. His bent knees were screaming.

When Will had all George's clothes off, Sal roughly propped him up under the armpits. Will threw open the shower curtain with a rattle, churned on the water, and came back to take one of George's sides. They strained to lift him over the side of the tub, and when that was done, they had to position him under the shower head.

"Get the wrench," Will said. "I'll hold him for a minute and let him go."

Sal maneuvered himself free, swayed over to the sink, and picked up the wrench. He hadn't realized a person could function so long without taking a breath. It felt like he hadn't taken one since they'd hauled George over from the dining room table. Sheet lightning flashed through the frosted bathroom window. Sal heard Will gasping and struggling. He stepped over. The lightbulbs above the sink flickered, and then Will swung himself out of the shower, releasing George.

George's head clipped the tiled stall, and the sound of his big body thudding into the tub was even more horrible. He looked like he was laid out cold, but Will's positioning was off. George's head hit too high. It was supposed to crack against the edge of the tub. Sal craned around while Will caught his breath. Maybe, if they were lucky, the fall had snapped his neck? He had no visible injury, no blood coming from his head.

All of a sudden, George had a fit of coughs and struck out weakly with his hands to raise himself. Sal jumped back and nearly lost his balance.

"Bash his head," Will said.

Sal couldn't stop staring at George. He was squealing like a pig to suck air into his lungs, struggling for his life.

"Do it, Sal."

Sal lurched over to the end of the tub. He was lightheaded and woozy, and now he had to judge a place to bash George in the head with the wrench. It had to look like damage from a fall. Meanwhile, George coughed out partially digested whiskey. It was the rankest stench Sal had ever smelled in his life.

"Sal, do it."

That vile stench triggered the malice Sal needed to do the job. He was putting George out of his misery. Getting him and Will out of the misery of having to see and smell the old guy's struggle. Sal shoved forward George's head and judged a spot to strike. He stooped down a little, got both hands on the wrench, and wound it above his shoulder. He heaved deep breaths, sharpened his gaze on a spot below George's crown, and he swung the wrench with enough force to shatter a brick.

The lightbulbs flickered, and Sal was plunged into darkness.

FOR A TERRIFYING moment, Sal thought he'd been sucked into the sightless void of hell for what he'd done. His ears were ringing sharply. Then the wrench slipped out of his hand and clattered on the floor, and Will's panicky voice warbled like Sal was hearing it under water.

"*The power lines must be down from the storm.*"

"*Don't touch anything. Just stay put.*"

"*Sal, you listening to me? Did you drop the wrench?*"

Sal shivered and awakened with a jolt. "Yeah."

"Stay here. I'm gonna get the flashlight from the bedroom."

Sal had no problem standing in place. He was blind and scared to move. He could trip over something and upset the staging of the scene. He might tumble on top of George. Had he pissed himself? He was going through hot flashes and cold flashes, and his whole body felt wet. He heard a spray of rain from the bathroom window. George wasn't making a noise. Was he dead?

A dagger of light pierced the room. Will had returned with his flashlight.

"It's just the electric. The phone lines are working. Tommy'll probably come up here wanting to know what to do. You need to get out of here while I call an ambulance."

Sal was in a panic on all sides. He didn't want to be seen when the paramedics showed up, but he didn't want to leave Will either.

"Is he dead?"

Will shone the flashlight on the tub and looked around. The strike Sal delivered had broken through skin and maybe more. Thick, dark blood oozed from the back of George's head and had gathered on the lip of the tub. Sal thought he might vomit.

"He looks dead." Will shifted the flashlight away. "I'll sort it out. You've gotta go."

Sal swallowed down his queasy spell. In the gleam of the flashlight, he finally felt like he had his legs on the ground again. But the situation was coming into focus.

He grasped Will's arm. "What're you gonna say?"

"Ow." Will pulled his arm away. "I'm gonna say what I told you. I heard him fall down in the shower and found him like this."

"You gonna say I was here?"

"Of course not. Stop bugging out." Will shone the flashlight on him head to toe and made him turn around to look at his backside. "You're clean. Just be careful going downstairs."

Sal could see his way out of the bathroom. He hesitated. "What're you gonna do with the wrench?"

"I'll hide it."

"It's got my prints on it."

"I'll clean it and get rid of it tomorrow."

"Maybe I should take it."

"You wanna walk out of here carrying a bloody wrench?"

Sal considered. He'd feel better taking care of the wrench himself, knowing it was gone for good. Could he hide it down the back of his pants in case he ran into somebody on his way to his room? He'd get George's blood on his clothes.

Before Sal could decide, Will pushed him along. "I'll call you later. Just trust me, Sal, and don't freak out."

Sal couldn't argue with him anymore. He stepped around Will to get out of the bathroom, and Will shone the flashlight to help him find the front door.

Sal carefully opened the door and took a peek around. Everything was shrouded in the night. He could just make out a silhouette of the outdoor hallway. Every room along the way was dark, and the parking lot was a pitch-black lake. Rain pattered down, but the worst of the storm had passed.

He took things slowly and cautiously, skimming his hand along the hallway rail as he walked. At the stairwell, he went down one foot at a time, glancing ahead and to the side and seeing nothing. He made it down to ground level, and he worked by memory to find his room. Every door looked the same, but his was three doors down from the breezeway with the ice maker and vending machine. Sal fit his key into the doorknob. He pushed it open and shut the door behind him with a sigh of relief that brought him to his knees.

Instinctively, Sal kicked off his shoes and peeled off his clothes, and in the thin aura of the battery-powered digital alarm clock on his night stand, he took everything to the bathroom. He threw his clothes in the tub, and then he stepped in and cranked on the shower. He was getting by with vague notions of what a person was supposed to do after he'd killed somebody. He felt absolutely filthy. Sal found his bar of soap and scrubbed himself from head to toe as best as he could in the dark. Then he rinsed under the shower spray. He wanted to be more thorough about it, but the jitters hit him again. An ambulance would be coming soon. They might bring the cops. Sal should make like he'd been in bed for a while.

He stepped out of the shower and realized he had soaking wet clothes laying in the tub. They wouldn't dry for hours. Sal wrung them out and shoved them in the cabinet under the sink. He'd deal with them in the morning. It was the best idea he could come up with.

He found his towel, dried off, and stepped carefully into his bedroom. No sounds from upstairs or outside as far as he could tell. He climbed into his bed, lay on his side, over the covers, and stared at his window that looked out to the parking lot.

They'd staged the scene pretty perfectly, and the power outage actually worked in their favor. That could've been the reason George lost his footing and bashed his head. Sal wished he had told Will to mention that to the paramedics.

Sirens gained up on the motel. Sal bounded over to his window. It was a hell of a commotion. First a fire truck and then an ambulance drove up to the parking lot. Through a blur of rain, Sal watched two men in reflective yellow suits climb out of a truck, and then a pair of paramedics joined them to walk upstairs. When they were out of his view, Sal sat down on the floor below his window and listened. For a long stretch of time, there wasn't much to hear except for an occasional bleep and fizz from radios in the emergency vehicles. Sal didn't budge from his spot. He prayed there wouldn't be any cops showing up.

Thirty minutes passed, and finally Sal heard some movement from outside. He craned his head to take a look. It was drizzly and dark, but he spotted two guys carrying a stretcher. Straining his eyes, Sal made out a big body fully covered in a blanket. They loaded George into the ambulance, closed it up, and pulled out of the lot with lights flashing. Then the mammoth fire truck coughed to life and groaned away as well.

Sal wasn't sure if it was too soon to say the coast was clear. It was a small town. Emergencies couldn't happen very often. Sal didn't know for sure about procedures, but the paramedics would probably be communicating with the police. When Hogan heard the news, Sal could bet he'd come straight over. Will might be right that he wouldn't be interested in opening an investigation that would bring in outside authorities, but the guy loved nosing around.

His alarm clock read one thirty in the morning. It was going to be a long night. Sal got up from the floor and lay back down on his bed. With no fan, the room was muggy. He shut his eyes just to rest for a moment.

The next thing he knew, he shook awake from the brring brring of his phone. He must've drifted off. Sal stretched over to his night stand and scrounged for the handset of the phone.

He didn't say anything at first.

"Sal?"

Will's voice. Hoarse and flat. Sal propped himself up at the head of the bed. "Yeah."

"It's over."

Sal wiped his face. He wasn't sure what Will meant. His brain was fried, and it took him a moment to form words.

"You okay?"

"Yeah." Will sounded dazed.

"How'd it go? With the paramedics."

"Fine."

Sal scratched his head. "They ask a lot of questions?"

"A few." Will's voiced faded away for a moment, and then pressured breaths came over the receiver. "Sal, there's blood. A lot of blood. All over the tub. I don't think I can clean it all up with just a flashlight. I'm going to have to wait until the morning."

"I'll come up and help."

"No. You can't."

Will sounded like he was freaking out. "They say they gonna call the police?"

"I dunno. I don't think so."

"I'll come up."

"No."

"Baby, I wanna be with you."

"Sal—"

"There ain't no one else coming by, so what's the problem?"

"Because it's not a good idea." Will exhaled a heavy breath. "I'm fucking spent, Sal. I just want a cig and to go to sleep. You do me a favor? I ran out of smokes. I'm pretty sure I left a pack under the counter in the diner. By the register. I told Tommy to lock up and go home for the night."

"You want me to bring you your smokes, but you don't want me coming up there?"

"Leave the pack by the door and knock."

Sal swung over to the edge of the bed. "I'll get 'em, and we can have a smoke together."

"Sal, please. Not now."

"I wanna see you."

"I don't want you seeing me like this. I got blood all over me, and my nerves are fucking frayed."

"I don't give a shit how you look."

"Please Sal." Will sounded tortured. "Just leave my pack by the door. We'll talk tomorrow."

"Baby—"

"Sal, if you really care about me, you'll get my cigs and leave it for the night."

Frustrated tears burned the back of Sal's throat. He wanted to go off on Will, but this was deep shit they'd gotten into. He took a moment to pull himself together. "Okay. Gimme like fifteen minutes."

They hung up, and Sal fumbled around in the dark to find clothes to throw on from his cabinet. Will wanted cigs, and maybe it would calm him down so he could process what had happened. Sal grabbed his ring of keys from where he left them on his dresser, and he stepped out of his apartment. He skulked over to the back door to the diner. Nothing was easy in the dark. He tried a half dozen keys before he found the right one, and then he had to take small steps into the back hall and feel around another door frame to make his way behind the diner counter.

Sal smelled the Pine-Sol he used to mop the floor and the sharp scent of the vinyl booths. He ran his hand along the diner counter while edging toward the middle. It reminded him of the big blackout in New York last summer. He'd been working at Joey's club that night. Sal remembered the lights and music cutting off out of the blue and the crowd of people laughing and howling, thinking it was a gag. That lasted a few minutes, and then guys started shouting, getting angry, and the bar staff had to calm them down. Sal remembered groping under the bar to find the flashlight, and then they gradually ushered customers out to the street so they could lock up.

Sal felt around the counter and discovered the diner's register. He stooped down to the undershelf. Feeling around, his hand landed on a small, lightweight box. He picked it up, flipped open the top and confirmed it was full of filtered squares. Bingo.

Just then, the jukebox came to life, sending Sal lurching backward on his heels and smacking his back into the rim of the order window. Lights flashed. Music blared. Sal righted himself and stared at the contraption like it had been possessed.

But it was just the power coming back. Through the front window, he saw the diner's neon sign zapping on as well. That might've calmed Sal's nerves, but the goddamn music was like a message from the afterworld. Doris Day riffing with a full orchestra.

When the red, red robin comes bob, bob bobbing along, along.

There'll be no more sobbing when he starts throbbing his old sweet song...

PART II

15

THREE MONTHS LATER, Sal was hauling rotted wood paneling to a rubbish pit at a lodge in the Thousand Islands. To say Will's dream property needed some work was putting things nicely. The place had been abandoned for twelve years. The roof of the main house had leaks in at least a dozen places, and the chimney had become a nest for bats. Most of the floorboards on the wrap-around porch would have to be ripped out and replaced, and they were going to have to get a new furnace and have an electrician rewire the entire place. The only good news Sal had gotten from the contractor was that the plumbing was reasonably intact. He'd shown Sal how to turn on the pump for the lodge's reservoir. But with no heating unit, Sal was taking cold showers and living on canned ham, Wonder bread, and potato chips.

Sal rolled his wheelbarrow around the back of the house and dumped its cargo into the pit. Later, he'd douse it with kerosene and enjoy the heat from the bonfire for a while before he had to tuck into bed under a sheet, afghan, and a musty sleeping bag that had been left in one of the cabins. It was only early October, but it got fucking cold up north, just across the river from Canada. The grass was white with frost in the morning. During the day, Sal could get by in a thermal shirt and jeans while keeping busy clearing out the rotting parts of the lodge. The nights were brutal, though, and they were only going to get worse. Wind swept over the giant, island-dotted Saint Lawrence River, and it drafted through a hundred places in the rickety house. It reminded Sal of some real low times when he had to sleep under the West Side Highway in the winter.

Sal threw off the last of the debris from the wheelbarrow and set it down. He swiped the sweat from his forehead with his shirt-sleeve, and he lit up a stale joint with his Zippo. His one lucky find since he'd moved into the place four weeks ago was a stack of jays the owners had left in the bedroom drawer. They were harsh, and the buzz wore off after fifteen minutes, but a man had to do what he had to do to get by.

He felt sometimes like he'd inherited Sherwood Forest. Giant pines and gray trunked maple trees, shedding red and yellow leaves, dominated the property. It spanned a quarter-mile along the rocky river shore and two hundred yards inland to the bordering country road. Sal had thought that Beacon was the boondocks, but that town was a metropolis compared to the Thousand Islands.

It was a rough place to live, but when Sal looked at it a certain way, he was a king. He'd never imagined owning land. He owned every one of them goddamn trees, every blade of grass, every boulder and pebble along the river, and every deer, chipmunk, skunk, raccoon, and bird squatting on his property. He'd never seen so much goddamn wildlife. He was a fucking pioneer, like Paul Bunyan.

Sal took another throat-scorching pull on his joint, and his mood lifted from the rush of THC. Yeah, when he looked at things that way, it wasn't so bad. There was work to do to get the lodge in shape, but he was making progress clearing out the rotting drywall and linoleum floor tiles. The last owners had left a lawn mower and yard tools, so he'd been raking leaves and trimming the grass in front of the main house. Once he got supplies from a hardware store, Sal would give the road sign a repainting, and he'd fix up the rail fence along the country road. The contractor was going to put in a new roof, rebuild the interior of the lodge, install a furnace in the basement and do all the electrical work. From there, Sal just had to figure out which cottages could be salvaged and which ones would have to be demolished and rebuilt. Gazing around, Sal could picture what it would look like when everything came together.

So long as Will sent him the money.

Sal took another swipe of his face. He ought to push away the bad shit that had a tendency to press into his brain and remember how lucky he was. He was a fucking business owner now. Nobody else profited from his labor. What he put in, he was gonna get right back, and while he had a long way to go to turn the lodge into a functional resort, it was gonna be mint when the work was done. The kind of respectable place he and Will had talked about. A year-round restaurant and bar with live music on weekends and a dozen tidy cottages for rent in the summer months. They'd take care of the place themselves and be rolling in cash. Sal just had to keep looking on the positive side and think long-term.

Otherwise, he was going to lose his goddamn mind.

A strange sound penetrated the forested grounds, which was unusual in and of itself, and then Sal placed it in his head. Car wheels crunching and spitting gravel on the driveway from the country road. Sal stubbed out his joint on the rim of the wheelbarrow and slipped it into the back pocket of his jeans. The only person who'd ever come by was the contractor. Sal eagerly pushed the barrow along the trail to the front of the house. It had to be good news. Will had paid the guy's retention fee, and he was showing up to start working on the roof.

When Sal made his way around, he saw it wasn't Andy Gulliver's pickup. It was a night-blue Chevrolet sedan he'd never seen in his life. It had pulled up near the lodge, and then the driver, in a checkered, camel business suit, stepped out of the car, shut the door, and walked along to the far side of the lodge as casually as he'd stopped by a roadside overlook. He looked too well-dressed to be a bounty hunter or a private dick, but still, Sal was on guard.

Sal left the wheelbarrow on the side of the lot and headed cautiously over to the guy. The stranger hadn't seen Sal, and he was angled away from him. He was tall and broad shouldered. Standard medium-length haircut for an upstate square. Not that old, though. Maybe in his late twenties. Sal came up to an arm's length from the suit, and he was still in his own world, gazing toward the little beach and dock behind the house. What the fuck was he doing there?

Sal raised his voice. "This is private property, pal. We ain't open for business yet."

The stranger turned to him. He wasn't shocked or ruffled in any way. He just looked at Sal with a moony smile on his clean-shaven face. He had a striking combination of light hair and dark brown eyebrows. It was off-putting, not in a bad way exactly, but it made it just a little harder to move the guy along.

"You work here now?" he said. "I've been stopping by the place for years on my run from Ottawa to Syracuse. Just for sentimental reasons." He hiked up another grin. "Somebody finally bought the place? I never thought it'd happen."

Sal nodded.

"That's super," the guy said. "It bummed me out, seeing the Frontenac's place falling into disrepair." He glanced at Sal a little shyly. "My folks used to take us kids up here every August. The week before Labor Day. Right before we had to go back to school. We'd rent cabin number nine." He pointed toward the east side of the property. "That's the second to last one down there. One of the two-bedroom units. We loved it. It didn't matter if it rained all week or it was ninety degrees and sunny. We were kids, y'know? Always found a way to have a good time."

Sal tried lining up a nice way to say he didn't have time to take a stroll down Memory Lane with a stranger. Before he could get out the right words, the guy went on.

"This one summer...heck, it downpoured every single day. But me and my brothers met some kids from Ohio, and we went fishing and swimming in the rain all week. Played freeze tag every night till it was too dark to see what we were doing. Drenched like fools! But those are the kinds of situations that make for the best vacation. When you're a kid, y'know?" He glanced at Sal. "The owner wouldn't happen to be around, would he? This might sound funny, but I'd love to look up that family from Ohio. We rented cabins together three summers in a row and swore we'd stay in touch after the place closed down in '66. I'd love to know if they kept Frontenac's guest registry. Wouldn't hurt to ask, don't you think?"

That was sounding fishy and got Sal's New York attitude coming back to him. "*I'm* the owner. Me and my partner. And there weren't no guest registry handed down."

The guy's eyes widened. "I'm sorry." He noticed the wheelbarrow a little ways off. "Gee, you must have your hands full. Doing all the fix-up work yourselves, you and your partner?"

"We got a contractor. I'm just clearing a few things out so his crew can do their business." It was a lie, but Sal didn't like being talked down to.

The guy reset with his big, affable grin and held out his hand. "I'm Todd Pulaski. Should've introduced myself before."

Sal looked at his big outstretched hand and couldn't do anything but shake it. "Sal. Sal Minovich."

"Nice to meet you, Sal. And congrats on buying the place. I hope you don't mind I drove up to take a peek. The old sign's out front, and I assumed the lodge was still abandoned." He lowered his eyes. "I shouldn't have assumed, I mean. You've done real well scoring the property. It's beautiful, isn't it?"

Sal fixed an I-don't-need-you-gassing-me-up look on his face.

"I'm sorry about barging in on you. I'll leave you to it." Todd made a half turn, hesitated, and then he came back at Sal again. "Can I ask you something? Are you reopening the place for cabin rentals? Or you got plans to turn it into something else?"

Sal couldn't help himself from bragging. "Check back in the spring. We're fixing up the kitchen and dining room, and we're gonna have a bar and grill with live music on weekends. In addition to renting cottages."

Todd beamed. "Out of sight. Sounds like you've got experience with the hotel biz."

He was looking for Sal to say something about that, but Sal didn't answer. His gut was telling him the guy was too mushy to be a hired PI, but he was poking around for information about the place for some reason.

"I wouldn't know the first thing about running a place like this. My beat is propane sales. You heard of Transatlantic?" He gazed at Sal's blank face reassuringly. "You wouldn't have unless you were in the business. I cover their sales territory in the North Country and Eastern Ontario. I pass by here every other Friday when I'm headed back from my Canadian customers."

Sal nodded along and glanced at Todd's sedan as a cue.

"You probably think I'm bananas, but would you mind me stopping by every now and then, just to take a look for old time's sake? I swear, I won't be any bother. It's just…I've got so many good memories of the lodge. Always makes me smile seeing the place."

The guy was red in the face and misty-eyed. Sal was stymied for a moment. He wasn't heartless. But whatever Todd was missing in his life that kept him coming back to his childhood vacation spot wasn't Sal's problem.

"I can call ahead so you can tell me if it's an okay time," Todd persisted. He brought out a pen and a business card from the inside pocket of his suit.

"We ain't got phone lines yet."

Todd's face deflated, and he tucked his pen and card back in his suit. But he wasn't the kind of person to be beaten down for long. "How 'bout I bring you something for the trouble then, the next time I come by? What's your poison, Sal? Canadian beer? Canadian whiskey?"

"I dunno."

"I always stop by the duty-free shop to pick up stuff for friends. What do you say?"

"You ain't gotta do that."

"It's no big deal. It's the least I can do for imposing on you like this."

Having some liquor would be pretty damn luxurious. It sure would make the nights pass by quicker. Sal was bored out of his mind, and he was down to his last twenty-four dollars. He'd left Beacon with nearly a thou, but he'd blown through that real fast over the past three months, having to pay for a motel room for the first two and buying things to make the place somewhat livable. Now he was scraping by on twenty bucks a week to get his groceries and generic cigarettes. Could be the guy was screwy, but Sal was feeling like it was an offer he couldn't refuse.

"Well then. That'd be all right."

"Which one?"

"Whiskey ain't bad."

Todd grinned ear-to-ear. "You got it." He reached out his hand to shake Sal's again. "Thanks Sal. You're one in a million. I'll see you in two weeks." He glanced around. "Bet you'll have made a lot of progress with the place. I can't wait to see."

Sal watched him stride back to his car and drive off with a parting smile and a handwave like he'd won the lottery.

SAL WAS LIVING in the boonies, and he didn't have a car. So, later that day, before it got dark, he hiked down the country highway to a Shell station where they had a phone booth. The shoulder of the road was narrow, and there wasn't a single street lamp on the mile and a half stretch. Drivers gunned it, coming off the thruway from Canada and not having to deal with a traffic light for miles. It wasn't Sal's favorite thing to do, plodding along the road like some hard luck bum. He was always paranoid about being spotted by local coppers who might take an interest in him, and more than once, he'd had to duck into the brush from a car that came barreling behind him. It was shit to tell the truth.

He got to the gas station phone booth, put two quarters and two dimes in the slot and lit up a cigarette. Will said he couldn't call collect no more because it would look suspicious. Sal didn't understand his point so well, and meanwhile seventy cents for a three-minute phone call wasn't cheap for a person with twenty-four dollars left in his pocket, and it was a dime for every extra minute. The line bleeped and droned and finally Will picked up.

"It's me," Sal said.

Will spoke quietly but sharply. "I thought I told you, it's better to call me on the other line after six." He said nothing for a moment, and then Sal heard the sound of a door clicking shut. Will must've grabbed the phone set from the front desk and closed himself up in the motel office. His voice came back, peeved. "You know I've got to stay by the front desk and keep this line open. People drop by at all hours from the listing in the paper."

Sal drew on his cheap cig, which had already burned halfway to the filter. "I ain't walking an unlit highway in the dark. It's a half hour in both directions."

"Whatever, Sal. You sound peachy. You calling to add more grief to my day?"

Sal scratched his stubbly chin. He only called three or four times a week, and they hadn't seen each other for three months. Was it a fucking crime that he wanted to hear Will's voice? "When you coming up here?"

"When I can. I've got a buyer interested, but it's peanuts he's offering. I'll probably take a loss one way or the other, but it'll look better if I hold off a little while."

It had been ninety-one days since George had croaked. Two days after they'd done it, Will told Sal to get out of town, and Sal hopped on a bus to Watertown with nine hundred or so bucks in his wallet and the name of a cheap motel Will had given him. Will had followed through with buying the lodge, but he hadn't even come up to see it. He just told Sal what to do and wired him four

Gs to pay a realtor for the down payment. Meanwhile, Will had closed the motor lodge for business a long time ago, and he was supposedly selling off George's properties. He said he'd have a quarter mil. "What's a little while?" Sal said.

"If I knew, I'd tell you. It's not easy, Sal. I've got his bills to settle. We're closing on his block of shops in Kingston next week, but that's barely gonna cover his unpaid taxes. And now his uncle's lawyer is fighting with mine. It's a fucking shit show I'm dealing with. I've got triple digit invoices for legal fees just to have my lawyer advise me I oughta pay off his uncle to get him off my back. So that's more money that'll be flying out the door."

Sal sucked in another toke. "What am I supposed to do? I barely got cash to live off for another week, and if we don't pay the contractor soon, it's gonna be too late in the season for him to replace the roof."

"I know. Just try to relax. Believe me, you're in a better place than me."

"*I'm* in a better place? There ain't no heat or electric, and it's fucking below freezing at night. I work all goddamn day guttin' the lodge, and I ain't got nothin' to show for it."

"The work's gotta get done, doesn't it? You knew that going in. You wanna trade places with me? I got George's tenants calling twenty-four seven. Every day I'm running back and forth 'cause I've gotta do the maintenance work myself. Not to mention all the harassing calls from his uncle. I lost ten pounds. It's a good night when I get three hours sleep."

Sal picked a paint chip from his fingernail. "Then why you still there?"

"I've gotta close things out. It doesn't happen overnight, and I can't do it from up there. I keep trying to make you understand that."

"This whole thing is bullshit," Sal blurted out. The operator's recorded message came on, and he had to find a dime from the pocket of his jeans to pay for another minute. His cig fell out of his hand in the process.

"What do you want me to do, Sal?"

"Don't treat me like a mook. You been hanging me out to dry."

"Who's hanging you out to dry? There's a reason you're up there, sitting on that lodge. I've got realtors and lawyers working on unloading his properties, and I've gotta be ready at the drop of a hat to sign off on the paperwork. I'm gonna make us big money, and as a matter of fact, I'm living without heat too. I'm getting by on his bank's line of credit. It's almost maxxed out, and I gotta use it so I can pay for gas to fix shit for his tenants so I don't have them making complaints to the state attorney general."

Sal felt hollow inside. Like he'd been played for a fool. Will had been singing the same song for three months. He brought out with some bite, "You sleeping with somebody?"

Will clucked. "You think I got time for that? You high?"

Sal had smoked another joint before he left out for the gas station, but that high had worn off a long time ago. Another message came over the receiver, and Sal had to throw his last quarter in the slot.

"I ain't paranoid or high."

"Then why would you say something like that? Christ, Sal, you never paid a bill in your life. I'm managing books all day so we can get something out of this, and you want to accuse me of spending my time fucking around on you?"

Sal swallowed a lump in his throat. "I'm sayin' I want you here."

"I know, Sal. I want that too. But put things in perspective. George's life insurance payout is coming through. I got the notice Monday, and they've got thirty days to send the check." He paused and lowered his voice. "It's three hundred grand."

"What you talkin' 'bout?"

"The life insurance. George had me as his beneficiary."

Sal's brain pinched up. "That's news to me."

"I told you about it. Remember? God, your memory's like a sieve sometimes."

Sal was just about one hundred and ten percent sure he

would've remembered George's three hundred-thousand-dollar life insurance policy. "So, now you're telling me you ain't coming up for at least thirty days?"

"It's the way things work. What do you think? A man dies, and poof, his estate cashes out the next day? I'm taking care of all these things, and *you're* the one complaining? I been through interviews with the coroner's office, lawyers, piles of paperwork, replumbing goddamn sewage lines. I'm fucking breaking. I didn't even tell you Loretta filed a complaint with the Department of Labor. She's claiming two thousand dollars in back wages."

Sal rubbed his forehead. "Buy me a bus ticket, and I'll come down to help."

"You know that's not a good idea."

"It's been three months."

"You gotta be patient, Sal."

"I'm tired of living up here by myself."

"I don't enjoy it either. But we're working on something big."

Sal's face hardened, and he shook his head. "Either you come up to me, or I'm coming down to you."

"You know we can't do that."

"All right. I'll hitch my way to Albany. Take the bus down from there."

"Sal, don't go funny on me. You show up, what's Hogan gonna think?"

"Why you mentionin' Hogan? You two been spendin' time together?"

"No. I mentioned Hogan 'cause it's not gonna look good for you to come back here for no reason. You're safe up there. You've gotta stick with the plan."

Sal was sweating now. "Where's the wrench?"

"What?"

"The wrench. The one you said you was gonna make disappear."

"I fucking scrubbed George's blood off it and buried it under eighty pounds of concrete in the cellar. I told you that. Why're you getting squirrelly?"

"What's Hogan shaken you down for so far?"

"He's not shaking me down."

"How many times you let him screw you?"

Will didn't answer.

"Nobody does that but me. You hear me?"

"I'm stressing, Sal. And you want to make me feel worse about myself?"

It sounded like Will was crying, but that didn't penetrate. "I'm your man, ain't I? I shouldn't be sleeping alone, shivering under three blankets every night."

"I'm doing the best I can. I don't know how else to say it."

Sal's anger went cold. "You got so much on your hands, could be time for me to do my own thing."

Will snorted. "What's that mean?"

"I got options. This salesman stopped by the lodge today." Sal blinked his eyes. "Not a bad looking guy. I done worse."

"What're you talking about? Sal, you shouldn't be talking to anybody."

Sal lit another cigarette, taking his time. "Why not? You ain't doin' shit for me."

"Why's a salesman coming by the lodge? Don't you have a sign up saying it's closed for the season?"

"I dunno. Come up and see for yourself."

"You're being childish. We both gotta tough it out for a few months until the payout comes through. That's what grown-ups do, Sal. You think I need this bullshit from you?"

The operator message cut in again. Sal didn't have any more coins. Before the call disconnected, he shouted into the receiver, "Wire me some goddamn money."

The phone clicked and died in a steady ring. Sal bashed it against the panel three times, and then he sank down to his knees and beat his fist against his head.

16

WILL HAD TO be lying. That's all Sal could figure. Maybe he wanted George's money for himself. Maybe he was working an angle, trying to pin George's murder on him, telling Hogan Sal had run off after doing it. It could be the two of them had planned to set Sal up to take the fall all along, and they were fucking and living on Easy Street now. Sal wasn't stupid. Will had never mentioned that life insurance policy before. He'd conned Sal, saying how easy the whole scheme would be, and now he had excuse after excuse for why he couldn't come up to get the lodge running like they were supposed to be doing.

Will wasn't going to get away with dropping him so easy. For a couple of days, Sal seriously considered going down to Beacon and setting the fucker straight on where they stood. Will belonged to him. Sal didn't care if he ended up in prison for going back to the scene of the crime. He'd even tell the pigs exactly what they'd done so Will would see he couldn't play him like that.

Sal came close to doing it, but as time wore on, his feelings modulated. Maybe it wasn't worth being locked up in prison for the rest of his life. Maybe Will would come around to appreciating what he was missing. Sal did a lot of thinking those days, leaving aside the grunt work that had to be done at the lodge. He stayed high most of the day and lay in bed just jacking off and feeling sorry for himself. Why did Will have to treat him like a dirtbag? Hadn't they had something good? Will promised once they got rid of George, they were going to be together.

Sal felt like he'd been exiled to Siberia. It was goddamn cold enough. His bedroom window had frost growing in the corners, and he saw motes of snow in the morning. Day and night, he was so fucking lonely, he thought sometimes it wasn't worth living.

He decided one day, if Will was gonna punish him, he'd punish Will back. He wasn't hiking a half hour to the phone booth to call him no more. If Will wanted to see him, if he even gave a shit, he'd get off his ass and make the drive up north. Until then, Sal wasn't going out of his way to do nothing for him.

Then day after day went by. Sal was down to his last five dollars, which would get him a carton of generic cigs and a loaf of bread. He started considering it was time to move on. He wasn't going to let Will leave him to starve. The Canadian border was only fifteen miles away. Sal could walk it, or even better, he could take one of the lodge's fishing boats and go straight across the river. Steal into Canada, make his way to a big city like Toronto or Montréal, and find a new hustle. Will could fuck himself as far as he was concerned.

One afternoon, Sal decided to look at what he had to work with in the moldering boathouse by the river. The place was pretty gruesome from who knew how many seasons of flooding, but amid the puke smell and debris, the owner had left six aluminum rowboats. A couple of them still had their gear and outboard motors. Sal even found a jug of gasoline, half full. He chose a boat that looked like it had the least wear and tear, and he dragged it out of the house toward the beach. He'd never operated a boat, but he had plenty of time to learn.

Sal almost made it as far as trying to attach the motor to the back of the boat. Then, faintly at first, he heard a voice up shore, and he turned in its direction curiously. Nobody was around as far as he could see, but then the voice came louder.

"Sal? You around?"

That triggered a recollection Sal hadn't thought about for quite a while. Was it a Friday? Sal had lost track of days. He shook out the thermal shirt he'd been wearing for a week. He hadn't taken a shower for that long either and probably looked like a homeless person. Sal had grown whiskers, and his wiry hair was overgrown and wild. A figure came around the lodge, just up a hill from where Sal stood. Todd. He gave Sal a big wave. Sal bowed his head and tramped over to him.

The guy was wearing a business suit like last time. He proudly showed off a box of liquor in his hands. Canadian Club whiskey.

"I make good on my promises," Todd said.

Sal hung back three feet in front of him. He was self-conscious about how he looked and smelled.

"I hope this isn't a bad time," Todd said. "I was passing by on my way back from Ottawa. You remember? I told you, every other Friday." He glanced past Sal, toward the beach. "You thinking about getting one of those old fishing boats in the water?"

"Just seeing what condition they's in is all."

"You been boating on the Saint Lawrence before?"

"No."

"I can tell you, you don't want to be taking an old dinghy out on the main waterway. The current is fierce, and the waves this time of year will have you capsized in no time flat." Todd pointed out some things. "We always stayed on this side of Wellesley Island. That's the big one that closes off the channel on the American side. You stay south of that, there's a lot of little islands to explore all the way over to Alexandria Bay. You've got Grindstone Island in the other direction. I caught my first bass over there when I was ten years old."

Given the circumstances, Sal didn't mind the guy's chattiness. He'd had no contact with human beings for two weeks, and Todd sounded like an authority on the matter. He might've saved Sal from drowning while trying to motor across the river to Canada. As Sal gazed at the enormous waterway, it pressed in on him that he'd be terrified on the open water, far from shore. Just looking out there gave Sal the creeps, like he was shrinking, surrounded by water.

"You fish?"

It took a moment for Sal to return his attention to Todd. "Just one time when I was a kid."

"Did I catch you in the middle of something, Sal? If you've got your hands full, I won't hold you up."

Sal pushed himself out of his funk. "Nah." He mustered up a grin. "I wasn't sure if you was coming back."

"Of course I came back! Like I said, I pass by this way every other Friday." Todd looked around the property fondly and breathed in the fresh air. "I've been looking forward to it. You have to catch me up on the progress you made with the place."

Sal glanced away. "I ain't made much progress." He considered his words. "Me and my partner, we ran into some snags. Nothin' serious. It's just slowin' things down a bit."

"Sorry to hear it. Say, I never asked you: Where are you and your partner from?"

"New York."

"New York City? That's something else. A couple of city boys."

Sal smiled a little.

"I've never been. But they used to get families from the city at Frontenac's place. They got people from all over." Todd glanced around again. "What kind of snags you dealing with?"

"Just waitin' on the contractor. There's only so much I can do myself." Sal scuffed his boot on the patch of dirt where he was standing. "I still ain't got no heat or electric."

Todd's eyes widened with concern. "You got a working fireplace?"

Sal shook his head.

"Christ, Sal. It must get below freezing at night this time of year. What's your contractor guy waiting for?"

"My partner. He's holdin' the purse strings if y'know what I mean." Sal considered that he didn't want to come off as a whiny loser. "But we're working it out."

"Hey. I brought sandwiches," Todd said. "Ham salad and tuna. In case you wanted to take a break. If you're busy, I can just leave 'em. Along with the whiskey, of course."

Their glances crossed. The guy looked real eager for company.

"A break don't sound bad. You mind if I take a shower first?"

"Not at all. You do what you need to do. Hey, you need anything from the hardware store over in Clayton? I can run over there while you're washing up. Pick up some lanterns or anything else you might need."

Sal didn't know why Todd was being so nice to him. It would've set off alarm bells if Sal wasn't so beaten down. He told Todd he could use some lanterns, and the guy gave Sal the box of whiskey and hopped in his car.

Sal went inside, stripped down, and gave himself a thorough scrubbing under ice cold water in the shower stall of the lodge's ground-level apartment. After, he shaved his beard with his last disposable razor, got his hair tamed with some gel, threw on some cologne and sorted through his clothes. His underwear was horrid, but he found a shirt and a pair of jeans he'd only worn a few times. Then Sal tidied up the little apartment in the few ways he could. Sweeping the dusty floor. Rinsing out the two mugs he'd inherited from the place. Using a worn sponge to wipe off the two-chair table in the kitchen.

LATER, THEY WERE chowing down on store-bought sandwiches at Sal's kitchen table and drinking cans of Dr. Pepper. Todd had picked up two camping lanterns and an economy pack of batteries from the hardware store and set them up in the kitchen. Sal had been getting by with a rusty oil lamp and candles, so it was a big improvement. Even better, Todd had bought him a propane stove with a kettle for heating up soup and his morning coffee.

Sal didn't need to say much at first. Todd could talk. He wanted Sal to know all the points of interest in the region: the miniature golf place a few miles south where he once won a Blueberry Slush Puppy for getting a hole in one; the big grocery store two towns over that had better prices than the little market down the road; a diner that Sal had to check out because they had the best burgers in the world. Sal just nodded along. The guy was as square as could be, but Sal didn't mind listening to his stories in exchange for the food and booze and the lights. Todd wasn't so bad to look at, either. He was built like a quarterback and had that All-American, clean-cut style. When Sal asked how he kept in shape, he said he never missed the morning routine his high school football coach had taught him, which involved a three-mile jog and push-ups, sit-ups and shit like that.

Todd got comfy, taking off his jacket, loosening his tie, and unbuttoning his shirt cuffs and rolling them up his forearms. He told Sal he was on the road four out of five days of the week. He didn't mind the work, but he was on his own a lot of the time, driving for hours and sleeping in motels off the thruway. He wore a gold band wedding ring, but he didn't mention missing his wife or any kids they might've had. Then he told Sal he'd been adopted. He didn't know anything about his birth mother or father. A couple in Syracuse had taken him in when he was a year old, and they'd become his family. While he was talking, Sal tore open the wrapping on the whiskey with a Swiss Army knife, poured two mugfuls, and handed the less chipped one to Todd.

"I guess that's why our summer vacations here were special to me," Todd went on. "It felt like I found the place where I belonged." He took a sip of his whiskey. "Don't get me wrong, Sal. My mom and dad always treated me like their own, but when you're adopted, it's different. For me, at least. Maybe it's in my head."

Sal pulled out his pack of no name cigarettes but stopped himself before lighting one up. "You mind?"

"It's your place. Go ahead."

Sal tipped the pack to his companion in an invitation.

"As a matter of fact, I've got my own." Todd reached behind himself to his suit jacket, which he'd draped over the back of his chair. He returned with a box of Marlboro Reds that sparkled in Sal's vision. "I always pick up cartons for my buddies at the duty-free shop. And every now and then, I'm in the mood for one myself."

"When you're drinkin'?" Sal said.

Todd smiled and drummed the box on the table to pack his cigs. "Yeah. When I'm drinking with my buddies." He opened the box and offered Sal a fresh, premium cig.

Sal took it and stretched his hand across the table to light Todd up with his Zippo. He clasped the back of Todd's hand with his palm while he was doing it, and he lingered with that contact. It was an old trick to see if a guy was interested. Not one hundred percent foolproof, but generally, if the guy didn't duck his hand away pretty quickly, it was a good indication he was open to getting down. Sal had caught a little mischief from the whiskey and maybe a bit of spite. If Will was going to freeze him out, Sal would show him he didn't give a shit. Todd's hand didn't move well after his cig was lit, and he blushed a little.

"It's ridiculous they've got you living like this," Todd said, glancing around.

Sal shrugged.

"They need to install that furnace soon. You won't make it through a Thousand Islands winter without one."

The big guy was worried about his welfare. That was sweet. Sal smirked in a flirty way. "It's pretty cold in bed. That's for sure."

"It got cold at night, even in August," Todd said. "None of the cabins were heated, of course. We slept in sleeping bags, under the covers. Every morning, we bitched about the cold showers in the bathhouse."

Sal sat back a little with his legs spread in his tight jeans, watching Todd take another gulp of whiskey. "You sure loved this place."

"I did. Every summer, from when I was ten to fifteen, we came up here. I told you about meeting that family from Ohio. One of the sons, he was the same age as me. We were best buds. Spent day and night together. We even shared the same sleeping bag."

Sal tapped the ash of his cigarette into the ashtray that was between them on the table. He had an intuition about what Todd was saying. "Must've been nice to have a friend like that." Todd's gaze fell, and he went for another sip of whiskey.

"Yeah. Well, we fell out of contact. A lot of things changed after the Frontenacs closed down the place." Todd sipped his drink and fiddled with his cigarette. Something was eating at him, and then he said it. "My parents and my younger brother died in an accident. Hit by a drunk driver. I was sixteen years old."

"Fuck."

"I'm sorry. I shouldn't be dumping this heavy stuff on you."

Sal gazed at him like it was no imposition at all.

Todd pushed back his hair. "So, yeah. That happened. Me and my older brother moved in with our grandparents. Jeff was never the same. He started getting into trouble. Y'know, with drugs and drinking. Then one night, he took off with our granddad's Buick, and he never came back." Todd downed the rest of his drink. "No goodbye. No note. That's kinda cold, y'know? But I guess he had his reasons."

"What kinda reasons?"

"I don't know. I've been taking it personal, but I've been trying to think about it logically in my head. He could've met a girl. Maybe they decided to run off together. He was really mixed up after the accident. He could've been deeper into drugs than we knew, and he needed to sell the car to pay his dealer or something like that."

Sal refilled Todd's mug. After that story, the guy could use another stiff drink.

"My grandparents went to the police to report him missing, but when they heard they'd have to press charges to get an investigation going, they backed off. We looked for him ourselves.

Tracking down his friends. Checking with every relative in the family. My grandparents called hospitals and took out an ad in the paper. Nothing. So, unless he turns up after ten years, we'll never know why he left." Todd sipped his drink and looked up at Sal. "Thanks for listening. I'm sorry to be such a downer. I really didn't plan on telling you all that."

Sal waved him off. "You ain't gotta apologize. We all been through something, ain't we?"

"So, what's your story? I talked your ear off all night."

Sal took a long toke on his cigarette, deciding how much to say. The guy seemed like a sweetheart, but not many people would have a high opinion of a history like his.

"I ain't seen my family for a long time neither. My pops took off. My mom had a talent for attracting deadbeats. I been on my own a long time, getting by with this and that."

"It can't be so long, can it? What are you? Twenty-two? Twenty-three?"

Sal smiled. "Twenty-eight."

"Get out of here. I'm twenty-eight. I thought I was a lot older than you."

"Nope."

Their glances met while they were both smiling, and then they looked away and sat in silence. Sal noticed it had gotten dark outside. The kitchen was shadowy but for the lanterns Todd had bought for him.

"You probably want to get on the road if you're gonna make it back to Syracuse tonight," Sal said.

Todd looked at his silver wristwatch. "Seven fifteen. It's just a little over an hour and half back to Syracuse. A straight shot down Route 81 from Watertown. So long as I'm on the road by eight o'clock or so, I'll be fine."

"Your wife ain't gonna wanna know where you been all this time?"

Todd scowled. "You trying to get rid of me?"

"No."

"Good. 'Cause I like watching you. I mean, *talking* to you."
Todd's face burned up, and he snorted a laugh. "I don't drink
whiskey. I think it's gone to my head already. And you look as
sober as a judge. I'm not leaving until you catch up with me."

Sal poured himself some more and threw back a big gulp to get
the lonely hunk smiling again. Todd undid the top two buttons of
his shirt and told Sal more stories about the lodge. Sneaking beers
with his brothers after dark. Going swimming in the middle of the
night, setting off firecrackers on the beach, playing truth or dare
with some girls from Long Island who were staying at the lodge
one summer. It sounded like the perfect teenage dream. They went
through two-thirds of the bottle of whiskey and most of Todd's
Marlboros. Then Todd said he had to take a leak, and Sal gave him
a lantern and pointed out the way to his little bathroom, which
was through the bedroom.

Todd swayed over in that direction. He was definitely feeling
the liquor, but Sal heard him stumble along and close the bathroom door, confirming that he'd found it. He reached into Todd's
pack of Marlboros and lit himself another smoke.

It was batshit crazy the situations he got himself into. Just a
few hours ago, he'd been considering taking a virgin voyage across
the water to Canada, and now he had some married square
bringing him sandwiches and whiskey and probably wanting to get
down his pants. It wasn't a bad thing, but as much as Sal was pissed
at Will, he missed him. Will ought to be there with him, getting
drunk and snuggling up together for the night. Was Will even
thinking about him? Was he cozied up with Hogan and having a
big laugh over how they'd set him up?

Sal stubbed out his butt. A good amount of time had passed,
and Todd hadn't returned from the bathroom. Sal didn't hear any
sounds coming from back there. Had he passed out? Sal waited
another ten seconds or so, and then he stood up from his chair and
went to see if Todd needed some help.

Weak light fanned out of the crevices of the bathroom door
from Todd's lantern. Sal could've called out to him, but he chose

instead to edge up to the door and see what he could hear. Todd was tipsy and kinda depressive-sounding, so for a dicey moment, Sal worried about what he was doing on his own.

The door rattled. Sal stepped back so he didn't look like a creep, but before he could move too far, the door swung open. Todd stood slumped in the door frame, backlit from the lantern he'd left in the john. He squinted in Sal's direction.

"That you, Sal?"

Sal stepped into the pool of light. "Yeah. You was taking a long time, so I was coming to see if you was all right."

Todd snickered drunkenly. "You were coming to see if I was all right?"

"Yeah." Sal studied him. Todd was acting strange. Maybe it was the booze. He took a wobbly shuffle toward Sal and clasped his shoulders.

"That was nice." Todd's head bobbed in front of Sal. "I like you, Sal. You like me?"

Sal got a hand around Todd's wrist for leverage. He'd been with drunken tricks and had things go south before. "Yeah, I like you."

Todd's face came so close, Sal could smell the liquor on his breath. Warm, swampy heat saturated his shirt, and his body was trembling a little.

"'Cause I could really use somebody to like me," Todd said.

His voice was strained. Sal thought he was falling apart. Then Todd nuzzled against his face, gentle and tentative. He brushed his lips against Sal's and went in for an open-mouthed kiss.

EARLY THE NEXT morning, Sal woke up with an urgent need to empty his bladder. He had to climb out from under Todd's thick arm and the bedsheet, afghan and sleeping bag to get to the bathroom. It didn't wake the big guy up. Sal stepped quietly, bare feet on cold floor boards, and carefully shut the bathroom door behind him. Then he stood at the toilet and let out a heavenly stream.

He yawned and peeled back the vinyl drape on the little bathroom window. It was bright outside, well past sunrise. Sal didn't know what time it was when he and Todd had finally passed out, but it had to have been pretty late. As the fog lifted from his head, memories from last night came back to Sal.

Todd had been all over his jock. He wanted Sal to fuck him. The guy was sloppy drunk and giving off a clingy vibe, but Sal had never been good at saying no. Especially in the state he'd been. He hadn't had anybody wanting him for months.

The sex hadn't been anything special. What Sal remembered better was what happened after. Rather than knocking the big stud out, getting him off had somehow given Todd a second wind, and he wanted to stay up talking in bed and having smokes and taking slugs from the whiskey bottle. He confessed that the kid from Ohio he'd mentioned was the first guy he'd ever slept with. It had him mixed up for a while because he didn't want anyone knowing he swung that way, but he'd been in love with the kid. His heart was ripped apart when the Frontenac lodge closed down. That one week in August every year was all they had. They wrote letters back and forth for a while, and then the kid stopped writing back, right after Todd told him about the accident that killed his parents and younger brother. But Todd wasn't looking to get back in touch with the guy to rekindle their relationship, he wanted Sal to know. He was just curious about how his life had turned out and thinking they could reminisce about their summer vacations.

Todd told Sal he'd fooled around with other guys after that. Nothing serious. Just cruising a park in Syracuse after dark and meeting guys in a shopping mall bathroom. But he never met anyone who wanted more than getting off quick together while they could get away with it. That made him wonder if it was possible to find love with a man. Sal said he'd been wondering the same thing, which in retrospect might've been the wrong thing to say. Sal still had Will on his mind.

He sat his bare ass on the cold toilet seat while he was recollecting. Todd was a good guy, but Sal wasn't looking to make what happened last night a regular thing. He felt a little bad about that as he remembered the deep stuff Todd had shared with him.

After high school, Todd got a job delivering propane tanks. His grandparents' neighbor ran the business. When he was twenty years old, Todd asked the woman who kept the books to go out on a date, and they got married two years later. He only liked her as a friend, but it seemed like the right thing to do. His wife was twelve years older than him and eager to start a family. Todd was able to get it up enough to get her pregnant twice. They had two girls – Polly, who was six, and Marcy who was four.

As they passed the whiskey bottle back and forth, Todd told Sal he had no regrets, but he always felt like something was missing from his life. He'd done well with his career. The neighbor sold the propane company to a big corporate, multinational energy firm, and they offered him a job in sales. He started making bank and bought a nice three-bedroom house for his family, a new car, and a station wagon for his wife, and anything she needed to raise their two girls. But that's when he started looking for what he was missing again.

He had to travel all over the state and up to Ontario, and he found highway rest stops where guys screwed around. In Ottawa, they had a gay newspaper with personal ads. He answered one from a guy who said he was looking for more than sex, and for a few months, he met up regularly with an older, married gym teacher at an elementary school. Todd hoped their relationship would give him what he was needing, but that guy was false advertising. He never wanted to do more than fool around in his car or check into a low budget motel once or twice.

Todd broke down in drunken tears, and Sal stretched his arm around him to calm him down. Todd said he'd thought about asking his boss if he could change his sales territory to Toronto or Boston since there were more men like him in those big cities. He didn't think his wife would mind. Since the girls had come along, their marriage was on autopilot, and she didn't want any more kids.

"*You* lived in New York," he said. "Are there men out there who want more than a fling?"

That got Sal thinking about Will again, so he bullshitted his answer. "I dunno. I had a couple of what you might call 'serious relationships.' They all been messed up in the head, or maybe I ain't been enough for them, so it ain't worked out for me. But it could be different for you."

Todd rolled toward him on his side and laid his thigh over Sal's. He gazed at Sal like a puppy dog. "Maybe you and me could have something. I like you a lot, Sal."

Sal froze up.

Todd grinned at him. "What? I'm not your type?"

"It ain't that. It's just…I dunno."

"You're not looking for something serious?"

Sal didn't answer.

Todd ran his hand down Sal's side and sank into the space between Sal's legs. "It's okay. It's nice having fun like this, isn't it? I get up here every other Friday. We could play around and get to know each other, don't you think?"

He didn't really let Sal answer. Todd turned onto his side and tugged at Sal to put it in him again. Sal busted the guy's nut a second time, and then Todd finally went to sleep.

Sal got up, went to the sink and splashed cold water on his face. He felt like a jerk, but he didn't really have a reason to feel like a jerk, did he? He'd been begging Will to come up so they could be together, and the kid had done jack shit. As for Todd, he was a closet case who was just buying Sal's time. Sal had heard all kinds of sob stories from tricks like that. It was part of the transaction, and he'd be fine going back to his life with a wife and kids until he needed to get off again.

Quietly, Sal opened the bathroom door and looked in on Todd. He was still buried beneath the covers like the Loch Ness monster crowning in the bed.

Sal stepped lightly to the kitchen and went through the pockets of Todd's suit jacket. He found a leather wallet and flipped it open. The guy was flush with cash and credit cards. He had wallet-size photos of his daughters too, but Sal didn't spend time looking at those. He pulled out a ten-dollar bill. Todd had a lot more twenties, tens and fives so he probably wouldn't notice and he certainly wouldn't miss it. Then Sal pried out a twenty. Todd was loaded. He wouldn't miss that either. He'd had a drunken night, and the next time he opened his wallet to pay for something, if he even noticed he was short some bills, he probably wouldn't be so sure of himself.

Sal glanced at the bedroom. Not a sound coming from there. He took the ten and twenty and hid them in a drawer in a kitchen counter, under a plastic tray the owner had left for utensils. Then Sal went back into the bedroom and got under the covers. The bed was nice and warm from Todd's body heat.

17

THIRTY DOLLARS WASN'T much, but it tided Sal over for a few more days. At the store where he got his groceries, he picked up Cup O' Noodles and instant coffee since he finally had a little stove, and he treated himself to a carton of Camels, which surprised the old lady at the cash register who'd rung up his generics every other time he came to the shop. Sal hadn't figured out what he was doing, living in a dilapidated lodge that was basically a squat, but he could ride things out until Todd came back in two weeks.

Sal was thinking his best move might be to work Todd for money. He wanted a relationship, and he'd seen that Sal had cash problems. Next time, Sal could come clean about his situation minus a few details. It probably wouldn't take much to get Todd offering to help him out. If he rented Sal an apartment, they'd have a cozy hideaway for fucking when he was traveling. Once Sal had a liveable place to get through the cold months, he could assess the situation and figure out contingency plans if Todd got screwy. He seemed like a big-hearted fella who wouldn't hurt a fly, but Sal had been with plenty of guys who started out that way and went wacko. Anyway, working Todd would get him a decent place to live in the short-term. Sal would be happy to have a room in a crappy boarding house so long as it had heat. It was getting to be torture taking a shower when he could see his breath inside the house. At some point, the pipes were going to freeze over, and he'd have no water at all.

Then, one morning while Sal was heating his instant coffee on his little stove, he heard the sound of a car and looked out the window. A blue and white USPS Jeep was coming down his driveway. Soon enough, he had a postal stiff clopping up the stairs to his porch.

The uniformed guy looked shocked when Sal opened the door.

"Morning. I got a letter for Sal Minovich."

"That's me."

The postal worker looked Sal over in his dingy thermal shirt and jeans. "Then it's my lucky day." He handed Sal a letter. "There hasn't been a mailbox on the highway for this address since the Frontenac's closed up the place. You the new owner?"

Sal nodded.

"You gotta buy a mailbox. They've got them over at Clayton Hardware."

Sal thanked him for the information, and the prick stepped back to his stupid Jeep and took off. Sal couldn't wait to shut the door before inspecting the letter. Handwritten, it had Sal's name and the lodge's address. A pre-printed return address: G.F. Management. Sal had seen that title on envelopes in Will's office: George's company name.

Sal stepped back inside, closed the door, and ripped the envelope open. He pulled out a money order written out to him. Five hundred dollars. There was a folded note along with it.

Dear Sal,

This was the best that I could do, but hopefully it will get you through a few more weeks. I wish it could be more, but things got complicated down here. Why'd you stop calling? I miss you. Let me know you're okay.

Love,
Will

Sal felt like the biggest scumbag who ever lived. It wasn't ratio-
nal. Will had left him to rot for months, but that signature from
Will's own blue ballpoint pen: *Love, Will*, got Sal's heart breaking.
Shortly after, he was having a panic attack.

Five hundred dollars wasn't chump change. Meanwhile, Sal
had written Will off and fucked another guy just three days ago.
He'd been a bastard, and there was no way to explain himself
without Will going nuclear and probably breaking things off. Sal
had behaved like the low-class hustler Will thought he was from
the start.

Sal sat down at the kitchen table and covered his face with his
hands. He'd just never tell Will what he'd done. Sal had only slept
with Todd 'cause he was angry and feeling desperate. It wasn't
worth mentioning to Will, and for the first time, Sal was glad they
were hundreds of miles away from each other. Todd would be out
of the picture by the time Will came up. Sal just had to make sure
of that.

Sal stood and paced around, beginning to feel a little lighter.
Maybe Will was close to wrapping things up downstate. Maybe
he'd collected on that life insurance policy, and he'd soon be up to
live with Sal at the lodge.

He threw on layers of shirts and his suede jacket, and he made
the long trek over to the Shell station payphone. He had plenty of
time to think about what he was going to say, but one thought
bled into the next, and by the time he reached the payphone, he
was just as anxious as he'd been when he left the lodge. He dialed
Will's number, and it rang and rang. Sal tried a second time with
the same result, and then he stepped out of the booth and drifted
over to the side of the gas station to have a smoke.

Will must be out and about. How the fuck was he supposed to
know? Sal clutched himself in his jacket and layered shirts. The gas
station's outdoor thermometer read thirty-two degrees. It was only

November, and he had to shove his hands into the pocket of his jeans every ten seconds or so.

Sal had a second cigarette before trying the phone again. Then he plodded back to the booth and dialed the number. After nine rings, Will finally picked up.

"It's me," Sal said.

"Sal?"

Sal had been bracing for Will's attitude, but he sounded frazzled. "Yeah. It's me."

"You got my letter with the money?"

"Just this morning." Sal swiped his nose. Why did Will sound so stressed?

"I don't have much time to talk. Things went a little sideways down here. You okay?"

"Yeah. What's going on?"

"The life insurance company put a hold on my claim. They want to do an additional review." Will broke off for a while. "I'm scared, Sal. They know something's off. I think they're going to figure out what happened."

Sal tried to be breezy. "You said the coroner's report says George died by accident."

"It does. But I don't like the claims agent. He drove over here all the way from Hartford. He said it was standard procedure when the cause of death is accidental, but he kept asking the same questions over and over again. He wanted to know why George adopted me, and I had to lie 'cause what am I supposed to say while he's looking at me like I'm some kind of pervert?"

"What did you say?"

"I told him he took me in when I was sixteen but didn't get around to filing the paperwork till last year. Then he asked me how come George took me in, and I said my parents couldn't afford to take care of me. He's staring at me like I'm hiding something, and it's all I could come up with."

Sal could feel Will breaking down. "Baby, that ain't so bad, is it?"

Will answered, angrily, "He's doing a fucking investigation. Jesus, Sal, do I have to spell everything out for you? He's gonna snoop around."

"Why you gettin' twisted? That don't prove nothin'. The police done their investigation, and the case is closed, ain't it?"

"They could reopen it at any time. There's no statute of limitations for murder. The guy's gonna want to talk to Hogan, and as soon as Hogan finds out about the life insurance, he's gonna be all over me to see how he can make out."

Sal laughed, though it was more from nerves than anything else. "You're talkin' crazy. The guy's an insurance agent. If anythin', he's tryin' to put the squeeze on you to see if he can get a cut of the money."

"I don't think so. He's a straight arrow. His company either knows something's off or they don't want to give the money to a queer. It's one or the other. I know it. I don't know what I'm supposed to do."

Sal felt tight all over. He tried to inhale some air. "Get out. We got a place to stay."

"I don't know, Sal. How's it gonna look if I run off in the middle of George's life insurance investigation?"

"Who cares? We can go wherever we want. California. Florida—"

"We've got shit. The lodge is mortgaged, and I'll be two months delinquent next week. I'm not just gonna have his insurance company looking for me. The bank, too."

"So, we hop the border to Canada or Mexico. How you doin' yourself any favors stayin' down there?"

"I need to put some money together—"

"You're always saying that. You're either leadin' me on or you're takin' things too serious."

"You don't think this is serious? The agent mentioned your name, too."

Sal skipped a beat. "How d'you mean?"

"For my claim, I had to give them a list of people who were on the premises that night. They must've run your record. I told the guy I didn't know anything about it, and I don't know where you went after I had to lay off the staff."

Sal's jaw clenched, and he raked his fingers through his hair. "What're you sayin', baby?"

"The insurance company knows you've got a rap sheet. If I've got any chance of collecting my claim, it's not gonna be from running up to see you a few months after George died."

Sal twisted a strand of his hair. "First, you're sayin' they don't want to give you the payout 'cause you're queer, and now you're sayin' they think I'm responsible?"

"I don't know."

"What did you tell them about me?"

"I didn't say anything."

"You tryin' to pin George on me?"

"No–"

Sal shouted. "That why you sent me money out of the blue? To get me comfortable 'fore the cops come lookin' for me?"

"I'm not trying to get into a fight with you. Jesus, Sal. This is the first time you called me in what? Three weeks? And now you're going at me like I'm trying to get you in trouble? Where have you been while I'm under cross-examination. I'm fucking falling apart."

Sal leaned his forehead against the glass booth. "Baby, none of this would've happened if you came up here in the first place. It's bullshit. You don't need that life insurance."

"It's three hundred thou."

"And look what it's got you. Nothin' but trouble. You're fuckin' things up."

Will said nothing for a long stretch. He came back with a sharp inhale like he was snorting back tears. "Maybe you're right. I'm going crazy down here."

"Of course I'm right. We's supposed to be stickin' together."

"But Sal, if I leave now, I only got a few hundred dollars. What are we supposed to do with that?'

"You got *me*. We'll figure it out. You been thinking too much about the money."

"You think I should just give up? Leave it all behind, and we can try someplace new on our own?"

"I been telling you that from the start. I been waitin' all this time for you to come up here with me."

Sal heard silence on the other end of the line, punctuated by anguished breaths. "I wish we'd never done it. Why'd we do it, Sal? I thought it was gonna make things better, but ever since, my life's never been so screwed up. I got nobody, Sal, and it feels like it's just a matter of time before they lock me up for life. I wouldn't survive prison. So, what am I supposed to do?"

"Stop thinking crazy. Baby, it's simple. Pack your stuff and drive up here. We'll figure things out from there."

"Can you come down and help me? I got this motel to close up for the winter, and all these documents to look through. I can't even think straight."

Sal almost told him he'd be on the next bus to Beacon. That's what his heart was telling him to do. But hadn't Will said before Sal shouldn't come back to town? Was Will losing it, or was he drawing Sal into a trap? For an eerie moment, Sal's paranoia deepened. Did Will have someone listening to their conversation?

"Sal? You still there?"

"Yeah. Listen, you gotta show me there ain't no funny business going on. Come up to me."

"What funny business? I'm falling apart."

"Then pack your shit and drive here."

"Why're you being so mean?"

Sal slapped his palm against the window of the booth. "I ain't being mean. But I ain't gonna be the fall guy neither."

"You think I'd set you up?"

Will's voice was so hollow and incredulous, Sal came close to caving in. There was a post office in Clayton, which was the nearest town to speak of, just down the road another mile or so. He had plenty of time to get there before it closed at five o'clock, cash the money order Will had sent him, and walk or hitch to Watertown where they had a Greyhound station. Buses only came by once or twice a day, but he could probably catch one in the morning and be in Beacon by tomorrow night. That wasn't so long for Will to wait, was it? Sal just wanted to take him in his arms, get him to pull himself together, and then they could go anywhere.

Unless Will was lying through his teeth and had a squad of federal marshals waiting for him.

"I gave you my trust. Now you gotta show me yours," Sal said.

"What're you talking about? I laid everything on the line for you."

Sal grinned madly. "For me? Sounds like you only wanted me to help get George out of the way so's you could get his money."

"I'm trying to get the money for both of us."

"I ain't stupid. You're askin' me to come down there when I got a warrant for my arrest. Which people knows about according to you. So, you tell me what's going on?"

Will said nothing for a stretch. "All right. I shouldn't have asked you. I'm just freaking out. I've got a right to do that, don't I?"

Sal didn't know what to do or say. Will's voice was pained. He sounded sincere. Another silence passed, then Will finally came back to him.

"I can try to get up to you. I gotta figure it out. I'm taking George's Oldsmobile to the dealer on Friday. He's gonna give me a couple hundred, but then I'm not gonna have a car."

"What 'bout his truck?"

"I was hoping to sell that, too, but I can't find the paperwork. The radiator started overheating, so I'm lucky to make it over to Newburgh driving it, let alone three hundred miles up to you."

"So, take the bus. That's a better idea, anyway, ain't it?"

Will heaved a breath. "I guess I could do that. With all the shit I've gotta do to tie things up down here, it's gonna take a week or so. Maybe by next Friday."

Sal came close to going off on him. A week or so? He'd been waiting for Will for four goddamn months.

The operator's message came on, and Sal had to scrounge out a dime. That gave him a moment to reset. The only thing he wanted in the world was to be with Will, and if there was a chance they could be together in a week, well, he might be the biggest dope who ever lived, but Sal's heart needed to believe that.

"Just do what you need to do, and I'll get us set up for traveling. I'm gonna take care of you, baby. Soon as you get up here."

18

SAL CASHED the money order later that day at the post office in Clayton. It was across the street from a strip mall, which was perfect for picking up things he and Will would need. As he was flush with cash at the moment, he asked the postal clerk if there was a taxi service in town, and the lady was nice enough to look up a phone number and write it down on a scrap of paper. Sal thanked her and headed to the stores.

He went into a bait and tackle shop that also sold sporting goods. They'd need some money for traveling, so Sal hunted down the best bargains he could find for winter jackets, a tent, heavy-duty boots, outdoor cooking gear, and thermoses. He lugged his haul of purchases to the grocery store next door and got a cart. There, he loaded up with canned stew, baked beans, bottled water, and five cartons of smokes.

He made out pretty well with three hundred and thirty dollars still in his pocket, and he spotted a pay phone right outside the grocery store. Sal pushed his cart over to it, fished out a dime, and punched in the number the postal clerk had written down.

A gravelly voiced dispatcher who could've been a man or a woman took down his pick-up spot and destination. Seven dollars, the dispatcher told Sal, and he'd probably be waiting a half hour. It was highway robbery in Sal's opinion, but with four big, heavy bags on his hands, he didn't have a choice.

A full hour later, a shit brown Pontiac sedan with a taxi sign on the roof finally pulled into the strip mall parking lot. The gruesome, bearded driver gave Sal a smile that showed off his few remaining nicotine-stained teeth. He popped open the trunk and did the lighter part of helping Sal get his bags inside. Sal hopped in the back and sank into a smelly, well-worn cloth seat. The driver lit up a smoke, turned over the ignition, got his oldies radio station playing, and steered them onto the road at a leisurely pace.

Sal noticed the guy peeking at him in his rearview mirror. Small town people expected conversation. Sal was still getting used to that.

"Probably kept you waitin' a while. Molly tell you I was all the way over in Alexandria Bay?"

"No, she didn't."

The driver chuckled. "*He*. Molly's short for Molinaro. Anyways, he shoulda told ya. He got me going everywhere from Fort Drum to Massena today." The driver looked ahead and took a tug on his smoke. "This time of year's the worst. Molly only got one driver working days 'cause he don't got volume like he do over the summer. But we still got customers, don't we? I'm only s'posed to be working till seven so I'm doin' him a favor picking you up. Not sayin' it's your fault, but fair is fair, y'know?"

Sal looked out the window and said nothing. He was happy to be in a car rather than trying to lug his bags along the shoulder of the road for five miles, especially now that it was pitch black outside. But he wasn't in the mood to talk with a fleabag cabbie who had a problem with his boss. His car stunk like a movie theater after the *Rocky Horror Picture Show*, and he drove thirty miles per hour when the speed limit was fifty-five.

The driver peeked at him again in the rearview mirror. "I ain't taken fares to the old Frontenac place in a long time. They got a new owner there?"

"Yeah."

The driver drew on his cig, and his beady eyes returned to Sal in the mirror's reflection. "They hire you to clean out the place or something?"

Sal considered his words, and then his pride got the better of him. "I'm the owner. Me and my partner. We got a work crew starting next week. My car's in the shop."

The driver looked impressed. He tapped his hand against the steering wheel in some kind of nervous excitement. "I could tell you weren't from 'round here. Where you from?"

"Jersey."

The driver laughed, stupidly and shook his head. "That's a long way from home. How you like living up in north country?"

"It's all right."

"Probably colder than what you're used to."

Sal shrugged and didn't answer. The car ride was feeling like an eternity. The guy was such a hick, he thought coming from New Jersey made him a celebrity? And why'd he have to drive so slow? His oldies station was playing a corny Big Bopper hit, which didn't help, either. It was like they'd been sucked into a time warp. The ancient car rattled and shimmied as they rolled down the highway. Maybe it wasn't safe to drive it higher than thirty miles per hour.

"I pass by the Frontenac lodge every day. I didn't know there was new management."

Sal let that go, too.

"You say you got a work crew fixin' up the place? It don't look like it been touched since Frontenac's daughter closed it down. You got electric?"

"They're turning things on at the end of the week," Sal lied.

The driver made a woeful face. "You livin' there without electric? You got the furnace workin' on oil? I probably ain't gotta tell you, it gets cold at night this time of year."

Sal was thinking that was none of the guy's business. He said nothing at first while the Big Bopper sang *Chantilly Lace* on the radio. Then he responded to set the nosy local straight.

"I came up here early to get the lodge in shape, but it ain't no big deal."

The driver blinked and looked away again. He drew on his smoke, likely brewing new ideas for conversation in his head.

"I was born 'cross the river from Jersey. The Bronx. Home of the Bronx Bombers. My family came up here when I was little so it feels like my hometown, y'know what I mean? My wife lived here all her life. The winters ain't for pussies, but we wouldn't live anywhere else. You got the river. The islands. The Adirondacks just a short drive away." He glanced at Sal. "You'll get used to it. It'll be nice to have the Frontenac place back in business. I was sayin' to Molly just the other day, there oughta be more places for people to stay on this side of the river. A lot of people, they drive straight over the bridge and spend the summer on the Canadian side. It's cheaper when a dollar gets you a dollar and a quarter so I can't blame 'em. But we lose a lot of business if you follow what I'm sayin'."

Sal avoided eye contact. A kindergartener could follow what the old dope was saying. Meanwhile, he could've jogged home faster than the guy was driving. They finally passed the gas station where Sal had called Will.

"That Frontenac lodge was something," the guy went on. "They was booked solid every summer, and they got families from all over the place. New York, Boston, Philadelphia. Folks from all over the country, y'know? It's a shame what happened." He fixed on Sal in the rearview mirror. "You probably heard, didn't you?"

"All I know is they went out of business."

The driver's eyes shifted. "Yeah, they went outta business. You ain't heard the story?"

He was going to tell Sal one way or the other so Sal played along, giving the guy a glance.

"Guy Frontenac owned the place for twenty years." The driver stubbed out his cigarette in the dashboard ashtray and lit another. "He was French Canadian, but he married a gal on this side of the border. You heard of Denmark Lumber? His wife was from the family that owns it. They's still around. Over in Oswegatchie. Anyways, that's how Guy got the money to buy that plot of land and start his cabin rental business. This was back in '42 or '43 when I was a teenager. You think this place is country now, you shoulda seen it back then. They had one motel over on Wellesley Island, and they hadn't even finished the thruway up to Canada."

The guy was shit at telling stories. Sal wasn't doing too well pretending he was interested.

"People used to say Guy was a schemer. Y'know, it looks that way when you come from another country and marry a girl from one of the wealthiest families this side of the river. But Guy weren't no freeloader. He had good business-sense, and he was a hard worker. He done a lot of the construction for that lodge himself. And he was a family man. His wife Laurie ran the front desk. Guy had his uncle and his cousin working in the kitchen, and he had his two sons and his daughter helping out when they was grown. Pretty soon, it got popular with tourists. Guy got his own billboard on the thruway when they finished it in '59. You had your bass fishers stayin' there, families over the summer, and people passing through from Canada, or the other way around. Guy knew what he was doin'."

Sal looked at the cabbie, impatiently. "Yeah? So, what happened?"

"It ain't no secret, but it ain't the kind of thing people like talkin' about neither, if y'know what I mean. The bank don't tell you when you're going through the paperwork?"

"No." Will had handled all of that. Sal was hoping the guy would come to the point.

"Figures. Well, like I said, it ain't no secret. It was all over the papers in '66. Guy's daughter Stella, she was the eldest, just twenty-two years old, she had a boyfriend who Guy was grooming to manage the place. Ted Bowman. He was from one of the old families 'round here. They still own a lot of the businesses in Clayton. Ted was a big shot player on the high school hockey team. One of them popular kids, y'know what I mean? Guy took a liking to 'im." The driver drew on his cigarette. "I never liked Ted personally. Y'know when you can tell that something's off with a person? You can't quite say what it is, but it's just this sense you get. Well, to get to my point, turns out I was righter than I ever wanted to be.

"One night, Ted gets his hunting rifle and blasts the faces off Guy, his wife, the two younger brothers, and Guy's uncle and cousins. Like Charlie Manson! He flipped or something. Or maybe it was a dispute over money. The fella swallowed the muzzle of his rifle and blasted his own brains out, so ain't nobody ever gonna know. Stella, the daughter, she's the only one who survived. You can't blame her for shuttin' down the lodge and puttin' it on the market after that, can ya? She seen her family massacred. They say she moved up to Montreal to live with Guy's parents. I dunno how you recover from something like that."

Sal had goosebumps. If the guy was telling the truth, he was living in the site of a slaughter. Did Will know? If he did, he should've mentioned it to Sal.

The cabbie came back in a reassuring tone. "It was all over the newspapers, like I said. I says to my wife, they ain't never gonna find a buyer for the lodge after that. Hey, maybe it was better you didn't know."

Sal chewed on his finger. It was disturbing what the guy had told him, but he didn't like the cabbie talking to him like he was a child.

"Listen, I ain't a superstitious person like a lot of people 'round here," the cabbie went on. "It ain't doing nobody no good leavin' the place to rot. Somebody gotta buy it and give it a new start. You couldn't ask for a better location, and all it takes is a little work to get the lodge fixed up and the cottages running again. The massacre happened over ten years ago. People forget about these things after a while."

"I don't believe in curses, if that's what you're talkin' 'bout. We got big plans for the lodge. Once we get the place renovated, we're gonna have a restaurant and bar with live bands on the weekends."

"Live bands?" The driver chuckled. "Ain't that a kick, Sally-boy."

Sal's glance shot up. He could only see the top of the driver's head in the rearview mirror. "What did you call me?"

"What's that?"

"What did you just call me?"

"Sally-boy. It's just a nickname, ain't it?"

A shiver passed through Sal. "How'd you know my name?"

The guy grinned like it was nothing. "You gave it to the dispatch, didn't ya?"

"No. I didn't."

"You must've. Hey, I'd walk out of the house without my keys if my wife hadn't made me this to remember them." He raised his wrist to show Sal a coil bracelet with a set of keys.

"The dispatcher didn't ask my name. I woulda remembered."

The driver snorted out a snicker. "Then I guess I'm the Amazing Criswell. How 'bout that?"

Sal gazed out the window. It could be, in all his excitement that day, he'd forgotten that he'd given his name to the dispatcher. Sal didn't think he would've forgotten something like that, but it could've happened. He was anxious to get home. The driver creeped him out. Thank God, they were almost at the lodge. Sal saw a Ho-Jo's billboard along the road, which was just down the bend from the place.

Another big band flourish came over the radio.

"You remember this one, Sally-boy?" The driver turned the knob on the volume.

Hairs stood up on the back of Sal's neck. Dean Martin singing that goddamn red robin song. Sal lost his shit.

"Turn it off."

The driver ignored him, or maybe the music was too loud for him to hear.

"Turn it off," Sal shouted.

The driver glanced into the rearview mirror. "What's that, Sally-boy?"

Sal leaned forward and clasped the back of the driver's seat. "Let me out. Right here."

The guy looked at him mirthfully. "The lodge is just up the road."

That song was making Sal feel like walls were closing in on him, and George, in phantom form, was hovering someplace near, come to claw out his heart. "I said, let me the fuck out, right here."

"Jeez, pal. Take it easy."

"I want to get out," Sal snarled at him.

"I'm telling you, you're almost there."

Sal beat his hands against the back of the driver's seat, and then he kicked it. The guy pulled over to the shoulder and finally turned off the radio. Sal shoved open the door and stepped out, sucking in shallow breaths like he'd just run a marathon. The open countryside, pitch black as it was, was paradise compared to his confinement in the car.

He heard the driver open the trunk, yank out his shopping bags and drop them on the ground. Sal pulled out his wallet and fumbled to find a five and two singles. He came around the back of the taxi and shoved the money on the driver.

"You some kinda mental case?" the driver said.

Sal pointed his finger at him, threateningly. "Piss off."

"Don't be callin' for rides no more. You got yourself on Molly's blacklist."

The guy got back in his cab and drove off in a huff. Sal collected his bags and lumbered down the road the fifty yards or so to the driveway to the lodge.

19

SAL CONSIDERED HE might be losing his marbles. That could happen to a person who was continuously under stress, couldn't it? He'd known some guys who'd lost it living on the streets. A few years back, he'd run into a hustler he used to hang with when bad weather kept the tricks away. Donny, his name was. He'd been a good guy, just had a hard life. They spent some winter nights together talking about their plans to get out of the game. Donny said he had a cousin who was going to get him a job helping out in his tattoo studio. They lost touch when Sal shacked up with Joey, and the next time he saw Donny, he was staggering down the middle of Tenth Avenue, barefoot, in filthy clothes, talking to himself and swearing at cars dodging around him. He hadn't even recognized Sal.

There was also a kid named Lou, Sal remembered. He'd been a real knockout with black hair and crystal blue eyes. Sal had envied him 'cause Lou was the first kid a john would call over to his car on the West Side Highway. He once boasted that one of his regulars paid him two Cs just to watch him take a shower and strut around his apartment.

Then something happened. Lou disappeared, and the next time he showed up at the piers, he was a different person. He looked like he'd aged ten years, and his easy smile was gone. Lou wouldn't say where he'd been or what he'd done, and he started going off on people out of the blue, saying they were looking at him funny and threatening them with a box cutter. Lou told Sal one night he was being followed by the CIA, that they'd implanted something in his head so they could track him, and all this other weird shit about aliens that the astronauts brought back from the moon. A few days later, Sal heard that the guy had carved out his own eyeball and been taken to Bellevue.

Sal was getting antsy remembering. He could handle being broke and living on the street, but his biggest fear was going insane. He had to keep it together. Think like a normal person. That red robin song–it was nothing so unusual, was it? George had been singing it because he liked it, and naturally, he'd put the record in his jukebox. Could be Hogan heard it, and it stayed in his head, making him whistle it one day. It was an oldie you didn't hear too often, but that cabbie had been listening to an oldies radio station. These things could be coincidences. They weren't a reason to think George had come back from the dead to drag Sal to hell or some crazy shit like that. It was a happy song about a harmless little bird. Sal was letting his mind run away from him. Will would be coming up soon. They'd get on the road and leave behind the creepy lodge with its shady history and what they'd done to George.

He tried calling Will the next day, and the next, and after three days of trekking over to the gas station to phone Will at different times, Sal gave up. He wasn't happy, but Will had said he had a lot to do tying up loose ends. Sal just had to sit tight and wait for him. He kept busy with little projects – clearing out the debris from the house, raking leaves, and washing the bedsheets in the tub so they'd be clean when Will arrived. Then one day when he was scraping paint from the railings of the porch, he heard a familiar rumble coming up the driveway.

Todd's Chevy sedan. Sal's shoulders pinched up. He'd lost track of days. Was it Friday, already?

Todd parked in front of the lodge, popped his trunk, and brought out a big grocery bag. Sal set down his scraper, dusted himself off, and came down to meet him. He had a big smile on his face. "I got you some groceries. And your Canadian Club."

Sal said nothing. It hit him all at once that he was in for big trouble if Will happened to show up. Todd hauled over the grocery bag and went in for a kiss. Sal turned his head. "I ain't had time to clean up. But come on inside."

Todd's smile deflated. He followed Sal into the house, and Sal pointed out a spot on the counter to set down his bag. He was impressed Todd had the guts to try kissing him in broad daylight, though that wasn't going to make the conversation they needed to have any easier.

"Did you forget this was the Friday I was coming by?"

"No," Sal lied. "I jus' didn't know what time you was comin'."

"If you had a phone, I would've called to let you know. We'll have to figure out another way to communicate. Smoke signals?"

Sal started unpacking the grocery bag. A loaf of bread. Some Campbell's soups. Kraft Macaroni and Cheese and a box of Hostess Fruit Pies.

"I didn't know what you like so I got a little of everything."

"Thanks." Sal opened the cabinet above the counter to find a place to put the food. It was pretty full with cans of stew and baked beans from his own trip to the grocery store.

"You stocked up," Todd said.

"Yeah." Sal got jittery as he unpacked more of the groceries. It would be just his luck for Will to drive up at that moment. Todd had bought a lot of stuff, including a carton of Marlboros and a giant box of chocolates, Sal noticed.

"I got those at the duty-free store," Todd said proudly. "Hey, if you don't feel like making anything, we can go over to the diner. Or I can pick up a pizza. There's a place in Clayton that's not bad."

Sal didn't know where to put the smokes and the chocolate. He felt like he should hide them somewhere so he could pretend he'd bought them special for Will, but that was a shit thing to do in front of Todd. He left them on the counter, brought out his coffee mugs, and started working on opening the whiskey.

"We drinking already?" Todd said with a goofy smile.

Sal poured the drinks and brought them over to the kitchen table. He took a seat, and Todd plopped down in front of him. His worried face was telling Sal he had an inkling of what was coming.

"You're a good guy, Todd, but this ain't gonna work," Sal said.

Todd fixed on Sal for an explanation. Sal wished he knew how to explain things without hurting the guy's feelings. Todd was the most decent person he'd ever met. If Sal had the time, he would've offered him another bang to thank him for the groceries and let him down easier. But he couldn't risk having Will show up while Todd was there. Sal looked him in the eyes and did the best he could.

"Listen, it ain't you. It's me. It ain't the right time. You understand?"

Todd turned around his mug of whiskey but didn't take a drink. "I thought...you're not married, are you?"

Sal shook his head.

"Did you meet someone else?" Todd gulped. "Was there someone else to begin with?"

That would've been the easy and honest way to explain it. But Sal was wary of getting into the subject. The less anybody knew about him and Will, the better. "Nah." Sal took a sip of liquor.

"Gosh, Sal. I'm just lousy at this, I guess. I read into things, and I'm always coming up with the wrong story." He scratched his ear. "Did I come on too strong?"

"No."

"Is it because I'm married? I never should've gotten married, you know, being like this."

"It ain't got nothin' to do with you," Sal said. "You're a ten outta ten. Believe me, you can do a lot better than me."

Todd sulked. Then he sighed, and worse, he came back to Sal looking desperate. "Listen, Sal, I think I did something to screw this up, but if you tell me what it was, I can change."

Time pressed down on Sal. He got to thinking maybe the reason Will hadn't answered his phone was because he'd cleared out of the motel and was on his way to see him. He should tell Todd he couldn't stand him so he'd leave in a hurry, hating him. Sal was about to do it, and then Todd wept into his elbow. The sight and sound of it was awful. Two minutes or more must've gone by, and all Sal could do was sit there like an asshole.

Gradually, Todd huffed back his tears and cleaned himself up. "I'm sorry. I'm making a fool of myself. I'll get out of your hair." Todd stood up.

Sal stood as well. "You ain't made a fool of yourself."

Todd ducked his gaze, but he lingered for a moment. A tight grin drew up on his reddened face. "Sal, you got any advice for a guy like me?"

Advice? Sal had no idea what he was talking about.

"You know, how men like us are supposed to live?"

Sal looked Todd in the eyes. "I ain't the kind of person you should be looking to for advice."

"You've got experience, don't you? I'm just tired of going through the heartbreaks all the time. I've got to be doing something wrong, don't I?"

Sal came over and gave him a quick hand on his shoulder. "There ain't nothin' wrong with you. There's just somethin' wrong with the rest of us."

Todd's brow pinched up, but before he could ask more questions, Sal gave him a hug and a pat on the back and walked him to the door.

Todd stopped short of heading out and gave Sal a sheepish grin. "I was going to tell you, my boss gave me that transfer. Starting in the new year, I'll be working out of Toronto."

"No kiddin'."

"Guess that would've made it tough for us to see each other anyway."

Sal gave him a sober nod.

"To tell the truth, I'm pretty terrified. But it's time, isn't it? I've gotta live my life for me."

Sal smiled, quietly, and clopped him on the shoulder. "Somebody gonna be real lucky when you find him." He looked at Todd firmly. "Just be a little careful. Don't let nobody take advantage of you."

Todd stood there speechless for a moment. Then he glanced at Sal one last time and got into his car and drove off.

SAL HAD JUST started putting away the rest of the groceries when he noticed a steady, souped-up growl gaining up on the house. He swung over to the window over the kitchen sink and perched on his toes. Somebody was coming up the driveway on a motorcycle. The driver was wearing a helmet, but it had to be Will. Sal recognized the purple Kawasaki.

He quickly took account of what had to be done. Wash out the two mugs, put them away. Stow the Marlboros and the chocolates in the bedroom drawer. Christ, if it had been a couple minutes earlier, Sal would've been in deep shit. As he came out of the bedroom, Will was already tramping up the stairs to the front deck.

Sal threw open the door for him. A little achy part of him had doubted that Will would ever show up. But here he was, looking beautiful and bad-ass in a sheepskin jacket, studded, brass-buckle leather belt, flared jeans, and brown leather lace-up boots. He had a rucksack thrown over his shoulder along with a single strap leather saddle bag. Sal was fucking trembling. He couldn't stop himself from throwing his arms around him. He was sucking back tears. He wasn't sure that he could trust that what was happening was real.

Will broke things off. "I drove six hours straight, and it poured all the way from Binghamton to Syracuse. I'm freezing and fucking exhausted."

Sal took his rucksack off his hands and ushered him into the house. "You want something to eat? Or you wanna get out of your clothes first? I got whiskey, baby." Sal's breath caught in his throat. "I'm so goddamn happy to see you."

Will didn't answer, and when they got to the kitchen, he looked around, appraising things. "It's gonna be dark as a crypt pretty soon, huh? No electricity." He rubbed his hands together. "No heat either, of course."

Sal fetched one of the battery-powered lamps that Todd had bought him, set it on the counter and turned it on. It must've been four or five o'clock in the afternoon. The sun set at about five-thirty, but clouds had rolled in and it was practically like night already.

Will was taking careful inventory of the kitchen. "Some guy was pulling out of here when I drove up."

"Yeah." Sal put on an easy shrug. "Some dude who used to stay here when he was a kid. He wanted to take a look around."

"You let him?"

"No. We talked like sixty seconds. Out front. He was just curious about the new owners is all."

"What did you tell him?"

"Nothing." Sal went to help Will out of his jacket. "You wanna get comfy, baby? You had a long drive. Let's get you out of your clothes and warm you up. I got towels and blankets."

Will drifted away and fixed on the bottle of Canadian Club on the kitchen table. "You've been drinking? I hope you didn't blow all the money I sent you on booze."

Sal took his pack of Camels out of his pocket, hopped up on the counter to take a seat, and lit a cig. Will's moody bullshit was coming back to him. Sal wasn't going to slave over him if he was going to be a prick.

Will took off his wet jacket and threw it down on one of the table chairs. He turned to Sal. His mustard, crew neck sweater clung to lean body, probably through a combination of rain and sweat. The jacket, sweater and belt were new, expensive-looking items of clothing, and his trendy satchel wasn't cheap neither.

"You're 'happy to see me?'"

Sal had no idea why the kid was copping an attitude. He glanced at him and nodded.

"I hope so. I stole my brother's bike to make the trip."

Sal drew on his smoke. "And now you're here. All's you gotta do is relax."

Will snorted out a laugh. "Relax," he repeated. "We don't have time to relax."

Sal studied him. What was the rush?

Will looked back at him fiercely. "We fucked up, Sal. The insurance company denied my claim and sent a complaint to the county sheriff. Between your criminal record and the stupid shit I said about George adopting me, they're recommending a reopening of the investigation."

"What they got to reopen?"

"They say Hogan took too long to photograph the scene and interview me. They say the coroner's report doesn't rule out foul play."

Sal took a dry swallow. "So, what's that mean? The cops ain't trailing you, are they? You can't loosen up for one night, and then we figure out what we're gonna do in the morning?"

Will stepped around the room. Sal's temperature was spiking. Had Todd's aftershave lingered in the air, or was Will noticing the position of the chairs at the table?

"That 'dude,'" Will said. "He the salesman you told me about?"

"No. He was nobody."

Will grabbed Sal's pack of cigs and sparked up a smoke. "He the guy you've been fucking?"

Sal slid down from the counter to face him. "You blew me off for four months, and this how you gonna talk to me?"

"Don't lie to me, Sal."

Sal drew up close to get his arms around the kid, and Will shoved him away. That raised the beast in Sal. He came at the kid, nostrils flaring, bullying him against the wall. Both their chests were heaving with violence. "I ain't been fuckin' nobody. How 'bout you?"

Will struck out his hand, and Sal caught it. The goddamn pretty boy was smirking. Sal fought to wrestle him around and pinned Will's arm behind his back. He inhaled the scent of his sweat-damp hair, grabbed him between the legs of his tight jeans, and ground his hard-on against him. Will reached back with his free hand and yanked a fistful of Sal's hair so hard, Sal's eyes teared. He threw his weight into Will and sealed his chest against his back.

Will bucked like a wild animal. The back of his skull smacked Sal's forehead, and the screaming pain got throbbing stars blinding his vision. Angrily, Sal pried open the brass buckle of Will's belt and the buttons of his fly. Will battled to twist out of his grip, but Sal was stronger. He braced Will's arm, which was bent behind his back, and got one hand inside his waistband. Then he pulled his jeans and briefs down his legs so he was bare-assed.

Sal groped his luscious bottom, breathing raggedly against Will's ear. "This what you gonna make me do?" He sucked his finger and forced it inside Will.

Will cried out in a guttural moan and shrank into himself for a moment. Sal pumped his finger in and out of his hole. Will was *his*. He was gonna remember that and appreciate that Sal had been waiting four months, goddamn dying to get some affection from him. He leaned into Will hard to hold him still and used his free hand to pluck open his button-fly, and then he yanked and shrugged to free himself of his pants and underwear.

Sal kicked the kid's legs apart, bowed him over a bit, and hunted to find his opening with his pounding cock. Sal thrust inside that spot. Will wailed and tore his arm free, and then he arched his hips and slapped his palms against the wall to brace himself.

"Aw fuck, Sal."

Sal punched his hole with all the angry pent-up need that had been building inside him while he'd been on his own. Quickly, he was close to bursting. He wrapped his fist around Will's cock and beat him off just before his own load came scorching out of him. Sal locked his arms around his chest. His feet were scuffling to keep his legs under him. He just wanted to melt into Will and disappear forever.

Will nudged out of Sal's embrace and stumbled to the kitchen sink to crank on the faucet and clean up with a dish rag. Sal leaned against the wall, catching his breath. His eyelids were clenched shut, and sweat was pouring from his brow. Will came back to him and clasped his shoulder blade. Sal's body bloomed and simultaneously, he winced back tears.

"Hey. You think I'd forget about you so easily?"

Sal couldn't answer. He was goddamn ruined from what they'd done and all the emotions that had led up to that moment.

Will slid his hand along Sal's hip. "That was exactly what I needed." He kissed Sal lightly on the forehead. "Now we've gotta get a move on."

Sal caught his hand to bring his arm around him. Will tugged himself free and chuckled softly. "I'm serious, Sal. We don't have time to sit around."

He put the cold, wet dish rag in Sal's hand, pushing him to clean up. Sal looked at him, not understanding.

"We've gotta get a jump on the cops. I know it sucks, but the quicker we get out of here, the better."

Sal pulled up his jeans and briefs. He was still confused. "You just got here."

"Yeah, and earlier this morning, I was supposed to show up at the police station to meet with a detective from the county sheriff's office. They were probably going to arrest me."

Sal swiped his face. "What're you talkin' 'bout?"

"The county's looking into George's death. Because of that insurance agent. And now I skipped town to be with you, but we're not safe here."

Sal stepped past him, threw open the cupboard, and grabbed a mug. He plopped down on a chair at the table, twisted open the

Canadian Club, and filled the mug three-quarters. He took a guzzle and looked up at Will defiantly.

"We don't have time for you to be acting pissy," Will said.

"You been here thirty minutes. How they even gonna know to look for you here?"

"They've got all of George's financials. I used money from his company to make the down payment on this place."

Sal's knee bounced. He took another draw of whiskey. "We can take it easy for one night, can't we?"

"You want to take it easy? You been listening to anything I'm saying?"

"You're gettin' too stressed." Sal pushed out the other chair. "Sit down and have a drink with me."

"It went to shit, Sal," Will shouted. "You've been up here all this time, and you don't even know the half of it. I been through hell."

Sal stared at him in disbelief.

"And what have you been doing besides drinking expensive whiskey and sleeping in till noon? Probably fucking around. Don't tell me. I don't wanna know."

"You told me to leave town."

"Oh sure. You could've stayed, and we'd both be in jail because of your police record."

Sal raised his voice. "Which you known 'bout from the start." He controlled himself a little. "We coulda left together. Four fucking months ago."

Will turned from him. His big man attitude was gone, and now he was weeping in his hands.

"Baby, come over here." Will didn't move. Sal stood and stepped over to him and gently held his shoulders.

Will glanced at him with watery eyes. "I know it's my fault. You don't have to rub my face in it."

Sal guided him over to the table and got him seated on his lap.

Will wiped his face with the sleeve of his expensive sweater. "We're in deep shit now. What're we gonna do?"

Sal massaged the kid's neck. "I'm gonna take care of you." He linked his arms around Will and rested his chin on his shoulder. "We got each other. We can go anywhere. Do anything you want."

"I've got two hundred dollars in cash and George's silverware from Greece. Altogether, that's four hundred, if we're lucky. We were supposed to have a quarter mil."

"And I got three hundred. It's something. We just take things step by step."

"We're fucking fugitives, Sal. Everyone up to the FBI's gonna be looking for us."

Sal held Will tighter, luxuriating in their cozy embrace. "Then we go to Mexico. Make our way someplace from there."

"We can't get to Mexico on a stolen bike with one helmet. You even have a driver's license or a passport?"

Sal had a doctored ID card he used for cashing checks. He'd heard that you could take your chances at the border. Sometimes they didn't ask for an ID if you said you were just taking a day trip. He tried to explain that to Will.

"And if they do ask for our IDs, they'll run them through a database and turn us over to U.S. authorities," Will said.

Sal remembered something Todd had told him. "We got a border fifteen miles from here. On a weekend, they're letting tourists through, no questions asked."

"No questions asked when the county sheriff probably put out an A.T.B. for me." Will looked around like he was thinking of something. "They still have boats here?"

"Yeah. They're dinky. They're for fishing on the bay, not crossing the waterway."

Will's eyes lit up. It got Sal feeling edgy. "They're aluminum, with one good two horse-power motor between 'em."

"My dad used to take us out on one of those. I know how to operate it. We used to go all over the Hudson River when I was a kid."

Sal was liking the idea less and less. He was scared of being out on the water, and Todd had warned him about the Saint Lawrence River at this time of year.

"We do it tonight before the weather gets bad, we can make it to the Canadian shore and disappear."

Sal clasped his leg. "We gotta do it tonight? Tomorrow's a Saturday. We can ride across the border on your bike."

"The bike's stolen. I don't even have the registration. I'm not taking chances crossing an international border with it." Will broke away from Sal and paced around. "The boat's the best way. We motor over to Canada, we just need to find our way to Ottawa. George knew some guy up there. Another slumlord who was always telling him how he used guys who jumped the border to do construction work. He can help us get fake IDs."

Sal fired up a cig from his pack. Some things were making good sense to him, but some things weren't. Did they have to leave that night? In a fragile little boat? It seemed to him, it wouldn't hurt to sleep on it, maybe test out one of those boats in the daylight before trying to ford the huge river in the dark.

Will drew up in front of him. "We've gotta leave tonight. It doesn't take long for the Dutchess County Sheriff to make a call to the local cops and get a squad car over here to check things out. I don't want to go to prison. I'd rather die on the run."

His face was pained and desperate. Sal just wanted one night when they could snuggle up together in bed. But if Will was right about law enforcement closing in on them, what could he say?

Will brushed his fingers through Sal's hair. "You need a haircut, but it's sexy." He grabbed his satchel. "I'll take a quick shower and change. Then we can pack up whatever you've got. We'll need warm clothes and food for a couple of days. I brought a map. Ottawa doesn't look so far, but I don't know how long it'll take on foot."

Sal pointed out the bathroom and took a long toke from his cig. He had a terrible feeling about trying to take a boat across the river.

20

SAL FOUND THE best boat in the boathouse and dragged it to the beach. When the chips were down, Sal had pulled off a fair share of escape acts in his twenty-eight-years, and no matter how messy the circumstances, they'd always aroused something of a thrill. At seventeen, he hopped on a train to New York's Pennsylvania Station to leave home for good. He had no idea how he was going to live, but he was kissing off his mom's asshole boyfriend and starting his own life. A few years after that, some thugs tried to put the squeeze on him at the hustler bar where he'd been tricking, and he had to set up in new territory, relying on his instincts for survival and some luck. Sal also thought about his exit from New York after the Castelli brothers killed Joey Delvecchio.

The Chinese letter for crisis means both danger and opportunity. A hippie street kid had told Sal that a long time ago, and it had stuck with him.

Sal came out of all those situations intact, and probably even better than he'd been before. He'd never done an escape act as big as he was doing now, but that was kind of impressive in and of itself. He was crossing an international border in a boat. He was doing it with a guy he loved like mad, and they were going to have to use all their skills to make it in a foreign country as fugitives from the law. The world was vast, and the possibilities were infinite. Sal looked across the river's dark void, which echoed with a million rumbling waves and enveloped him in its icy breath. For a moment, he was enlivened by the boldness of his adventure.

Will came along with his rucksack and satchel, and Sal held up a lamp while he checked out the outboard motor and topped off the fuel tank. Sal looked on, clutching himself in his jacket and three shirts. He was also wearing a knit cap, thermal underwear, and his only pair of jeans without holes, and it was still damn freezing by the water. Will made sure the motor was secure, and then they pitched their bags of clothes and food into the boat, pushed it into the river, and climbed in.

Once Will spun on the motor, it kicked up a racket. But the boat didn't make much progress from the shore, and waves were coming in. Will hunched over the motor to see what was going on, and then the boat rocked at an extreme angle. He fell into the water.

As soon as Sal got his equilibrium, he lunged to the back of the boat. They were still in the shallows of the river, and he could see Will's silhouette and hear him cursing. It looked like he was only submerged up to his midsection. The damn motor was noisy, but it was just grinding uselessly. Sal reached out his hand and called to Will.

Sal was hopped up on adrenaline, so when he heard a distant siren, he discounted it as some product of his mind at first. Then he looked back to the lodge and saw red and blue flashing lights. He swiped his eyes to confirm it. The pigs downstate had coordinated an operation to arrest them in less than a day? Sal had thought that Will was being paranoid about that. He said he'd only skipped a voluntary meeting with a detective that morning. Sal cast out his hands to try to grab Will.

"You okay? Take my hands."

Will had turned to shore and wouldn't answer. Sal didn't know if he was in shock from the freezing water or struck to stone by the approaching raid.

"C'mon. We got time." Sal struggled to grasp him. The boat was rocking and drifting sideways, and Will wasn't doing anything to help himself. Sal grabbed the lamp to shine some light on the kid and break him out of his stupor. "Will. You gotta get in here."

Will finally looked his way. "It's over."

His face was scary. Pale as a ghost and utterly defeated. "No it ain't," Sal said. He struck out for Will again but only caught ice cold water in his hands.

"Sal, go."

Sal finally got a hand on the collar of Will's jacket and yanked him closer to the boat. In a blink, Will freed himself and stared up at him.

"You've got seven hundred dollars to start a new life. I'm going back. I'll bide you some time."

"What're you talking about? Just get in here. We can make it."

Will shook his head. "I'm the one who fucked it up. You were always right about that. I'll take the heat. Maybe it was supposed to end this way."

"What you mean? Baby, I'm right here. I ain't gonna leave ya."

Will gazed at him warmly and tenderly. Sal was spellbound. It was the most heartbreaking thing he'd seen in his life.

"You've got a future, Sal. You don't have to ruin it for me." Before Sal could speak or even think, Will wrapped Sal's hand around the tiller of the motor and tripped some kind of switch. The boat jumped and surged forward, away from Will. Sal's stomach leapt to his chest. He let go of the tiller grip, which stopped his forward momentum.

Sal stared back to shore. He might've only shot out ten or twenty yards, but in the dark, it looked like a huge distance. A bright kaleidoscope of lights had exploded around the lodge, and in the flashes, Sal caught sight of Will trudging out of the water and onto the beach. It felt like time had stopped, and all Sal could do was watch the only person he'd ever loved moving farther and farther away from him. Then Will disappeared like a blip in the dark.

A primal moan rose from Sal's throat. What was he supposed to do? He wanted to drag Will back, escape with him, but he barely knew how to work the outboard motor. Even if he managed to drive the boat to shore, there wasn't time to catch Will. It wasn't fucking fair. It wasn't supposed to end like this. Tears bled from his eyes. He felt like dying.

A megaphone screeched, and an authoritative voice chattered in the distance. They caught Will. Sal still didn't know what he should do.

The noble thing would be to get back to shore and turn himself in. Maybe it would take some of the blame off of Will. People got good lawyers, didn't they? He and Will might get off with light sentences. But Sal was helpless in his dinky boat, which was drifting farther from shore, and maybe he was a little bit scared of pigs and handcuffs and spending the rest of his life in prison. He hated himself for it, but he scrounged the lamp from the hull, set it between his legs, and examined the grip of the tiller. There was a trip switch to press and twisting the grip looked like the way to get the motor to accelerate. Sal probably deserved to be swallowed up by the freezing river and drown for what he was doing, but he churned on the motor and used the tiller to point himself out to open water.

He told himself, he'd come back for Will. He'd get to dry land on one of the islands, lay low for a night, and figure things out from there. A lump pitched in his throat, and then he was bawling. Will sacrificed himself to save his butt. Didn't the kid know his life wasn't worth living without him?

PART III

21

THAT NIGHT, SAL made it to Wellesley Island. It was the big island before the main channel Todd had told him about. There, he dragged the boat onto a rocky beach. As best as he could tell in the dark, it was wilderness all around. He was wet and shivering and seriously worried he might freeze to death. But a drive for survival spurred him on. He'd never been in quite so dicey of a situation, but he'd made it through a lot of winter nights in New York. He unloaded the boat and hid it in the pine woods where it couldn't be seen from shore. Hiking inland, he found a spot beneath the tree cover that was relatively flat and dry and seemed to be far removed from civilization. He used the lamp to hunt through his provisions. He needed to warm up and pitch the tent to stay dry. Miracle of miracles, the propane stove worked, and Sal huddled over it to thaw his hands and feet. Then he broke open his bottle of whiskey, took some slugs, and got to work setting up the tent.

Sal had never thought of himself as an outdoorsman, but he learned that night he could hack it. He heated up a can of beans and fed himself with his hands, and then he burrowed in his tent with the sleeping bags and his whiskey. A few slugs of liquor later, exhaustion claimed him, and he plummeted into a blank, dreamless sleep.

The next thing he knew, he was peeling his face from the sleeping bag with a vague sense that someone was calling out to him. Sal sat up, disoriented by the claustrophobic tent he barely remembered from the night before. Pale sunlight filtered through the canvas. A damp chill drew goosebumps over his neck. Someone was hollering at him outside the tent.

"Sir, I'm going to need you to come out of there."

It sounded like it wasn't the guy's first time asking. There wasn't much Sal could do besides smooth himself out a bit and present himself. He unzipped the tent flap and climbed out.

A park ranger in a brown hat and uniform stared at him from no more than a yard away. He was wearing a utility belt, holstered with a short-range radio.

"Sir, you can't camp here."

Sal's head and body were working on a time delay. The nightmare of what happened with Will was only slowly coming back to him.

"Sir, do you need some assistance?"

Sal straightened out. "No." He cuffed his chin and swiped it. "I'll pack up. I got a place over in Clayton. I was just getting away for the night."

"I need to see your ID."

Sal tried to pluck out options. "I ain't got my driver's license with me. Like I said, I'll be outta your way."

"Sir, this is a state park, and we've got signs that this section is closed off to visitors this time of year. You're gonna have to give me your name and address so I can write up a ticket."

The prick took his job too seriously. While Sal was best off playing things cool with any type of authority, he was confident he could blow off some small-town wannabe cop trying to throw his weight around. The guy looked like he was younger than Sal.

"I boated over here last night. I'll be gone before you know it." Sal started gathering his camping supplies into his rucksack. The park ranger wouldn't let up, however, and Sal realized things looked bad. Last night, he'd spilled out two bags of groceries and all the winter gear for him and Will around the tent.

"Name and address, sir."

Sal ignored him and kept packing his things.

"Listen, if you don't give me that information, I'm going to have to radio this in to the sheriff's office."

Sal went about emptying the tent so he could break it down. He wasn't saying shit.

Eventually, the ranger stepped away. Sal could hear him having a conversation on his radio. The bags were packed. Sal just needed to bundle up his tent. Whatever was going on over the radio was stressing him out. He did a sloppy job of stuffing the tent into his rucksack, and then he got it hitched over his shoulders, grabbed the bags, and took off in the direction of the boat, as best as he could remember.

The ranger called after him. "Sir. Sir! You need to stay put."

Sal staggered through the woods, not looking back. Did he really need all the stuff he'd packed up? He didn't think so. It was slowing him down. He threw off his heavy bag with cans of food. It was just his fucking luck he happened to make landing at a state park closed for camping for the season. With some do-gooder park ranger stumbling upon him first thing in the morning.

He ended up at the shore without coming across the boat. Sal looked around the craggy beach and couldn't place a single marker from when he landed there the night before. It had been pitch-black, and he'd been working on adrenalin to get himself under the cover of trees and warm up. *What a bitch!* He was literally marooned on an island. The riverscape was gray and vast.

Sal threw off another bag and hiked up to the woods in one direction. When he couldn't find the boat, he doubled back the other way. He came up empty again and cursed himself out loud. He should've thought to leave the boat in a place he'd remember. He'd been so concerned with hiding it, he'd hidden it from himself.

Scrambling around, Sal lost track of any direction. The pine woods were thick and rugged and far from his recollection of the night before. He started worrying that he might've strayed far from where he'd beached the boat. He headed back the way he thought he'd come, and then he worried he'd gone too far in that direction. It was a goddamn comedy, but not so funny. He was wasting time. That park ranger had notified the local 5-0. He was no good to Will if he got arrested. The kid had turned himself in so Sal could have his freedom, and less than twenty-four hours later, Sal was fucking things up.

He rifled through the woods for what seemed like hours. Sal was feeling like he'd been sucked into *The Twilight Zone*, and it was impossible to say. By dumb luck, he finally stumbled upon the aluminum dinghy, nested in some underbrush. He gripped it from the stern and tried to drag it toward the shore. He had to use all his strength to lift it so the outboard motor didn't catch under the terrain. That worked for a yard or so until his arms and legs gave out.

He sucked in a dozen breaths and gave it a try again. Sal couldn't believe he'd managed hauling the boat so far from shore the night before. He bowed over himself for a while, and then little by little, he got the boat to the rocky beach. He was thinking he could motor to a minor island, hide himself, and wait for shit to blow over. He just had to get the boat in the water, and he could get far away from whatever trouble that park ranger was stirring up.

Sal was halfway to the water when it all closed in on him. A flashing coast guard boat appeared on the river on a clear trajectory to his spot on the beach, and upward on the shore, he heard the sound of a search party rustling through the woods. Sal sat down inside the boat and covered his face in his hands. His time was up.

SAL GOT TAKEN to the Jefferson County police station and ushered into a holding cell. The pigs had told him he was under arrest for trespassing, vagrancy, and resisting arrest, and they read him his Miranda Rights. Sal kept his mouth shut and went through the miserable business of surrendering his belongings, getting fingerprinted, and standing for a mug shot.

The upstate police station was tiny and didn't get much traffic. Sal had the cell to himself. He'd only noticed one other in the lock up area, presumably for women. Where was Will? They'd nabbed him the night before, hadn't they? All Sal could figure was that maybe the cops wanted the two of them separated. As he lay on a bench under a thin polyester blanket, the only positive thought he could come up with was he'd hopefully be seeing Will soon. Maybe they could get a lawyer together. It was pretty inevitable they'd be charged with George's murder, but George had a history of roughing Will up. A good lawyer could convince a judge they'd killed George in self-defense, couldn't he?

Sal was locked up in the holding cell for five days with no news about why they were keeping him for so long. Then one morning, a copper told him his arraignment had been scheduled. An hour before he was to appear before the judge, the jail guard brought him over to a boxy, windowless room with fluorescent lights to see his court-appointed lawyer.

Sal was happy to be out of the cell and able to talk to some-body about what was going on. His lawyer was a long-haired hippie type who couldn't have been much older than Sal. Troy McDonough. A minute into their conversation, Sal already had a bad feeling about the guy. He barely looked at Sal.

Troy went over the basics of the arraignment proceedings, and then he brought out a folder from his briefcase to explain what Sal was being charged with.

"This'll just be for the trespassing and vagrancy charges. They haven't booked you for kidnapping yet."

Sal narrowed his eyes. "I didn't kidnap nobody." He tried to read the document Troy had pulled out of his folder, but it was upside down. "Who they sayin' I kidnapped?"

The lawyer gave Sal a quick glance. "The complainant is

William Ganz." He sorted through his papers. "Here's the statement he gave to the police." He turned the document to Sal. "He says you were squatting on a cabin-rental lodge that he's renovating, and when he showed up to check on it last Friday, you forced him into a boat to cross over into Canada with the intent of dropping him in the river along the way."

The one-page typed statement swam in Sal's vision. A stupid grin spread across his face. "That ain't what happened. Will wouldn't have said that." Sal's knee started bouncing. He swiped his face and pushed his hair back, and then he fixed an angry, desperate look at his lawyer. "What the fuck is goin' on?"

Troy's whiskered face ticked. "It's all in Mr. Ganz's statement. He says you'd been threatening him, and you murdered his business partner George Filapoussis to get his money."

Sal felt like he was going insane. "Will said that?"

The lawyer leaned back in his chair. "So, you know this guy Mr. Ganz? Will?"

"Yeah, I know him."

"You two friends?"

That sounded much too casual for Sal's relationship with Will, but he didn't know how the lawyer felt about queers. "Yeah, we're friends."

The guy started scratching down some notes. "He give you permission to stay at his lodge?"

"Yeah."

"You two have a falling out or something?"

Sal shook his head.

"You got anything in writing about him giving you permission to live at the lodge? Like a rental agreement or a rent receipt?"

"No."

"So, you're saying it was a verbal agreement?"

Sal bowed his head. Waves of shock were immobilizing him.

"Did you say anything to the police about what happened last Friday? When Mr. Ganz alleges he found you living in the lodge?"

"He didn't just find me living in the lodge." Sal's voice was stunted. He couldn't say anything more.

"Did he ask you to leave?" Sal didn't answer. The lawyer reread one of the documents from his folder. "There a reason you took off on a boat?"

Sal said nothing.

"There's a report from one of the officers who apprehended you on Wellesley Island. They found some items matching Mr. Ganz's description. His clothing. Cash. Silverware belonging to Mr. Filapoussis. You got an explanation for any of that?"

Of course Sal did, but he was still struck mute and on the verge of tears.

Troy set down his pen. "All right. We can come back to that when you're ready. This is just an arraignment hearing, and like I said, the D.A.'s not doing anything with Mr. Ganz's kidnapping complaint. At least for now. The judge is going to want to know you understand the charges and your rights. Then you'll need to make your plea, and he'll decide on bail. We can ask for a reduction, but with these felony charges from downstate, it's almost guaranteed the D.A.'s gonna want you held without bail until they can transport you down there. You also skipped a sentencing hearing for solicitation in New York City. You want to tell me about that?"

Sal itched his neck. He was trying to appreciate the guy was just trying to do his job. But this was bonkers. "Where's Will?" he demanded.

"I don't know, Sal. But I strongly advise you to not have any contact with him."

"I didn't do nothin' to him," Sal swore. Frustrated tears bled from his eyes.

"It's a long shot, but if there's anything I can say to sway the judge to consider leniency with bail, it could be helpful. Are you currently employed?"

Sal shook his head.

"You have family? Or any people who would take you in and vouch for your character?"

Sal shook his head again. He was completely alone.

"All right," Troy said. "Let's get you through the arraignment. We'll make sure you get due process and take things from there." He looked at Sal firmly. "Since the charges in Dutchess County are more serious, they'll probably get you down there as soon as possible, so we won't be seeing each other for a while. But the court there will assign you another lawyer." He pushed his business card across the table. "Call me if you need any help."

Sal was rocked by disbelief. What was going on with Will? It didn't make no sense he told the cops Sal had kidnapped him. Had they roughed him up to coerce him into making the story up? Was this all the pigs' dirty work to pin George's murder on Sal?

22

AS TROY PREDICTED, at the arraignment in Jefferson County, the judge ordered that Sal be held without bail to allow his transfer to the Dutchess County authorities. The cops drove him down there to a slightly bigger courthouse where he was booked and arraigned for murder one and sent to the county pen.

Later that week, Sal met his public defender, Annie Rubin. She was a tough-looking, broad-shouldered woman who didn't wear any makeup and had a thick Bronx accent. She seemed like she wasn't going to feed him any bullshit. Sal opened up to her a little more than he had with Troy, though he was wary of saying anything that could get Will in trouble. He emphasized that she could clear up everything if she talked to Will. Annie said she'd look into it. When Sal tried the phone number for the motor lodge from the jail's payphone, he got a message that it had been disconnected. Sal was seriously stressing over the possibility that something had happened to the kid.

Meanwhile, Sal was facing a criminal court trial, back in the last place in the world he wanted to be. It was Hogan's jurisdiction, and no doubt, the corrupt lieutenant would be gunning to stick George's murder on Sal. Sal had nothing but time on his hands, and it got his head going to dark places. Hogan could've figured out what was going on and pressured Will to set Sal up. He could've sent his pig friends in Jefferson to catch Sal and Will, and once they got Will's statement, they might've disposed of him. Sal was freaking out so bad, he even considered that Will and Hogan were working together. He needed answers from Will, and there was nothing he could do while he was in the pen.

Prior to the initial hearing, Sal met with Annie again. First thing, Sal wanted to know if she had found Will, and the lady lawyer said the DA had entered Will's statement to the Jefferson cops into evidence, but he wasn't on their list of witnesses.

"The way I see it, that's a good thing for you," she went on. "The hearing's two days away, and they're going to need his testimony. It could mean the guy got cold feet."

"How 'bout getting him to testify for *me*?" Sal didn't like the addled look on the lawyer's face. "I'm telling you, this ain't like Will. He was turning himself in to them cops in Jefferson. Did you even try to talk to him like I asked?"

"Sal, he filed a complaint against you for kidnapping and attempted murder. He's not someone you want giving testimony. Now settle down. I'm trying to help you here."

She seemed to know something Sal didn't, so he sat back in his seat, trying not to lose it.

"I made some inquiries. The police have to enter into record every part of their investigation, and there's nothing from the Beacon Police Chief or the County Sheriff about talking to him since he made his complaint back on November 10th. I've got access to your case in Jefferson, and there's no further deposition from him up there either."

"Don't that mean he stopped talking to the cops 'bout me?" Sal sat up at the table between them. "I'm tellin' you, somethin' ain't kosher here. Will made up that complaint. What you oughta do is get a three-way meeting with him. He'll listen to me, and we'll figure this out."

"All that means is either the DAs can't find him or they think his testimony isn't going to help their case. From everything you told me, he's not going to help you either. And if the Dutchess DA can't even produce a deposition from him for your hearing, we've got a shot at getting your charges dismissed. You follow me?"

Sal knew what she was getting at, but he needed to know that Will was all right. "That make sense to you? Will just disappeared after tellin' them upstate cops I killed George and tried to kidnap him? They're fucking with somethin'. I know they are. Will was turnin' himself in."

Annie's eyes wandered, impatiently.

"Why'd they buy it, if they're on the level?" Sal persisted. "If theys looking for foul play, Will oughta be suspect number one. He got George's properties, and he was the sole beneficiary of his life insurance. So how're they coming up with a statement from him blaming me and lettin' him go?"

The lawyer scribbled a note on her pad. "I'll look into it. That could help you, too. If the judge doesn't dismiss the case based on lack of evidence, we can build an argument that only Will stood to gain from George's death. You said Will gave you George's silver-ware? That it was his idea to hop the border to Canada?"

That wasn't Sal's point, and he couldn't find the words to explain it to her. She looked at Sal from across the table. "I'm not going to sugar coat this, Sal. The DA's signaling he's not dropping the case until he's got somebody convicted of something so he can say he's doing his job. But with a lack of evidence, we can bargain things down to conspiracy to murder or criminal negligence, maybe. Instead of life in prison, you could get five to seven years with the option of early parole."

Having options for a lighter sentence wasn't a bad thing. But Sal was gutted over what could have happened to Will. Had the cops made him disappear? Sal remembered Will talking about George's Greek friends. Was it them who tracked him down to make him pay for killing George?

. . .

AT SAL'S FIRST hearing, he sat at the defendant table in his prison uniform and shackles, trying to make sense of the proceedings. The assistant DA and his cronies were doing a lot of talking among themselves, and when the judge told them for the third time they had to get things moving, the ADA smoothed himself out, stood, and said there'd been some developments in the police investigation and asked to postpone the hearing.

From there, Sal only made out bits and pieces amid all the legal gibberish. They weren't dropping charges against Sal, but a key witness had disappeared. They needed time to review evidence from the Dutchess County PD and asked for two weeks.

Annie did her best to jump all over the ADA's shaky performance. She argued for the case to be dismissed since the state had failed to produce the evidence they'd promised at the arraignment, and any further complaints against Sal required rebooking him under new charges. But the judge remanded Sal back to the county pen and set a new date for the evidentiary hearing at the end of the month.

After, Sal had a chance to talk privately with Annie in a little room inside the courthouse detention area.

"It's shit, Sal, but this is how things go when the DA's got someone with a criminal record in custody. On the bright side, we just bought ourselves some leverage. Their key witness is Will Ganz, and without him, their case is circumstantial at best. I'll give it a day, and then I'll call them to see about working out a plea deal."

"What kind of plea deal?"

"You testify against Will, and they'll have no choice but to drop the charges to accessory to murder. They can't try you on a complaint from a guy who won't cooperate in their own investigation."

Sal felt split down the middle. He sure wanted to get out of the pen as soon as possible, but he didn't want to testify against Will. If there was a chance that the pigs hadn't deep-sixed him, he could be out there somewhere, on the run from the law.

"How do the cops lose track of Will when he got turned down trying to collect on George's life insurance policy?"

The lawyer lowered her eyes and came back to Sal. "Will told you that?"

"Yeah. Three hundred thou. Will was the sole beneficiary. George adopted him."

Annie hesitated, looking like she was taking things gently. "Sal, the county sheriff got a report from the insurance company. He had a policy with the minimum benefit. That's fifty thou. It was paid in full to George's uncle in September."

Shivers snaked through Sal's body. He didn't want to believe it. Will said up and down he was holding out for a big payout.

"If George had any other beneficiaries, it would've been in the insurance company's report," the lawyer went on. "Listen, I don't know what the relationship between the two of you was, and I don't need to know, but the guy isn't doing any favors to you now. He's the reason you're in this mess. So how 'bout we work out a statement you can make to the police?"

Sal dug his fists into his eyes. He couldn't produce a word at first. Then he blurted out, "What's Hogan doing? He's gotta be involved in this. What's he said about George's death?"

The lawyer blinked. "Who's Hogan?"

"His name's on George's death investigation, ain't he?"

The lawyer brought out her pen and pad. "He the coroner? I'll have to look back. I read those records three, four weeks ago."

"Lieutenant Hogan. He's chief of police in Beacon. He was shaking George down for money." Sal covered his eyes again. He felt like he was going to pieces, and he almost couldn't say the next part. "He might've been involved with Will."

"How you mean 'involved'?"

"I don't know," Sal spat out. "Like he was pressurin' Will or something. Or maybe him and Will were workin' together, settin' me up to take the fall. But you're saying there wasn't any money from the life insurance."

"Besides the life insurance, did Will say George had other assets?"

"Yeah, but it was complicated. He was dumping George's properties. He said it would take a while to get his books in the black, but when it was done, he'd have a quarter mil."

The lawyer looked at Sal like he was a child. "Will told you a lot of things, didn't he? You ever see any of that money?"

"No. But it's worth looking into, ain't it?"

"Sal, I'm not a private detective."

"You're my lawyer, ain'tcha?"

"Yes, and as your lawyer, even if you had the money to hire a private dick, I'd tell you, you'd be throwing it away. This guy Will lied to you repeatedly. He lied to the police. You write it all down, every detail of his plan to kill George and the way he did it. We present that to the sheriff, and you can bet he'll look into what happened with George's estate. Frankly, they should've done that already."

"That's why I'm sayin', Hogan must be pullin' shit. Could be he stole the money from Will, and now he's workin' people to cover his tracks."

Annie drew in an impatient breath. "Sal, you want a sentence pled down to a couple years or maybe just parole? That's not happening with the DA based on some conspiracy theory about the local cops. Do you have a single person who would testify to what you're saying about this Lieutenant Hogan?"

Sal dug his fingers into his hair. A name came to his head. He blurted it out. "Al Shapiro."

"Who's Al Shapiro?"

"He was a friend of George's. He was murdered over in..." Sal snapped his fingers. "Highland Falls. Would've been four, five years ago."

"He's not sounding like the best witness for your defense."

"Look up the case and tell me if it sounds kosher. You ain't need a private dick to pull a police file, do you?"

The lawyer glanced at Sal twice. Then she stowed her notebook and pen in her beat-up leather briefcase. "I'll see what I can do. I'll be in touch in a couple of days. In the meantime, think about that statement, Sal. We're going to need it."

23

A WEEK LATER, Annie came back to Sal with the plea deal the DA was offering. If the Jefferson County court was willing to drop their charges against him, they'd take his plea for manslaughter in the first degree. That didn't sound so swell. The mandatory sentence was five to twenty-five years. But Annie was pushing Sal to take it.

She said it was the most the DA was willing to bend. Even without Will's testimony, they had a lock on the judge seeing the case through. The Beacon police had entered a bloodied plumber's wrench into evidence as the murder weapon, and they were saying it had been recovered under the bathroom sink of Sal's old room at the Beacon Motel. They had Sal's rap sheet and no documented residence for him since 1967, when he was seventeen years old and living with his mother in Jersey. If the case went to a jury trial, Sal was rolling the dice on doing better in terms of sentencing. He could end up with Murder One and twenty-five years to life.

Once Sal's head stopped reeling, he sank into a deep pit of defeat. No jury was going to care that he'd been set up. He was a vagrant and a prostitute. He had nobody to stand up for him, and maybe he deserved being locked up for a while. The fact was, he had helped Will send George to his grave.

Sal's voice was weak. "I gotta make some kind of confession?"

The lawyer leaned closer over the table. "Here's the thing. I think you'll like it. They don't even want a confession. They'll take what's called an Alford plea, which is accepting the charges without admitting guilt. That usually helps the judge decide on a lighter sentence."

Sal computed that. But something didn't feel right.

"They don't want my testimony against Will?"

Annie nodded. She was practically smiling. Sal kept staring at her, and she wiped her mouth. "I don't know where they're at with investigating him, but the important thing is they're willing to take an Alford plea. I can tell you that's better than waiting around for Will to come back into the picture and see what happens with dual trials based on he said/he said. It's not a bad outcome, Sal. You'll get nine, maybe ten years at the max, and you'll have it on your record, you never admitted responsibility for the crime. You'll be out of prison before you're forty."

Sal's eyes burned. He hid his face for a moment. "Will ain't coming back into the picture, is he?"

"I have no idea."

Sal peeked at Annie while his insides were disintegrating. "'Cause he's dead. They got rid of him and now they gotta pin George's murder on me, right?"

His lawyer shifted in her seat. "Sal, I've gotta tell you, you're thinking about this all wrong. There's no police conspiracy. Will fed you all kinds of stories, and he's probably doing just fine. Until he passes a bad check or gets pulled over for some routine highway investigation, and some cop in Wyoming gets a ping on him."

"He was turning himself in," Sal said.

"Yeah, that's what he told you. Along with getting George's life insurance policy and being his adopted son. He's an operator, Sal."

Sal didn't have the fight in him to argue any more. He looked away. He just knew what he felt in his gut. Hogan screwed Will over.

The lawyer's posture softened. "Listen, I'm no psychologist, but

I've seen a lot of situations like this. I think Will put in your head this idea that the cops are pulling the strings. Is he the one who told you about that friend of George's, Al Shapiro?"

Sal's eyes returned to her.

"You got my curiosity piqued with that story, so I spent some time looking through police files. There's no Al Shapiro who washed up on the Hudson outside of Highland Falls. But I ran into a clerk at the archives department who knew an Al Shapiro. He used to come in to apply for building permits at the office down the hall. A businessman from New York City who was developing properties up and down the river. That sound like your guy?"

Sal nodded.

The lawyer knit her hands together, looking pleased. "I called a pal of mine who works in the city. Just curious, y'know. He made some inquiries and got back to me just yesterday. Al Shapiro, a former stockbroker and an upstate real estate developer, died a year ago. Slipping in the bathtub in his Bronxville home."

What she was saying got icicles crawling up Sal's spine, but after all the shit he'd been through, he wasn't in the mood to be made out like a rube. His damn knee was bouncing, but he didn't say a word.

The lawyer slid back her chair and stood. "Just thought you should know. We've got a week to get back to the DA before the hearing. If you want to take the plea, you can let me know now, or take a couple days to think about it and call me."

Sal glanced at her with a fiery spark in his eyes. "I'll do it."

She told Sal she'd bring over the paperwork to sign later in the week and gestured to the guard outside the door that they were done.

SAL WAS BREAKING apart, but he couldn't break apart while he was locked up in the county pen with tough guys fighting to say they were the top dog. He went through his daily routine, staying under the radar, and when he could let his guard down, he disappeared into daydreams about that lodge in the Thousand Islands. He could've made it a hot joint with Will. A liquor license and rock bands every Saturday. Cabins rented through the summer. With the cost of living up there, they'd be living flush. They could buy one of those camper vans, and in the off season, take vacations to see the country. The Rocky Mountains. The Grand Canyon. Will would like that.

At the hearing with the judge, Sal gave his Alford plea. The DA accepted it, and the judge sentenced Sal to nine years with the possibility of parole in three. He was rounded up for the bus to Attica a few days later and bunking with a hard luck kid who stabbed a police officer trying to take him in for dealing heroin.

Living in a clink with guys with violent tendencies wasn't a lifestyle Sal had aspired to, but at least he didn't have to worry where his next meal was coming from and if he would freeze to death at night. Ever since he'd left home at seventeen, Sal had considered he might end up in prison. He wasn't shocked or angry, but it did give him a lot of time to think.

His mind opened up to the idea that Annie might be right about Will. He could've been the hustler of hustlers, working Sal from the very start. Will wanted George out of the way, and when Sal stumbled into his diner, he saw an opportunity. A guy who was attracted to him and didn't mind getting in on some action. Will played it cool, feeling Sal out to see how far he could take him. He bought Sal's trust with tearful stories about how hard his life had been and how his old man was doing him wrong. He gassed Sal up with his big plan to buy that lodge in the Thousand Islands. His coup de grace was that black eye. He could've given it to himself. Will made Sal believe he needed saving. He made Sal fall in love with him. It could've all been premeditated, every detail down to getting Sal to use that wrench to kill George so he had a weapon to tie Sal to the murder. Will could've even staged the blackout that night to disorient him.

Some parts of that theory didn't make sense, though. Annie

said Will was never going to get George's life insurance, so what was he getting out of the deal? It could be Will lied about how much money he got from selling George's properties, but even if that was the case, why'd he keep Sal around as long as he did? He could've told the pigs Sal killed George right after Sal left town and gotten them on his trail. Will didn't have to buy that lodge if he never intended to keep it. He certainly didn't need to come up there with the story about skipping out on a meeting with the county sheriff. Will had gotten into the goddamn boat to run away with Sal. Had something changed his mind at the eleventh hour?

One day, six months later or so, a correction officer told Sal he had a visitor. That got Sal hopeful for a moment, but then the officer said it was Danny Hogan. Sal considered refusing to see him, but the sad truth was, a visit from anyone was welcome. He was bored out of his mind and feeling claustrophobic in the sunless high security pen. So, he followed the C.O. down to the reception center. Across the glass divider of his visitation booth, Sal locked eyes with the lieutenant. The smug fucker had a big smile on his face.

"Sally-boy, how you doing?"

Sal sat down and didn't answer.

"You acclimating all right?" Hogan studied Sal's face. "Don't look like you had trouble so far. I bet a fella like you always finds a way to stay popular."

Sal stared at the crooked pig. If he came to gloat, he wasn't gonna get a rise out of him.

Hogan leaned forward, confidentially. "I came all this way to see ya. It was a five-and-a-half-hour drive! You ain't got nothing to say to me?"

"You wasn't at the top of my list of people I wanna see."

Hogan's eyes twinkled with amusement. "What's that, Sal? You got people lined up to visit you? Who you got, buddy? Beggars can't be choosers, can they?"

Sal sat back in his chair with his legs spread. "What d'you want, Hogan?"

"I know, you're mad. We never got around to go fishing together. But you was the one who was always too busy."

Sal rolled his eyes and fixed on the wise guy impatiently.

"Hey, I brought you something." Hogan dug into the inside pocket of his quilted pig jacket. He took out a thin gold necklace that was immediately familiar to Sal. Will's first communion cross pendant. Sal stared at it with a combination of heartbreak and horror.

"I was thinking, after all you done for Will, maybe you deserve this," Hogan said, dangling the necklace from one hand for a moment and then catching it tight in his fist.

"How'd you get that?"

Hogan smiled like the meathead bully he was. "Funny thing. I just found it, tangled in my bedsheets." He shrugged his eyebrows.

Sal shot up from his chair with a screech of steel against the concrete floor. He caught himself and tried to even out. "You're fuckin' lyin'."

"Easy, Sally-boy. You don't wanna get sent to solitary for bad behavior, do you?" Hogan looked away and rubbed his nose. "'Sides, it ain't like we got anything to fight over no more."

Sal sat back down, combed through his sheared hair and nibbled at the side of his finger. Had Will really been sleeping with the scumbag? Did Hogan come up all this way to rub Sal's face in it? The last thing Hogan said, he sounded strangely regretful.

"I done you a favor," Hogan said. "I known about your past. I ran your name through the state registry right after you started working for George, and did I squeal? It ain't my fault you're in here. I never said anything about you till the Dutchess DA gave me a call and told me he had you detained. I been real good to you, Sal. I filed a report on George's death back in July, and I coulda said George had a hustler on his payroll, but I didn't."

Sal wasn't feeling any warmer toward the lieutenant. Was Hogan making shit up? Why wouldn't he make trouble for Sal?

"Think about it, Sally-boy," Hogan went on. "You coulda been locked up a year ago. You think I didn't know everything that was going on at the Beacon Motel?"

Sal put on a poker face. "What do you mean by everything?"

Hogan opened his fist and pinched out Will's necklace again, hanging it from two of his knobby fingers. Sal couldn't look away from it, and then Hogan quickly closed it up in his hand. "You never really know *everything*, do you? Take you, for instance. You ain't really a cold-hearted murderer, Sal, are you? Sure, you done some cons and leeched off a mafia prince for a while, but killing people for money ain't never been your beat."

Sal said nothing. He had questions too, but with Hogan, he couldn't ask them straight out and expect to get an answer. He had to play along, see where Hogan was going, and find the right opportunity.

"You ain't gonna tell me, Sal? What you got to lose? The DA already put you away. He ain't interested in reopening George's case." Hogan took on an earnest expression, something he probably thought worked well in his line of work. "I'm gonna be straight with you, Sal. I already know. Will told me he had a plan to get George out of the way. So I just wanna hear from you, how'd you end up here instead of him?"

"Will told you that?"

"Mm-hmm."

"That's bullshit."

Hogan grinned in a not so happy way. "I known Will a lot longer than you. What did you think, Sal? You stroll into town and suddenly he belongs to you?"

"Will couldn't stand you. He thought you was a disgusting, phony loser."

Hogan's face compacted. He hid it for a moment, and then he swung back to Sal. "Watch your fucking mouth. I know guys in here." He jabbed his finger against the window. "I could have one conversation, and you'll get your throat torn out, bleeding to death while the C.O.'s look the other way."

Sal nibbled on his lip. That was probably a threat Hogan could deliver. But things were coming into focus, and he almost had the fucker right where he wanted him. He stared back at Hogan without saying a word. *Tell the truth. Will had you thinking he'd give up his ass for you? What else did he promise if you covered for him?*

Hogan blinked while some tacit knowledge sunk in. "I shoulda turned you in the first time we met. Was you working Will from day one? Waitin' for him to deal you in on getting George's money?" Hogan's face was scary red. Desperate. Riding the line between breaking into tears or striking out violently. "I swear to God, if you killed him, I'll come in there and strangle you myself."

Sal managed to chuckle. "You think I was playin' Will? Since I'm sittin' pretty in this luxury hotel?"

"What happened at that lodge in the Thousand Islands?"

Sal wasn't sure what Hogan was trying to get at. The lieutenant had to know Will gave the cops a statement that night, accusing Sal of kidnapping him and murdering George. What else needed to be said?

"You lured him up there, didn't you Sal? You was sweet-talking him like one of your johns, trying to get in on the big payoff when the cash came through for that plot in Sarasota Springs."

Something about Sarasota Springs was familiar, but Sal couldn't place it.

"I know the score, Sal. There ain't no point in playing dumb. Will told me how he talked George into going in on that invest-ment in Sarasota Springs with his rich friend. He set up the perfect heist. George's pal put up ninety percent of the money to buy it, but he asked George to list it as a purchase from his rinky-dink real estate company so he wouldn't get taxed for it. Then George's friend bites the dust, and Will pushes George to sell the plot to a big-time real estate developer. 'Cause Will's savvy, you know? He knows there's people with deep pockets circling that area because it's blowing up with new homes and tourism from the race track. They drew up the paperwork, and Will just has to wait for the money to come through. One million dollars cash, free and clear. George croaks, and all Will's got to do is collect the money. So, what happened to the money, Sal?"

Now Sal remembered George talking about an investment in Saratoga Springs. He took a trip up there just before that Sunday night when he and Will bumped him off. The same night George had bragged about landing a deal that was gonna pay big dividends so he could renovate the motor lodge. He'd been meeting with lawyers and arguing with Will about money. If what Hogan was saying was true…Sal felt like he was hyperventilating.

"You talkin' 'bout Al Shapiro?"

"Yeah, Al Shapiro. What's wrong, Sal? You're looking pale."

Sal swiped his face. His hands were fucking ice blocks. Something Will said flooded back to him.

You ever notice, people don't ask questions about things they don't want to know about? Even when it's right in front of their face.

"Where's Will? Did you come back to that Thousand Islands lodge and kill him after he talked to the local cops? Where the fuck is Will?"

It took Sal a moment to register that Hogan was talking to him. Shouting actually.

"I didn't know nothin' 'bout Sarasota Springs."

"You expect me to believe that? You was squatting at that lodge for four months, just waiting for Will to show up. I told you, I know everything. I'm the one who ponied up the four grand so Will could put a down payment on the place. So's we could flip it. You was watching Will like a hawk, and you're telling me you didn't know nothin' 'bout Sarasota Springs?"

Sal looked back at him, blankly.

Hogan pounded his hand against the counter. "You fucking greaseball. I know Will picked up the money. The same day he went up to check on the lodge. Will's supposed to call me to lemme know things went smooth and he's headed back." He glared venomously at Sal. "I'm the one who told the guys from Jefferson to swing by the lodge that night. So, you either gonna tell me where the cash went or where Will went."

Sal was so stupefied, all he could do was laugh. "He played both of us. You don't see it, you stupid fuck?"

The blood drained from Hogan's face. Sal must've looked the part of a mook who'd finally seen the light.

"That money was supposed to be for me and Will," Hogan said.

A funny thought occurred to Sal. "Yeah, and before that, it was for George and Will, and probably before that, it was for Al and Will."

Hogan snorted. He was tense, like he could murder somebody in the vicinity. But Sal was safely behind protective glass. He cocked a smirk at the lieutenant. "How long he been telling you he'd deal you in on the cash he was getting once George was out of the way?" Sal snickered. "He told me it was coming from George's properties. He told you it was coming from that deal in Sarasota Springs. He conned both of us, though he did you one better."

"You're the one who's not walking out of here when visitor hours are over."

"Yeah. He laid out all the pieces so I'd take the fall for George. Youse two had it planned when I started workin' at the motel." He studied Hogan. "That's what I'm thinkin'."

Hogan sat back and rubbed his face. "I ain't gonna lie to you. It was Will's idea."

That and a nickel will buy you a cup of coffee. Sal sat back and smiled devilishly. "He probably didn't tell you we was fucking. Sometimes three, four times a day. He couldn't get enough of it. I fucked him that same night he showed up at the lodge, sayin' we had to skip the border 'cause his claim on George's life insurance went south. He even sent me five Cs the week before so I could get gear for traveling."

The lieutenant turned his head. His ruddy complexion had gone ten times ruddier.

"So I got conned, but you got conned worse," Sal went on. "Will got you to put up four grand to buy that dump in the Thousand Islands, and you got nothin'." Sal laughed. "You didn't even get to fuck him, did you?"

"Fuck you," Hogan spat out. The douchebag actually looked pretty desperate. "What happened in the Thousand Islands, Sal? If Will was planning to run away with you all along, why'd he make up the story you were squatting and plotting to kidnap him?"

Sal replayed that night. Will had been rushing him along to pack up and get a boat ready to cross the Saint Lawrence. Probably because he knew Hogan would get the local coppers looking for him when he hadn't heard from Will. As for Will bailing on him, Sal didn't feel like saying anything special.

"Could be your pals scared him." He looked at the lieutenant squarely. "I didn't kill him. I told you, I never knew nothin' 'bout the money."

Hogan took that in for a moment. "I'm gonna find him, Sal. You tell me where you think he might've gone, and I'll make him pay for screwing both of us."

The only thing Sal could think of was the guy Will mentioned in Ottawa. But he didn't see the point in telling Hogan that.

"He ain't said nothin' to me. You gotta figure, by now, he could be halfway 'cross the world."

They sat in silence for a while. Then, Hogan stood. "Nice talking to you, Sal. I'll be looking forward to your parole hearing, in what? Three years? Maybe then, we can go fishing together."

Sal stood and waited for the C.O. to escort him back to his cell.

AFTER THAT VISIT, Sal had just about all the puzzle pieces fitting together in his head. When he stumbled into the Beacon Motel, Will had just knocked off Al, and he was hedging his bets on George or Hogan to help him run away with that million dollar deal in Sarasota Springs. Sal showing up with his criminal record gave him a third option to juggle, and he decided to dump George and play Sal and Hogan off each other while using them both at the same time. Sal had to admit it was genius. Though sometimes, he couldn't shake that there'd been something real with his connection with Will.

Maybe he was being a knob. It didn't make any difference in the end. Will used him as a patsy for George's murder. But he could've cut Sal loose a lot sooner than he did. He'd even gotten into the boat to motor across the river to Canada. He almost chose Sal instead of turning him in. Had he picked up that Sal two-timed him? That night, Will drove up in his motorcycle just as Todd was leaving.

These questions pressed down on Sal day and night. A person couldn't fake their feelings that well, could they? Maybe once, maybe twice, but Sal and Will had been all over each other for three months straight. Their relationship was twisted for sure, but the love had to be real. Sal should've felt like killing the kid, but he actually ached for him. If he could just have a conversation with Will, let him know he didn't have no grudge, maybe they could work things out.

One night, when Sal was playing Crazy Eights with three other inmates before lights out, a C.O. let the guys listen to music on a transistor radio. That usually started a fight over what station to listen to, but the vibe was mellow that night, and nobody complained when a guy tuned into *Dr. Love Coast to Coast*. Sal didn't mind neither. Even though the songs were corny, it took him back to a time when things were better.

The guys made wisecracks about the dedications, but like they say, music calms the savage beast, even when it's sappy songs by Anne Murray and The Carpenters. Everyone was having a great time that night. They all quieted down when Dr. Love's voice came on so they could hear his next dedication. Sal was shooting the shit with the guys he was playing cards with during a commercial break, and then the room went still when the smooth baritone of the disc jockey came back on the air.

"This next song is taking us back, and I mean way back, cool cats. I didn't know the producers even had it in the collection. But we've got time for one last ditty, and this one goes out to Sal from Will, and it's a funny one. Sal, if you're out there, Will picked this out special for you, and he says: 'At night, when I'm feeling lonely, I play this song and think of you. We could've been something. You were always my number one, but I couldn't trust you after you broke my heart. No hard feelings, baby." The disc jockey chuckled. "Somebody's gonna have to explain *this* one to me, but here you go Sal, with love from Will."

A jazzy flourish. A chill gripped Sal's heart. Dean Martin's croon came over the speaker.

When the red, red robin comes bob, bob, bobbing along, along,
There'll be no more sobbing when he starts throbbin' his old
sweet song...

Like someone had sawed open his skull to poke at parts of his brain, Sal couldn't help himself from smiling, real dopey, and then he was cracking up like he was on laughing gas. He jumped up on his chair and shouted the lyrics along with Dean. Sal was so hopped up on crazy juice, he went dancing around the floor, bumping into people, laughing in their faces and scattering cards and dominoes from tables. Sal couldn't see a reason not to do it. The world was just one big cartoon, wasn't it? It took three C.O.s with billy clubs to wrestle him down and restrain him, and then they cuffed him and yanked him along to a padded cell for solitary confinement.

ABOUT THE AUTHOR

Romeo Preminger has been called the master of the romantic thriller. He's the author of over a dozen books including the Southern Gothic *Arizona* series, the branded romantic thriller series *Guilty Pleasures Editions*, some naughty shorts called *Storybook Editions*, and two erotic romance standalones.

Romeo lives on the East Coast with his husband. Beyond writing, some of his favorite jobs on his resume are a brief stint as a zookeeper, an even briefer stint as a hot dog vendor, and a more substantial career as a counselor and advocate for LGBTQ+ youth. For more about Romeo, visit: https://romeopreminger.com or connect with him on Twitter at https://twitter.com/Preminger Romeo

Sign up for his mailing list for free stories, sales, and info on new releases:
http://eepurl.com/g5f64b

ALSO BY ROMEO PREMINGER

Want more Guilty Pleasures?

KILLER TWINS (Guilty Pleasures Editions, #4)

Mason thought he married the man of his dreams, but when he meets Erik's twin Lucas, who recently came out of prison for a murder he might not have committed, he's strangely drawn to the hard-luck guy. Then a slow drip of secrets from the past suggests that neither twin is what he seems to be.

FRAT HOUSE SECRETS (Guilty Pleasures Editions, #5)

Ethan Leavitt is on a mission to reinvent himself at college, but he never thought that would involve joining a fraternity. He suddenly has an amazing friend group, gay and straight, and he might actually find a boyfriend. But secrets lurk beneath all-American, inclusive Tau Alpha Theta, and Ethan's in for the terrifying thrill-ride of his life.